The Humane Algorithm

M

The Humane Algorithm
The Streetlighters Trilogy - Book One
by Trevor Wynyard

Published by
Manywhere ApS
www.manywhere.xyz

Paperpack ISBN: 978-87-972966-1-5
Ebook ISBN: 978-87-972966-0-8

TREVOR WYNYARD

THE HUMANE ALGORITHM

Manywhere

To my wife, Mie, and her patience.

01

Matt's little brother was the only one with a tassel. At the end of a long line of graduates, all in caps and gowns, Kevin beamed. Tall and lanky, he was the only one of his year to be awarded that special golden flurry of threads, the only thing that Matt had ever wanted for Kevin.

Years ago, Matt had flunked his own finals at high school. Being deemed unworthy of investment, even after such a perfect record up until that last year, had split his self-worth in half. Helping Kevin prepare and study for his finals had brought it all back—the sweat, the shakes, the rage, the tears. And then nothing. Only the empty feeling of a future with no prospect. No *streetlights*. Of course, he had never told his mother or Kevin how he had fled the test, overcome with anxiety. He needed to be strong; his father would have wanted that. So, he had made it seem like his choice to stay home and help out. Filling the void, fueling his sense of purpose.

The clouds were dark, hanging low over the football field, but had yet to shed their first drops of water. The stadium floodlights were off, gathering leaves and mold. Creepers had grappled with the few remaining bulbs that hadn't shattered by now. Standing in line, the graduates shuffled forward, waiting their turn to shine in the single spotlight allowed, fixed at the podium. Parents occupied row upon row of folding chairs, clapping proudly as their offspring filed past the principal, receiving their diplomas. Of course, that rolled-up piece of paper wasn't worth much, in Matt's opinion. Access to a low-end college education didn't hold any potential: scarce funding, degraded facilities and no electrical priority.

But that little tassel, distinguishing the exceptional, was the key to the best colleges across the country; the absolute best education in science, technology and politics. Each illustrious institution was a hotbed for the sculptors of the future, the pinnacles of human potential—a gateway to *the streetlights*.

Matt and his mother, Elizabeth, had come early to the ceremony in order to secure front-row seats. Matt could smell the recently cut grass, reminding him of his own graduation. His mother was wearing yellow, just as she had on his big day. Except for this time, there was a genuine reason to celebrate. During the speeches and songs, their three-legged stool of a family had kept close eye contact with each other, more or less ignoring the world around them. Kevin looked so promising as he stood in his dark pine-green robe, ready to conquer the world.

The line was nearing the end. Matt gripped his mother's hand and clenched it hard. He tilted his head towards her, keeping his voice low.

"We did it, Mom. Dad would be proud," he said.

Elizabeth turned and smiled.

"And last but not least, Kevin Turner," the principal said, raising his voice. The crowd roared.

Pride filled every fiber of Matt's body. It was hard not to feel that sense of fulfillment, knowing how much effort he had put into tutoring his little brother, pacing and persisting. Kevin grabbed the scroll and shook the principal's outstretched hand. But his lips didn't move. Matt watched him uneasily. He'd imagined this so many times: Kevin's smile was supposed to widen now. But it just sat there, frozen on his little brother's face.

Didn't he know what an enormous accomplishment this was? What was in store for him? The incredible destiny awaiting him?

Matt watched closely as Kevin lined up with the rest of the graduates. As one, they took their caps in hand and tossed them into the air, dotting the sky with their green mortarboards. Matt raised his arms in victory and finally caught Kevin's eye. There it was – the smile that Matt had been dreaming of.

And then Elizabeth dropped to the turf at the twenty-yard line.

Matt saw it in Kevin's face first. His sparkling eyes turned sharp, the dimples in his cheeks faded—and Matt knew. As his mother toppled outwards, away from the front row of chairs, Matt dropped to his knees beside her, reaching for her neck.

"Mom!" Kevin screamed, cutting through the noise of claps and hoots.

"Come on, not now," Matt whispered. He tried to find the artery at the side of her neck. With his fingers sweating profusely, veins seemed to melt with flesh. Out of the corner of his eye, he saw Kevin moving in a full sprint towards them.

The claps and murmuring tapered off.

"Mom!" Kevin screamed again. It tore through the sound of pennants flapping in the breeze. Every parent, teacher and bystander held their breath as Kevin reached his brother and fell to the ground at their mother's side.

"Someone get me the defib," Matt shouted to the crowd at large, but he got no response. "The defibrillator, by the stands! Someone!"

Kevin looked wildly up at Matt. "What's happening? Matt?"

Matt ripped his mom's button-down dress open and tore her bra apart at the seams.

"It's here. It's here." A member of the faculty came running with the AED.

"Is she gonna make it, Matt?" Kevin was staring, wild-eyed, at his big brother. Matt focused on his mom's chest as he turned on the machine.

"She'll be fine, she'll be fine—" he replied. He needed to keep his composure.

Elizabeth's arm twitched a bit.

"Stay calm. Follow these voice instructions—" began the mechanical male voice.

"Come on—faster," Matt muttered to the machine while he untangled the wires and stretched them towards his mother.

Then Elizabeth's shoulders jerked. Matt held the pads back.

"It's a seizure, not a stroke," said the teacher who had brought the defibrillator, putting his hand in front of Matt. Matt swept the man's arm aside and put his ear to Elizabeth's chest. He felt for her pulse again, and this time he found it.

Elizabeth's rib cage lifted; her mouth widened and heaved at the air to fill her lungs. Her eyes opened and locked onto Kevin.

"Mom!" Kevin threw his arms around her, holding her tight. "Are you all right?"

"You were so beautiful up there," she said.

"She's fine. She's fine," Matt said. He sighed and slumped back in the grass. As the tension released its grip on the crowd, the murmur and chatter returned, though more softly now. The teacher handed Matt a blanket.

"She needs to go to the hospital to get checked," he said. "Should I call for an ambulance?"

"No, no—please, I'll take her. Let me handle this." Matt got up, helped his mother to stand, and wrapped her in the blanket. "Let's go," he said.

They walked off the field, Kevin holding and supporting their mom and Matt three steps ahead of them, parting the sea of parents and guests. There were looks of approval on the fathers' faces while the mothers clasped their hands in front of their mouths. Matt felt the occasional pat on his back as he shepherded his little family along.

If you didn't know, it was hard to tell that Matt and Kevin were brothers. There was a significant age difference, and neither their hair nor their facial features were alike. Where Matt had the same dark hair and dark, intense eyes from their father Jeffrey, Kevin was red-haired and blue-eyed, the same as Elisabeth, and almost as angelic.

The teacher pushed past Kevin and Elizabeth and caught up to Matt, tapping his shoulder as they headed towards the parking lot. Matt stopped and turned to him, frowning.

"She needs medical attention," the man insisted. "Are you sure you don't want me to—"

"I've got it," Matt snapped, annoyed.

"Yeah, I know, you said, but I'm not sure you understand the potential severity—"

Matt grabbed him by the collar of his academic robe. Matt

was both taller and broader. He looked down on the teacher as he pulled him close.

"Listen," he said.

"But—"

"Listen, I said. I've got this under control." The teacher, whom he didn't even know, avoided his eyes. "Now take your little fancy dress and fuck off," Matt said, pushing him away.

The teacher stumbled a few steps back and fell to the pavement. As he got to his feet again, Matt continued to stare, waiting for him to leave. The teacher, shaking his head in disbelief, backed away. Matt turned and hurried to catch up to his family.

Walking across the parking lot, he was thinking about what to say to Kevin. How would he explain the situation? How would he reassure Kevin that nothing was wrong, that Elizabeth would be fine? After all, it should be Matt's burden to bear, not Kevin's. Family first, his father had always said.

"Kev, listen," Matt began as they arrived at their old maroon Ford pickup. "I'm gonna take Mom home, and you should go to the graduation party."

"But—"

"I'm gonna watch over her all night and make sure to call emergency services if something happens or she gets worse." Matt opened the door for their mother.

"I'm fine, Kevin," Elizabeth said, and hugged him once more.

"But I don't want to leave. I'm worried about you, Mom," Kevin said as he helped her into the passenger seat.

"You good, Mom?" Matt said, and Elizabeth nodded. He turned towards Kevin again and lowered his voice. "Listen to me, Kev. I understand. I really do." Closing the door, he took a few steps away from the truck, motioning to Kevin to follow.

"But go to the party. It's sanctioned and all. You have no clue what you're missing. There'll be music and lights, like a real old disco. All your friends will be there. And you're the star of the show! You *have* to go."

"I'm not the star…"

"Of course you are! You're the only one with honors. You have no idea what your friends would give to be in your situation."

Kevin shook his head and looked down at the asphalt. He kicked the rubble.

"Mom is fine. Look." Matt gestured at the truck, and Elizabeth waved back at him, smiling bravely. "She's fine—see? She didn't have any head trauma, and of course, she needs a check-up, so I'll take her to the doctor in the morning. But we can't take the risk of going to the hospital for no reason. What if they decide to charge us? We can't afford the energy deficit that would mean for us for months to come. Not with you needing to research for college. Dr. Aldridge will check her for free. He *knows* us."

Kevin looked uncertainly at his older brother.

"She'll be fine—I promise." Matt hugged him. "Go, Kev, and have a blast. Or whatever you call it. Take in the spectacle, enjoy yourself! Might not be till college graduation that you get another shot at one of these. This is *your* time. You worked your ass off for this. Now take it in."

Kevin gave him a weak smile and then nodded. "Thanks."

"I'll sleep near the tablet so you can get a hold of me if you need a pickup."

"Ha. I don't get drunk, Matt. We don't really do alcohol, or drugs either, for that matter."

Matt smiled indulgently. "Of course you do, just like we did when I was your age. But I get it. Just remember, I'll be one connection away. If you need me, call from a tablet anywhere, and I'll be there in a few."

"Sure. Thanks." Kevin shook his head. "But don't stay up waiting. Please." He went over to the truck window and tapped it. "Love you, Mom!" With a last wave at Matt, he darted off towards the football field where the marching band was striking up the first notes of the school's victory anthem.

"Take care in the dark," Matt yelled after him. He walked back to the truck, settled himself behind the wheel, and turned to Elizabeth. "You all right, Mom?"

"Yeah, I'm fine. Not sure exactly what happened, though."

Matt looked at his mother, who was staring blankly out over the parking lot.

"You know it's the second time now?" he said.

Elizabeth looked at him and shook her head. "What do you mean?"

"Never mind. We'll go see Dr. Aldridge tomorrow. Let's just get you home for some rest now. I told Kevin to go ahead and celebrate with his classmates. It's his big day."

"Yes. I know. It's his day. Thanks, Matt."

"Always."

"No." She reached across and took his hand. "Thank you for getting him this far. He couldn't have made it without your help. Your father would be proud if he were here. Especially of you."

Matt blushed slightly. "Thanks, Mom. But I'm not done with Kevin yet." He grinned. "He still needs to pick a college." He leaned in and gave his mother a squeeze. "Let's get you home." He started the truck and rolled through the parking lot, heading out into traffic.

02

The Turners lived in an apartment complex on the west side of Grid WDC, Sector 8-5. They had moved to the building when Matt and Kevin's father died. It was a run-down two-story brownstone, with AC units still attached to the outside. Most of the complexes hadn't seen repairs since the government had bought up all the cheap residence buildings many years ago. Now, it was subsidized housing for lower-income families. Take a government-approved job, and you'd get a roof over your head. Standards varied, but overall, the cheap rent allowed families to save money for a future home of their own.

Matt pulled up in front of the building's crumbling concrete walkway, pushing away thoughts about their beautiful old villa on the cul-de-sac. Lawns to play catch on, peaceful lanes perfect for learning to ride a bike. Friendly, hospitable neighbors who had been kind to him and little Kevin and helped out his mother and father from time to time. All of that was nonexistent here, he thought bitterly. Everyone kept to themselves in the name of self-sufficiency. Like everyone else, the Turners managed with less now.

Kevin, who had been just a baby when their father's accident had happened, knew nothing else, of course. Yet he had graduated with honors from high school, Matt thought proudly. So, despite everything, the neighborhood had done a decent job of incubating his little brother. It wasn't like living in the streetlights, of course, but few got that privilege.

Following the energy crisis, the government had enacted a nationwide shutdown of the unnecessary road- and traffic-related services, including all street lighting and most traffic lights. In the wake of this highly unpopular decision, traffic accidents had soared, but the car manufacturers had come to the rescue with a standard for automated vehicles. As the dust settled, some lights had returned, but this was not a consequence of popular outcry. Rather, it was implemented as a policy instrument.

Matt had kept dreaming, though. He longed for a house of their own, although now his focus was on getting Kevin into a good college and securing him a job that offered family relocation as a benefit. Maybe not the streetlights, but who knew. There was always hope. Everybody knew that the most prominent neighborhoods had streetlights, just one of the perks doled out to the important—the hardest workers and the people upon whose shoulders the future rested. Kids didn't dream as much about a profession these days. They dreamed about making it to the streetlights. Whatever your job, wherever you worked, no matter the business, making it to the streetlights was the number one goal. Whether you were a plumber or a politician, living in the streetlights signaled to everybody else that you'd made it. But getting there meant serving: society, government and nation. And if you served well, you would be selected for a spot under the glistening bulbs. Matt had flushed his own chances, he knew, when he'd chosen to care for his family. But that was what his father had preached: family first. And so it was for Matt.

He got out of the truck and went around to the passenger door to help Elizabeth out. Still wrapped in a blanket, she leaned on Matt's shoulder as she walked up to their block. He could see one apartment with its lights still on, which struck him as odd at this time of day. There shouldn't be a need during daylight hours.

"Go lie on the couch, Mom," Matt said, assisting Elizabeth through the front door. "Get some rest."

The apartment was in the same general shape inside as the building outside. Wall to wall carpets peeling back in the corners. Torn strips of wallpaper, with a few moisture stains. Whether it was white turned yellow or yellow just faded, none of them really knew; the color had remained the same over the years. One bare lightbulb dangled from the concrete ceiling in the entrance hallway. Off.

Matt looked at their E-Meter. A simple digital display with a spinning disc counted every watt spent. The first number tallied up the user's monthly total; the second was the monthly electricity limit. Each E-Meter sent its data to government analytics and received new limits; that second number would fluctuate all the time, and residents never knew the exact quota until the end of the month. Calculated by algorithms and adjusting for changes in weather, supply, and production efficiency, the amount of available renewable energy was never a constant. People who spend together should save together, the government had proclaimed as they issued E-Meters to every home and business across the country. By now, saving electricity was second nature for Matt: turning lights off when he left a room, unplugging unneeded electronics and always checking when he got home for unseen usage hidden in some standby appliance. He looked at the E-Meter and breathed a quiet sigh of relief. They were almost at the end of the month and had plenty to spare.

"I think we could save for a bonus this month, Mom," he called. "Did you hear me?" he said, popping his head through the living room doorway.

Elizabeth sat slumped down on the couch, the blanket halfway down her shoulders.

"I'll get you some water," Matt said. She nodded.

He headed into the dingy kitchen. The same torn wallpaper was stuck under the cabinets; the checkered linoleum was worn and scuffed. Matt could still make out a stain on the rug beneath the dining table leg from the first time Elizabeth had passed out. She had been doing the dishes when she collapsed, and her head had struck the corner of the table on the way down. Blood had flowed from the side of her head, but she had regained consciousness in seconds. Kevin was already asleep since he had a big test the next day, so Matt had called in a favor and driven Elizabeth to his friend Stephanie's house. He had scrubbed the rug and then washed and dried it in the laundry machines to remove the blood. This had sent the E-Meter soaring, but Matt had needed to make sure Kevin wouldn't notice. In the morning, he'd made up a lie about their mother leaving early for work.

"Did you like the speeches, Mom?" Matt returned to the living room with a glass of water. His mother, still on the couch, was now holding a picture from Matt's high school graduation.

"You look so alike," she said softly.

"We look nothing alike," he said, laughing, as he sat down beside her.

"Could you turn on the lights, Matt?"

He ignored her. "I liked the part where the principal mentioned the bright future we were heading towards. I could swear he was looking at Kevin."

"Could I get a bit of light?" Elizabeth was squinting at the worn gold-painted frame.

"No, Mom. Didn't you hear what I said? I think we should make an effort to save for these last few days. If the quota doesn't drop unexpectedly, we should be in for the monetary bonus this month. That could go into our savings, you know."

Elizabeth just sat and stared blankly at the picture.

"I—" she started, but nothing more came out.

"Mom?" He looked at her as she tried to find the words. "Are you all right?"

"He was just so—" She had a distant, dreamy look in her eyes. She blinked and looked around the living room. "Too bad it had to rain."

"What do you mean?" Matt said, puzzled.

"On such a special day, I would've loved for Kevin to get a bit of sun."

The sky had been dark, but throughout the day, the clouds had not broken. In the picture in Elizabeth's hands, though, Matt stood drenched in his graduation gown. The photo had been taken twelve years ago. Matt tilted his head, trying to catch her fleeting eyes.

"What color was Kevin's robe, Mom?" he asked. "Do you remember?"

The school colors had changed from ruby to pine after a merger.

"His—"

"Mom, look at me! What day is it?"

"It's Kevin's graduation day." She locked onto his eyes.

"No—what day of the week?"

"Friday?"

"It's Thursday. Graduations are always held on Thursdays," Matt said, sinking back into the couch.

What the hell was wrong with her? Why did she have to get sick now?

"We'll go to the doctor in the morning. I want him to take another look at you," he said.

"But I'm fine, Matt," she said.

"No. You're not, Mom. Kevin doesn't need this now; he needs to focus on picking a college. It's important that he finds a good fit. I don't want him worrying about you while he's looking at courses and trying to decide." He stared at his lap and then met his mother's eyes again. "I don't want him ending up like me."

Elizabeth didn't respond. She was back to looking at the picture.

Matt sat back on the couch beside her. He looked across the coffee table at the old armchair, his father's trusty old seat, where he'd watched his old man devour the news every night. It was the only piece of furniture from the old house. Young Matt had dragged it all the way across town from their place on Pine Road. Just getting the heavy thing up on the pushcart had almost finished him, but he had persisted, and now, when they were all in the living room together, it was his to sit in.

He got up and took a couple of steps towards the kitchen. "I'll cook tonight. What do you want? There's macaroni and cheese or eggplant lasagna for the microwave. Which one do you prefer? I'm not going waste electricity cooking on the stove when Kevin's not home," he said. "Where's your citizen card, by the way?"

"In my purse, I think. Why?"

"Just want to make sure we don't forget it tomorrow."

Matt went into the hallway and found her handbag. Rummaging, he found her wallet. As he took it out, he saw a folded piece of paper with company letterhead. He pulled it out and opened it, and his eyes widened in horror.

Matt stormed back into the living room.

"What the fuck is this?" he lashed out, waving the letter in his hand. "You lost your job? Why didn't you tell me?"

"I'm sorry. You shouldn't have seen that."

"Why? Why didn't you tell me? I need to know something like this."

"Let me explain, Matt, please—"

"Were you just gonna turn a blind eye? When was this?" Matt skimmed the letter again, fast.

"A couple of months ago. I don't know." She stood up and grabbed Matt by the shoulders. "I'll get another; don't you worry. I just didn't want to burden you with any more. You seemed so preoccupied with Kevin's graduation, and I didn't want to spoil that. I didn't want to ruin his finals. You two were so busy preparing, and I…" She swallowed. "I didn't want to interrupt. You know I hate to bring bad news, and as time went on, I must have just forgotten."

"How could you *forget*, Mom? It's not like doing the laundry or shopping for groceries. How the fuck could you forget something like this?"

"I don't know, Matt. Please, calm down," Elizabeth said.

Matt skimmed the letter again for a third time. "Wait—why *did* you get fired?" he said.

"I—I started to forget things. Couldn't keep the calendar in order, forgot appointments and so on. I guess they saw no other option."

Matt sat down in his father's chair. His mother had always been a secretary and was known for being conscientious and meticulous in her work. He could see why an impaired memory would compromise that; he also knew it was unlikely anyone would hire someone her age now.

"Listen," he said. "I don't want Kevin to find out, all right? We'll go to the doctor tomorrow and see if he can figure out what's causing all this."

"All what?" She stared at him, puzzled.

"Your—" He broke off, searching for the kindest word he could find. "—Spells."

"Okay, Matt. Whatever you think is best."

Matt began tearing the letter to pieces. "And I'll see if I can get *my* old job back at the community center. At least I left by my own decision," he said darkly. "We'll have to contact the government and arrange to sign over the apartment contract from you to me if it comes to that."

He leaned back in the chair and leaned his head back, resigned. "You're gonna have to make a plate for yourself, Mom. I'm not hungry anymore." He plunked his feet up on the coffee table and reached for their tablet. "I'm gonna watch some shows, see if anything's on. I need to get my mind off things. You can join me if you want." He tapped a finger on the tablet. "I promised Kevin I'd sleep with this in case he needs me tonight."

Elizabeth picked up the pieces of the letter and trudged out of the living room.

Matt pressed the power button on the tablet and connected with his thumb.

03

Matt put a brief note on the kitchen table. Kevin had come home during the night, so Matt decided to let him sleep in. He accompanied his mother out the door.

Elizabeth stopped at the sidewalk, staring at the maroon pickup. Matt had saved for ages to buy it used from the dealer. Their old car had been wrecked in the crash that killed Mr. Turner, and the insurance payout, thanks to the *Energy Efficiency Act*, had been so minimal that they hadn't been able to afford a new one.

"Get in the truck, Mom. We're already late," he said crossly. He climbed into the driver's seat and reached across to open the passenger door.

"Sorry, I just—" she started, but didn't finish. She buckled herself in. Matt shook his head, turned the ignition, and pulled out from the curb.

...

The waiting room at Dr. Aldridge's was standing-room only. With subsidized healthcare, there was no way to get appointments. The government had done this to keep expenses down. They figured the longer people had to wait, the less likely they'd be to visit with minor, insignificant problems. And they had been correct. The number of visits had dropped, and so had the number of prescriptions needed. Medical companies had been furious, but legislation following the *Energy Efficiency Act* had reduced the size of many sectors and had been easy to pass, considering the public pressure.

Matt swiped his mother's citizen card on the tablet at the little booth.

"Any open wounds, suspicion of contagions, or issues requiring urgent medical attention?" the secretary asked.

"No," Matt replied. He knew from previous experience that a *yes* only got you directions to the nearest emergency facility, and it wasn't like he was lying.

"Sign here." The secretary pointed to a field on the tablet form without looking up from her book.

"Mom," Matt said and stepped aside so she could confirm her identity with a fingerprint.

They found a spot on the floor, up against the wall. He laid out his jacket for his mother to sit on.

"It's gonna be a while, I guess," he said.

Elizabeth sat down. "Are you sure all this is necessary?"

"Yeah, Mom. I'm sure," Matt said.

He looked around at the people waiting; some had scarves covering their faces, and there was a lot of coughing going on. Matt could still smell the sanitizing detergent. He'd been here many times, but over the years, attendance seemed to have grown. Dr. Aldridge took only patients who were on government-subsidized healthcare; it was the only way he could live with himself, he'd once told Matt. The Turners had stayed with his practice even after they'd moved; Dr. Aldridge was as close as you could get to a family doctor.

It had been months since their last visit, and Dr. Aldridge had guessed back then that Elizabeth had suffered a concussion from the fall, but otherwise hadn't been able to pinpoint the source of her blackout. Now, as he sat, waiting, thinking, it dawned on Matt that he had been seeing small changes in her personality. He'd been so busy helping Kevin with college applications that her shift in demeanor had gone under his radar. But now, given time to reflect, he realized that she seemed more hesitant and insecure than how he remembered her. She was no longer the mother he and Kevin had grown up with, always gregarious and cordial.

"Ms. Turner? The doctor will see you now," the secretary called.

■ ■ ■

"Ah, Ms. Turner. Please, take a seat. Matt, pull that chair up, will you?" Dr. Aldridge said as they entered his examination room. "So, it hasn't been long since we last saw each other. I'm guessing you're not well?"

Elizabeth sat down and regarded the doctor. "Oh, I'm fine, thanks," she said. "It's just that Matt's a bit worried, so I promised I'd come and see you."

Dr. Aldridge smiled. He was a bulky man, with a large brown beard to match his frizzy hair. It now showed the occasional streak of gray. He wore a sunflower-yellow shirt and a green Hawaiian tie beneath his occupational-issue white coat. He looked over to Matt.

"You don't strike me as the worrying type," he said. "Has there been another incident?"

"She had what I think was a seizure yesterday," Matt said. He looked at his mother, who was staring out the window. She didn't seem to take any notice. "And she's been distant. Like that," he said, nodding at her. "I haven't noticed it before, but I think she might have been like this for some time now," he said.

Dr. Aldridge looked over at Elizabeth again. "Ms. Turner? Would you mind telling me about yesterday?" he said. "How would you describe, in your own words, what happened and how you felt?"

"Oh, it was such a nice day. Kevin graduated, you know. He looked so happy and—" Elizabeth began.

"No, Mom, he wants to know about your—" Matt interrupted, but the doctor waved a dismissive hand at him, so he sat back.

"I've been so lucky with these two," Elizabeth continued. "They're so grown up now, and Kevin's off to college soon."

"Thank you, Ms. Turner. Would you mind helping me with a few tests?" Dr. Aldridge turned to his computer and typed a few words. He stood up and gestured Matt towards the door. "I need your mother on her own for this one."

Matt got to his feet and followed Dr. Aldridge to the door.

"I'm going to run an extended search of her journal," Dr. Aldridge said to him in a low voice. "I only have access to our own files and logs, but I want to request her prior medical history to see if anything might help me confirm my suspicions."

"What do you think is—"

"It might take some time. The servers are not the fastest. Meanwhile, I'll do some memory tests."

"Sure. Is there—"

"Be with you in a second, Ms. Turner," Dr. Aldridge said out loud before turning back to Matt. "I'll also do some blood work.

We can get the results from those with in-house equipment. So, you're going to have to wait a while, but try not to worry."

Dr. Aldridge nudged Matt out the door and closed it behind him.

■ ■ ■

Half an hour passed before Elizabeth came out, all smiles, and joined Matt. She sat down beside him in a now-vacant chair.

"So?" Matt asked.

Elizabeth looked at him, trying to figure out his question.

"So, what did he say? What did you talk about?" Matt tried once more.

"Oh, we just talked about how things were going with you guys. He showed some picture cards, and we talked about them, and so on."

"But did he say what was wrong? Did you get any results? Do we need to wait for blood tests?" Matt tried to dig for information.

"Oh, yes. Another half-hour or so." Elizabeth looked over at a painting of a giraffe on the opposite wall. "Remember that?" she said, pointing. "You used to love that one."

Matt looked at it. Kevin had loved animals when he was a toddler, but Matt had never taken an interest, as far as he could remember. He sighed.

■ ■ ■

Finally, Dr. Aldridge came out to the waiting room.

"Ms. Turner? Would you be so kind as to wait here? I'll just have a quick word with your son, if you don't mind."

She didn't seem to notice. Matt looked from his mother to Dr. Aldridge, but the doctor just shook his head and beckoned him into his office.

"You need to sit, Matt."

Matt sat down in the patient's chair, feeling a cold sweat trickling down his back. "What's wrong with her, Dr. Aldridge?" he said.

"Call me Ben, please."

"Can we get a prescription or what? How long will it take before she's back to normal?"

"No, I'm afraid we can't. You need to relax and take your time to understand what I'm about to tell you," Dr. Aldridge said.

"Is it dementia, then?" Matt blurted. "Can't we just get some meds for her?"

"Matt, please," Dr. Aldridge said. "You know I have a long professional relationship with your family. I want to help, but I can't do that if you don't listen."

Matt slumped back in the chair. "Sorry. It's just—" he began, but didn't make it further.

"Do you know what Alzheimer's disease is, Matt?"

"Yes. Is that what this is?"

"Yes—no. Well, not exactly." Dr. Aldridge laid out a graph on a piece of paper before him. "This is the average progression for a patient with Alzheimer's. This is time, and this is general mental cognition." He pointed at the axis with his pen. Then he drew a nearly vertical line. "*This* is your mother."

Matt just stared at the paper. It was like a kid had drawn some random line on the graph; it didn't seem to belong there. At the top of the mental cognition axis was a single word: *terminal.*

"It looks like your mother has an extreme form of rapidly

developing Alzheimer's. To be honest, I haven't heard of anything like this. Normally, after diagnosis, a patient with the disease goes on to live anywhere from three to ten years, some even more. But the symptoms your mother exhibits, like the seizure and the epilepsy, are only evident in the ultimate stages."

Matt just stared at the paper. He was trying to find a reply, but his thoughts raced and whirled. *Was she going to die? Could he stop it? What would he say to Kevin?* Matt tried to ignore the turmoil in his stomach and keep his composure.

"Matt, are you there?" Dr. Aldridge said, trying to catch his eye.

"Yes, sorry. I—"

Dr. Aldridge looked at him, expecting more of a sentence. Matt reached for a box of tissues and wiped his forehead.

"Do you need a glass of water?"

"No. Thanks. I … uh… What can I—" He cleared his throat. "Is there any—"

"I'm going to be forthright because I need to be sure you understand the severity of the situation. Your mother is dying."

Matt's blood flow zipped towards his toes.

"If she continues progressing like this, she will probably die within a month. There's no way for me to tell," Dr. Aldridge said. He looked more closely at Matt. "You're going pale on me, Matt. Put your head between your legs, like this."

Matt put his head down. He could see Dr. Aldridge's shoes as he crouched next to him. As Matt's ears leveled with his knees, he regained the feeling in his limbs, and the dizziness retreated.

"Here's some water," Dr. Aldridge said, handing him a cup. "Better?"

"Yes, thanks." Matt took a big sip.

"Listen. There might be treatment options available for her. There have been tremendous advances in gene therapy, for Alzheimer's in particular. But I cannot sit here and promise you anything. And given that gene therapy is an advanced treatment, she'll need Grid approval."

"Okay, so how do I get that?" Matt said, collecting himself.

"Given more time, I could refer you for an assessment, but the waiting lists for those are months in your healthcare bracket. So, the only viable option is for your mother to go queue up at the Central Grid Hospital. They have an emergency intake of patients each day. That would get her a faster assessment and a way to apply for treatment."

"Great," Matt said. "Do you have an address? Do I have to take a reference or something?" Matt said.

"Yes indeed. Here, take this." Dr. Aldridge handed him a brochure but didn't let go. "And Matt? You need to be wary." He released the brochure. "I've heard of people who don't make it inside getting swindled in their desperation. There are multiple underground and unauthorized medical facilities in the big cities. Just be wary, Matt: none of those have licenses, and most of their staff are not even doctors. Use your own best judgment, and try not to get carried away by emotion."

"Thanks," Matt said, looking at the pamphlet.

"One more thing."

Matt stopped reading and looked back up.

"When I did the extended search on your mother's journal, I stumbled on some blocked entries. I didn't have proper clearance to go in and view them. Do you know anything about this? Most of them were made around the time when Kevin was born."

Matt thought for a moment. "I suppose they're about the fertility treatment she underwent at the time. I don't remember much about them, other than she had a ton of appointments and some stays at a clinic," Matt said.

"Yes. That could be... Those types of appointments shouldn't be blocked, though," Dr. Aldridge said, and paused. "Anyway, your mother is waiting. I hope everything gets sorted. Let me know when you're back, okay?"

"Will do. Thanks, Dr. Aldridge. I mean it," Matt said, and got to his feet.

Dr. Aldridge simply nodded.

Matt walked back out to the waiting room. Elizabeth stood up as he approached.

"That was quick. Is everything all right?" she said.

He embraced her and held her close in his arms. He laid his head on her shoulders. "I love you, Mom," he whispered as he tightened his grip.

"Love you too, Mattimouse. Everything okay?"

"It will be, Mom. I promise, it will be," Matt said.

04

There was a black sedan parked outside their apartment complex. Its shiny finish told him it was not from this part of town. The police cruiser next to it was a regular sight, though. Matt heard muffled complaints from inside the maze. Some poor bastard being dragged away for something illegal, he thought. Common practice where they lived.

"Come on, Mom," he said, helping her out of the truck.

As they approached their flat, Matt broke into a run. The yells sounded like his brother's voice. He let go of his mother's hand and dashed towards their front door. He couldn't make out the words, but it was Kevin. The door was open.

"You have no fucking right to do this!" Kevin yelled. Matt crossed the threshold as his brother was thrown to the floor by two burly police officers. One of them pointed a taser at Kevin and pulled the trigger. Kevin jolted on the floor and froth bubbled from his lips. The second officer raised his stick at Matt, while the first reached for his holster.

"Stand back, sir!"

Matt flung up his hands. "Wait, take it easy. I live here. That's my brother."

"They are taking our home," Kevin mumbled, raising his head from the floor. He spat a mix of saliva and blood onto the carpet. He tried to push himself up but fell back again, his muscles still twitching.

"Let me handle this," Matt told him. "There must be some kind of misunderstanding…"

He turned to see a woman emerging from the living room. Her raven-black hair was pulled back into a tight bun. She wore a pencil skirt, a fitted blazer with square shoulder pads, and a shirt whose collar was buttoned so tight it barely left her room to breathe—all dyed in a deep, rich government blue. She wore sturdy glasses with yellow-tinted lenses. Matt could just make out the flickers of light reflecting in her eyes.

"Identify yourself," she said, sharp and snappy.

"I'm Matthew Turner. I live here."

Elizabeth came through the front door now, and the officers unholstered their firearms again. Matt raised one hand in defense and, with the other, dragged his mother close to him.

"This is my mom, Elizabeth Turner. She's the legal tenant. We just came from the doctor."

"Do you have some identification?" the blue-clad woman said.

Matt reached inside his jacket pocket to find his and Elizabeth's citizen cards. He held them forward. The woman examined them.

"What's happening, Matt?" Elizabeth said.

"Step forward for retina confirmation," the woman said.

"Just do as she says, Mom," Matt said, taking a step forward and raising his jaw a bit. Elizabeth followed suit.

The yellow-tinted glasses flashed for an instant, and the woman's focus adjusted to the side, her pupils scanning lines of text. Matt had seen shows about this government eyewear, which provided contextual information based on the wearer's surroundings while assisting in hostile environments. And probably more besides, Matt reckoned. Of course, this technology was available only to officials and government personnel.

"So, Ms. Turner," the woman said when she had completed her scan, "I have to inform you that the WDC and the government of the United Grids have opted to evict you and all residents at this address. The absence and/or negligence of a government-regulated job forces the Grid to withdraw the benefit of a subsidized home, as per your residential agreement. Do you understand?" she said.

"What? Have they have fired you?" Kevin said weakly. He rolled onto his back, revealing his bruised face.

"My mom's sick," Matt said, ignoring Kevin. "Isn't there any way of postponing this?"

"No. Application for work leave is not done at the government level. That is for the workplace to handle," the woman said.

"What's going on?" Elizabeth looked from the officers to the official, to Kevin and back to Matt.

"Mom, don't worry. Let me handle this," Matt said.

"Ms. Turner, I'm from the government," the woman said. "I'm here to ensure you vacate this apartment. We need to give it to a family who contributes."

"What? I don't understand," Elizabeth said, still looking at Matt.

"Mom, wait here with Kevin." Matt turned to the woman in blue. "Can I have a quick word with you in the kitchen?"

The woman nodded and followed him just out of earshot.

"You have two minutes," she said.

"So, we just came from the doctor…" he started.

"You already said. Get to the point."

"My mom has some sort of terminal, progressive Alzheimer's disease. The doctor said she needs to get medical attention at the Central Grid Hospital. My brother doesn't know, and since he has to start college at the end of the summer, I would prefer keeping it that way." Matt glanced past her towards the hallway. "He graduated with honors, so it's quite important. Mom didn't tell us about her termination, so I've had no time to find work, and now she needs to get to WDC-0-1 to begin treatment."

The woman seemed to be listening to him now.

"Is there any way we can keep the apartment?" Matt said. He noticed her foot tapping.

She looked at him, tilting her head a bit, sizing him up.

"Well," she said reluctantly. "You could volunteer as a nuclear remedy worker. The government is running a program where workers clean up radioactive spills in the southern grids, caused by terrorist attacks," she said. "If you did this, it would also give your mother a better chance of admission if she needs to go to the hospital."

"Wouldn't that require me to join the government labor forces? And to live near the site camps?"

"Yes, that would be a requirement. You could let your brother go, but I suspect he's not of legal age yet. At the moment, it's the only unskilled job available that would make your family eligible for continued residence here."

"Can't you bend the rules?"

"No. Not unless you have a job that's on a government-approved list."

"So you're throwing a dying mother and her children onto the street? Have you no soul?"

She took a quick step towards Matt, squared off and locked eyes with him.

"What do you think happens if I don't follow procedure?" she barked into his face. "Do you think *I'd* get to keep my job? Do you think *my* family can survive with no income?" She stared into his eyes and didn't flinch. It was the first time she had exhibited any kind of emotion. "What mother would *I* be then? Not taking care of my own three kids, all about to start school? All of whom are more dependent than your college-bound brother? Remember—the government is giving you an option here. *You* are the one unwilling to take it."

Matt regarded her silently.

"I didn't make the rules—democracy did. And we both have to live by them, or else we both risk eviction—and worse! So do me a favor; feel free to unload all of your troubles if you need someone to lend an ear, but don't you try to lecture me about compassion."

Buckling under her piercing stare, Matt looked down at the kitchen floor. Somehow, *he* felt ashamed.

"That's what I thought," she said briskly. "I'll give you until Monday morning, but I have to change your citizen status now. Then the sanitation crew needs access."

"Thank you," Matt said, not daring to raise his eyes.

"But if you haven't found a job or softened to the idea of a few years in a hazmat, I'd suggest you start packing. 'Cause I won't have pity when Monday comes. Then you and your lovely family will go straight to the community centers—and just see where that gets you."

A lightbulb went on in Matt's head. "Would a *job* at a community center make the cut?"

She stared at him. "Yes. That's on the list. Now, are we done here?" she said.

Matt nodded in silence and followed her out of the kitchen.

The woman gestured towards the two police officers as she marched back into the hallway. Elizabeth was crouched beside Kevin, helping him to support himself. He spat out some more blood. One of the officers paused as he passed them. Matt cringed; he already knew what was coming, having seen the police at work many times at the community center.

The officer turned and brandished his taser rod.

"No, don't!" Elizabeth screamed.

A quick swish struck Kevin across the face, sending blood spattering across the wallpaper.

"Don't you ever resist, kid," the officer snarled. He raised his stick once more and held it aloft for a second. Matt moved towards his brother, but the officer whirled on him. "Back off," he barked. Matt crouched, shielding Kevin with his hands.

"Move your hands," the officer said.

Matt hesitated.

"So be it." The officer swung down one last time, hitting Matt in the back and sending him sprawling to the floor. Without another word, he turned and strode out of the apartment. Matt heard the woman and the other officer follow him, and then the door shut behind them.

Elizabeth clasped her hands around Kevin's face and stroked his forehead.

"Are you all right, Kevin?" she said. "Look what they've done to you."

Matt stood up and arched his back, then helped Kevin to his feet. Blood was dripping from the wound across his cheek.

"I'll see if we have some bandages," Matt said. He placed a hand on his waist to assess his injuries.

"I will go straight to the local police department and demand an excuse first thing Monday. They shouldn't get away with this harassment and brutality," Elizabeth said.

"You know that's how it is, Mom," Matt said wearily. "There's nothing we can do. It's within their authority, and the law protects them from us. I hate it, too, but unless you convince politicians that the government needs to allot more resources, this is what we get. Why don't you go rest in the living room, and I'll take care of Kevin."

Matt supported his brother into the kitchen and helped him to a chair.

"I'll just clean these up, and then you need to rest, too, Kev."

Kevin nodded and rubbed his jaw. "Don't think anything's broken," he said. He gasped as Matt cleansed the wounds and lashes with alcoholic gel. "Matt?" he said quietly. "What's happening?"

"I don't know, Kev. They want to evict us, but I'll see if I can't figure something out."

"I meant Mom. What's happening with Mom?"

"She's sick," Matt said, waiting to see the response on Kevin's face. "It's nothing dangerous, but Dr. Aldridge told us that we should look at getting her treatment at the Central Grid Hospital in 0-1. I know she seems out of it sometimes, but it's nothing you need to worry about. I'll handle it—don't worry."

"Are you sure?"

"Yes, I promise. He said there have been tremendous advances in therapy to help people with her condition, so she should be healthy again in no time." He turned and pulled up his shirt, exposing his back. "Would you mind pressing near my spine?" he said.

Kevin prodded a few places as Matt clenched his teeth and flinched in agony.

"That's enough. I'll go get some painkillers," Matt said. "Also, I think we're out of food. Can you keep Mom company in the meantime?"

"Yeah, sure. What about here?" Kevin said.

"What about what?"

"What will happen to the apartment?"

"I have some options. I might have to go away for a while and work for the government. But before I decide, I'll see if I can get my old job back, and then we'll be fine."

"Didn't you say you hated that job? Something about your boss turning a blind eye?"

"Yeah. But he has some good qualities, too. I guess it wouldn't be that bad, and if that's what I need to do so that we can keep the apartment, then so be it. I'll just have to keep my mouth shut when I'm at work and treat the wasters like everybody else does."

05

"The system's denying your citizen card, sir," the clerk said.

"What? Try it again, please," Matt said.

The clerk continued to gaze at him with annoyance for a few more seconds. She had dyed pitch-black hair, neck long, with an undercut to reveal sides of saturated hot pink. A pale green bubble of gum peeped out of her mouth and then burst with a pop. At her throat was a silver chain, on which hung a little pendant that spelled the words *Fuck it* in romantic serifs. She swiped his card again. The beep resounded down through the line of waiting customers.

"Is there a problem?"

A broad little man, bald on top, short on the sides, in a uniform matching the clerk's, came up behind Matt. A gun was holstered in his belt, and a lapel badge identified him as the store's owner.

"This gentleman's citizen status says 'Non-resident,' boss," the clerk said, raising her voice to be loud enough for everyone to hear. She peered at Matt.

"I'm sorry, son. We cannot allow you to buy anything here," the owner said.

Matt looked down at his groceries, now piled at the end of the conveyor belt. The cupboards at home were nearly empty.

"None of it? That can't be," he argued, "I live just down the street. And there's plenty of money on my account. I checked yesterday!"

"It's not about the money, son," the owner said. "Go to the community centers and get your groceries from there. They do not allow us to sell to non-residents." He said the last word as if it tasted bad.

"So, I can't get any food now?" Matt said. Looking around at the other customers, he threw his arms out wide. Their eyes were sharp, their faces puckered. Not a glimpse of sympathy anywhere.

"You have to put all this back, or I'm going to have to—"

"Get out of here, *waster*!" someone down the line yelled. Matt turned to see who had said this, but they all looked indistinguishable.

"Listen, son. You're holding us all up, wasting time and resources, so it's the last time I'm going to ask you..."

Matt grabbed his basket and started tossing items back in it. The owner stood and watched him as the clerk motioned the next person up.

Matt trotted down past the line. People turned their heads as he passed, following him with their eyes. He couldn't muster the courage to glance back. Head bowed, he looked at his meager pile of groceries. The food was one thing, but the painkillers for his brother—he wouldn't know where to beg for those. He began his long, slow meander through the aisles.

The silence was eerie. There were other shoppers around, but their noises faded into the background. As he put a gallon of juice back in the cooler, the Muzak, off tune, crept up and down

Matt's spine. The soles of his sneakers squeaked against the polished tiles at the refrigerated displays, stopping at every other cover as he returned yet another microwaveable dish. The faint humming of the electrical circuits grew to a thunderous roar inside his skull.

Above him, surveillance cameras winked in their black domes of glass. There was no way for Matt to know which way they pointed. Maybe they wouldn't notice. Maybe they wouldn't look. He stood in the pharmacy aisle, removed the box of Kevin's painkillers from the basket, and put it back on the shelf. Then with a flicking and flipping of his fingers, a fumbling sleight of hand, he brought them out again, tucking them into his sleeve with his thumb and index finger and shielding them from the nearest camera.

He walked casually to the breads now, holding the basket in his left hand and clutching the package in his right. The thin corners of cardboard carved their way deeper and deeper into the grooves of his palm. Lobbing the sandwich toast back onto its shelf, he spent a little time prodding to get it to look nice. Meanwhile, he brushed his leg, sliding the painkillers into the pocket of his pants. A quick dip with his thumb and Matt was sure the package wasn't sticking up.

And now, the last, irrevocable step awaited.

Walking unnaturally slowly, breathing heavily, and avoiding eye contact with the rest of the shoppers, Matt once more went towards the checkout line. He felt the pack of painkillers pressing against his thigh; its edges were damp with sweat now. He had never given a thought to the president's inauguration speech, but in this moment, Matt understood the protesters. He felt ashamed. Alienated.

We monitor, we analyze, we optimize.

The queue had emptied. There was only the popping sound of bubblegum.

We contribute, we moderate, we separate.

The clerk's head was tilted down towards the magazine in her hands. Her eyes followed him from under thin black eyebrows.

And in technology we shall trust.

"Have a nice day, *sir*," she said as Matt passed.

He nodded. The hairs on his arms vibrated as they stood to attention. A droplet of sweat trickled down his neck. He closed in on the revolving door. Only a few yards to go now. He kept his pace steady, not turning to look behind him, not giving any hints as to what he'd been doing…. And then he was out the door, stepping from the cool, climate-controlled, fluorescent interior of the store into the humid dense summer heat. He could see the last rays of sun dancing through a birch at the opposite side of the road. Exhaling the suffocating staleness cramping his lungs, he heaved great gulps of the fresh, vibrant air.

"You forgot the pills in your pocket, son."

Matt slowly raised his arms. "Easy," he said. He remembered the gun, and that the man had a license to use it.

"Didn't I tell you to put everything back?" the store owner said.

"Please don't shoot," Matt said.

"Then don't try anything stupid. Turn around, and let's go to my office."

■ ■ ■

The light from the table lamp stung his eyes. Like in one of those old movies with interrogations and gruff detectives, it was enough to make Matt squint and avert his gaze.

"What were you doing, son? You don't want this shit on your record. You're too young to get a tag like that," the owner said, parking his body in a chair behind the table between them.

"I didn't know that I was a non-resident—I swear, sir. We're about to lose our apartment on Monday if I don't find a job. I need food and medicine for my family. We're all out," Matt said.

"Why don't you take handouts, then? Why try to steal?"

"I can't. They don't give out painkillers at the centers. Because of the addicts and the homeless." Matt stared at his lap.

"But stealing and getting caught doesn't help your family much, now, does it?" The man lowered the lamp so that Matt could see his face. His pudgy, dewlapped cheeks wobbled every time he opened his mouth.

"Didn't plan on getting caught."

"Don't get cheeky with me, son."

"Sorry, sir. I was out of order." Matt sensed the kind of authoritarian patriarch who demanded respect from anyone younger than himself.

"What's your name, son?" the man said.

"Matt—I mean, Matthew. Turner, sir."

"I'm Hank. Nice to meet you."

"Likewise, I guess."

Hank sized him up. Matt was his near opposite. Tall, broad-shouldered, fit. No slouch, no pear shape.

"You look like a man who could manage hard days of work, Matt," Hank said. "You retarded?"

"What? I beg your pardon?"

"I'm sorry, is that not proper anymore? Listen, I couldn't care less what you young folks think of me. I fought in Iraq. I helped win those last barrels of oil. I earned my place in society. So, excuse my language, but are you incapable of using your brain?"

"No, sir," Matt said.

"Then why don't you have a job?"

"Had one. Lost it because I spoke up."

"Moxie. I like that," Hank said. The word reminded Matt of his father.

Hank adjusted his gut so he could lean forward over the table. "Now listen up, Matt," he said. "I own this store. I fought through and adjusted as the energy crisis hit. So, I would argue that it is safe for me to say that you are stealing from me. And I can't have that, now, can I?"

"No, sir." There was a pause, but Matt was unsure if he needed to respond further. "I apologize," he tried.

"Now, Matt, I've noticed you around my shop. Hauling groceries, always by yourself. You have kids?"

"No, sir. Just me, my mom, and my little brother."

"Ah, family man. I like that, too."

Matt nodded. Hank sat watching him. Matt, unsure whether this was a prompt to talk, decided not to.

"Here's what I'm gonna do, Matt," Hank said at last. "There's a set of dumpsters out back. Plenty of excellent food in those. It's destined for the prisons, feeding the inmates, but I couldn't care less for those pieces of shit. They already blew their chances, but I'd hate to see you do the same. As for the painkillers? I'm gonna buy them for you and your family."

Matt's eyes widened in surprise. "Thank you, sir," he said, too taken aback to come up with anything further.

"Only doing what any decent man would," Hank said gruffly. "Government doesn't allow for much charity anymore, so we owe it to ourselves to help protect our fellow citizens now and again. Now, I can't give you a job, even though I would very much like to. That would mean I'd have to put somebody else on the street, and I'm not going to do that," Hank said. "Need to keep in line with the average number of employees, or we risk the entire business. But I do my fair share of insubordination." He gave Matt a wink. "And hopefully, one day, somebody will get the best of those sleazy fucking politicians."

Matt had to bite back a smile.

"I'm sorry—I'm rambling now. You a politics man, Matt?"

"Can't say that I've ever given it much thought," he replied, but what a lie that was. "I had to drop out of school after my father died to keep the family going," he said, following the lie with a half-truth.

"There are those family values again. When the electricity comes back and the machines take over? That'll be all that's left. Family." Again, Matt was startled by how much Hank sounded like his father.

Hank leaned back, getting comfortable in the flimsy swivel chair. He looked around at the desk, back up to Matt. He sniffed and scratched his nose.

"I don't have any left now. Family, that is. They all left me to rot when push came to shove. My nephew got a fancy new job in government and a home in the streetlights."

"I'm sorry to hear that, sir." Matt kept at the *sirs*. Better to be polite to a man like Hank.

"I tried to call once, but you know how it is. They asked me to come, but I know they didn't want me to. Courtesy, that's what it was. Nothing more. So, I decided not to go." He cleared his throat and changed the subject. "Have you seen the street-lights, Matt?"

"No, sir."

"Well, me neither. Sometimes I doubt they even exist. One of them conspiracy theories I read online. Anyway, I'm sorry. Starting to babble again. Haven't got much company, so it's been nice to have someone to talk to." He got to his feet. "You go fill a couple of bags out back, and I'll fix the medication. You should be able to get home in time before all those homeless people crowd the streets."

"Thank you, sir. I don't know how to repay you, or explain how grateful I am," Matt said.

"You don't have to. And you can call me Hank."

A few minutes later, Matt was on his way home carrying two shopping bags bursting with food and supplies. It should last them until Monday at least. He had already made up his mind not to tell his mother or his brother about the incident at the store. There was no need for them to worry.

06

Matt spent Saturday morning at the park. He liked to go outside whenever the weather allowed. Being crammed inside the walls of the apartment felt gloomy, even in broad daylight. His old boss wasn't in on Saturdays, so there wasn't much to do but wait.

He sat on a bench, looking out over the pond. Often, kids would come by and play with their boats or splash the water with branches from a nearby weeping willow. Sometimes he wondered what it would be like to go back to being a kid. Those had been simpler times, with no real sense of past or future; living in the now. He often wondered what dreams kids longed for these days, and what obstacles life would line up against them. He noticed a little boy in a green shirt with an alligator print. He was playing with a small group of other children who were putting paper boats in the water, dragging them along the bank on strings tied to sticks. The government had prohibited children from playing with digital toys since they used up energy and resources that were better spent on adults, and so simpler toys had made their resurgence.

He watched as the boy lost his grip; the boat drifted to the middle of the pond, its stick out of reach. The boy wept like he was shattered; his father ran to his side but failed to calm him down. When would this kid's father die? Matt wondered. His mother? It was inevitable for the little boy to experience it, unless, of course, he himself should die before his parents did, but Matt wouldn't hope for such an event. So how would he react? Would he be strong, like Matt, take up the fallen torch and shine a light through these times of darkness? Or would he crumple, begging for the world to pull him from the depths of his bottomless sorrow, expecting others to rectify this inevitable wrong? There was no way to know.

The boy stopped crying and ran away across the grass. He began to climb the willow; his father held his breath as the boy went farther and farther up, pushing the limits of his courage. The father was merely a helpless bystander now, hoping his child would be sensible and take a safe path back down the tree. What a sense of wonder, that kid, Matt thought. What a determination to explore, leaving safety behind.

■ ■ ■

The door was ajar when he came back. Kevin was still lying on the couch, where Matt had left him, sifting through massive amounts of college information on their tablet. Matt went into the kitchen. Elizabeth was nowhere in sight; there was no note on the countertop, a spot she often used for messages. Her room was empty, but her clothes lay beside her bed.

"Kev?" Matt said, sticking his head back into the living room. "Have you seen Mom?"

"Isn't she taking a nap?"

"Nope. Have you been out?"

Kevin looked up from the tablet in his lap. "No. Why?" he said.

"The front door was open."

Matt hurried out the door, Kevin following right behind him. They split up and began looking around the building complex, calling out for Elizabeth.

"Anything?" Matt said as they met up again at the main gates.

Kevin shook his head. "Where could she have gone?" he said.

"I don't know. She rarely leaves without telling us. She couldn't have taken the truck. I have the keys in my pocket," Matt said.

They began searching up and down the street.

"The park?" Kevin said.

"I doubt it. I came back from there."

"Should we split up? Look in town?"

"I think so. You take the suburbs, and I'll head downtown," Matt said. "Two hours max, then we convene back here."

I need to keep calm. I need to focus. Don't break down. Don't lose it. It will only worsen the situation.

In times of crisis, feelings were best left at the backseat so that reason could take the wheel; his father had always preached this, and Matt had taken it to heart—even more so now that their family was Matt's responsibility.

It was a bit of a walk to the shopping district. A lot of old businesses stood empty, left in clouds of dust by the churning cogs and roaring engines of the mega-stores at the outskirts of town. There was nobody around; almost no traffic went through these streets anymore. The inefficiency and inaccessibility of the narrow, cobbled lanes had laid them to waste.

Matt roamed alley after alley until a honking horn broke the monotony. Rushing back to the main street, he saw a car in the middle of the road, still honking, and in front of it, his mother. Elizabeth stood oblivious in her pajamas as the car tried to edge around her, her bathrobe wrapped around her shoulders and bedroom slippers on her feet. Matt rushed over, apologized to the driver and laid a hand on his mother's lower back, nudging her forward. Once they'd crossed the street, Elizabeth stopped.

Matt tried to pull her forward again, but her attention was riveted on a display window packed with handcrafted baby dolls. She gazed, spellbound, into a myriad of glass eyes that peered back out. The details were so lifelike, with deliberate tiny imperfections; every iris had its own unique hue; each glass marble held a galaxy of endless depth.

Matt tugged at her robe. "Come on, Mom. We should get you home," he said.

Elizabeth didn't seem to notice, and as he grabbed her arm, she wriggled free.

"It's my second pregnancy," she said.

Matt sighed. "Let's go, Mom. You need to get home and get dressed."

"It's going to be a boy. My firstborn is a boy, too, though he never plays with dolls. This time is going to be different. They told me my two would be nothing alike. But that was the whole point, I guess, and that's why I'm not scared."

Matt stood and looked at his mother as she rambled on.

"Can I help you with something?" An older woman poked her head out of the glass door beside the immense window.

"Oh, no," Matt said. "My mother is just reminiscing, I guess."

"You're welcome to pop in for a cup of tea," the woman said.

"Thanks, but we ought to get home."

"Ah, Matt," Elizabeth said. "Don't they look beautiful?"

The older woman nodded at Matt, gave Elizabeth a curious glance, and closed the door behind her.

Matt looked at the dolls again. They were meticulously made, all with individual details in their anatomy. Different weights, variations on fingers and toes, little nuances in their hand-painted complexions made them all distinct from each other, even though they were all clearly babies.

"I guess so, Mom. Will you come home now?" Matt said.

"All so different, yet all made by the same woman. I want to get one for Kevin. So it's ready when he comes." Elizabeth rubbed her belly. "Which one do you think? We could guess which one he will look like and then get that one?" She giggled a bit.

"But Mom, Kevin is already here."

"I think he will look like that one." She pointed to a red-haired doll in a pair of overalls. "Don't know how much he'll get from me, but I'm so curious, aren't you?" she giggled again.

"Come on, Mom." Matt took her by the hand and pulled her away from the window. This time, she followed.

Halfway home, Elizabeth stopped again. She looked around, then down at her clothes and her slippers, then up at Matt.

"Where are we?" she said. "What am I doing here?"

"You don't remember, Mom?"

"Remember what?"

"How you got here?"

"No. Why am I wearing my nightie?"

"Mom, you're sick. Your memory is failing."

"What? … No." Elizabeth looked at Matt, waiting for him to

speak. He didn't. She looked in confusion at the sidewalk, the cars passing, the trees lining the street and back to Matt.

"How long have I…"

"I don't know, exactly. But it's getting worse now. Progressing fast, they say."

"But what's wrong with me?"

"They don't know for sure. But I'm gonna take care of it, Mom. I'll make sure you get well," Matt said. He put his arms around her and hugged her tightly.

"Matt?" she said, still holding on. "I'm dying, aren't I? Be honest with me."

"Yes, Mom," he whispered in her ear. "You might be."

He felt her clasp tighten, her fingers digging into his back, a little splash as she let a tear fall onto his neck.

"But I won't let that happen, Mom. I'll fight—I'll find a way. I'm not ready to lose you. Kevin isn't ready to lose you." His voice cracked with emotion.

She let go, taking a hand to her eyes, wiping a couple of tears.

"I won't let it happen, Mom," Matt said, as if the words alone could make it true.

"I'm so proud of you, Matt. All that you've done, all that you've given me. I'm so glad that we had you. Your father would be proud."

"Thanks, Mom," Matt said. He was quiet for a moment, thinking. "I'm gonna need your help, Mom."

"Anything."

"I can't have Kevin know. He's not ready for this, and he still has college. I don't want him to falter like I did. It's an enormous opportunity, and we both need to keep him focused. Can you help me with that?"

"Yes, Matt. Whatever you say."

"You can't tell him you're dying, Mom. He won't be able to focus on school, and I can't have that. *We* can't have that. And Dad wouldn't have wanted that. We need to make sure he takes full advantage of this opportunity we helped give him. Honors and all. Can I count on you, Mom?"

"Always, Matt. But is there anything I can do?"

"We have to make up a story about why you wandered off."

Elizabeth nodded, and they began to walk again. As they went, they pitched ideas for a believable story. It was hard, with the pajamas and robe, but finally, they hit on a plausible tale: Elizabeth had spilled her coffee, and with no clean clothes and the household out of detergent, she'd gone shopping. Kevin never did the laundry, so Matt was sure that he wouldn't argue that part. But just to be sure Kevin would buy the story, they agreed to let Elizabeth herself tell the lie: Kevin, always wary of his brother's motives, was less prone to doubt their mother, they agreed.

Back home, Matt made a pot of tea while Elizabeth put on some proper clothes. They were sitting in the living room together when Kevin came through the door. He was overjoyed and almost wept with relief at seeing Elizabeth safe; he told them about his fears of her getting hurt, of his flashes of doubt that he would never see her again. He told them about where he had looked, what he had seen, people he'd asked. It was almost like when he had come home from field trips in elementary school, giddy with excitement, his words tumbling over one another.

Elizabeth eased their made-up story in, weaving it around Kevin's thoughts. Matt sat back in his chair, dropping in an eventual comment about their mother's hazy memory, each time quick to reassure Kevin that this had all been only a minor nuisance and that the problem with her memory would be swiftly resolved once Elizabeth got her treatment. Kevin seemed to buy every single bit they served him.

That evening, Matt stirred a homemade casserole on the stove as they all watched a game show on the tablet. Later, Matt relaxed in his father's old lounger, enjoying the view of his mom and little brother guessing along with the stars on-screen—people from the streetlights, of course. It delighted Matt every time he and his brother outsmarted the celebrities. He felt a sense of belonging and a certainty that their family was destined for a spot under ever-glowing lightbulbs, among equals. He yearned to help Kevin through college, fully expecting his little brother to soar above the competition. He wanted all of them to claim the spot he knew their family deserved. A place among the stars. A place among the streetlights.

07

On Sunday morning, Matt drove off to the community center. He dreaded the place.

After the energy crisis, social service hubs, established by the government, had sprung up across the country. Each served two primary functions: providing necessary housing and administering supplies to people without jobs that benefited society.

The primary goal had tanked years back. None of the buildings had had anywhere near the capacity needed to provide ample beds, and most now functioned as halfway houses, giving people a last shot at an unlikely redemption—that is, until their stay expired and they were turfed out to meet their inevitable demise in the streets. Now, every community center across the country was a sort of hub from which the homeless emanated, attracting criminals and drug dealers preying on the destitute and scattering out into nearby neighborhoods.

The centers' secondary goal had fared a bit better; most of them still provided handouts of food and clothes, donated through charity but controlled through a rigid system of rationing. Non-residents, the official classification for the jobless-turned-homeless, lived beneath the poverty-level calculations instrumented by the government social, healthcare and environmental offices. With food in your stomach, clothes on your back and a roof over your head, the American Dream could still be attained. Or, that's what the politicians kept declaring.

Having worked in one of these centers for a little over a year, however, Matt had never heard of anyone turning their circumstances around once they hit basement level. And as the number of homeless people continued to rise, many radicals had put forth the idea of removing even that meager safety net for good, since so few of these "charity cases" had any hope of paying back their debt to society. It was a waste of funds and resources, they'd insisted. And so, the term *wasters* had been coined.

The center where Matt was headed now was an old hotel, out near a large strip of abandoned offices. Matt parked and started across the parking lot to the front door. Since it was a Sunday morning, the place lay quiet. A couple of rusty oil barrels, used as fire pits by a group of homeless the previous night, were shedding their last columns of smoke. It was still too early for the morning shift to get around to cleaning outside; needles and glass shards littered the ground and a nearby set of public benches.

Inside the building, the marble tiled floor lay almost bare. Excess furniture had long since been removed; a front desk was built from the same immovable marble slabs. A single bell sat on top. Snoring emerged from the dormitories one floor up the spiral staircase to the left.

Ding. Matt laid his hand on the bell to dampen the reverberating echo.

He looked towards the kitchen; there was a smell of frying bacon on the cusp of burning. Bacon was served only on Sundays, he knew, and only if the nearby supermarket donated any outdated cuts.

"Matt? It's been a while. What brings you back?" A man stood in the kitchen door, rubbing a large metal pot with a dishtowel.

"Is he in? I need to talk to him," Matt said.

His former co-worker nodded and pointed up the staircase. "In his office. You know where it is," he said.

Matt went up the stairs and walked down the hall, passing the open door to the dormitory. Most of the residents were still fast asleep. People slept in when they stayed at the community center. The nightly commotion outside made it impossible to shut your eyes before midnight, and by then, most inhabitants were drunk on alcohol brewed from garbage or intoxicated by more potent, more addictive, substances. Also, most people saw no reason to get up.

Matt made his way to the boss's office and stopped in the open door, knocking two times on the frame.

Mr. Sorensen looked up from behind his desk. "Matt! What a surprise. Come on in and have a seat," he said. A former bodybuilder, Mr. Sorensen was still tall and sturdy, although time and desk labor had caught his muscles off guard, adding a few pounds here and there, making his stature more prone to the power of gravity.

Matt sat. "Thanks," he said. "I'm sorry for the way I left last time."

"Don't worry about it, Matt. In my line of work, you get used to the shouting and the names," Mr. Sorensen said. He winked at Matt. "What brings you here?"

"I kind of need to ask you a favor."

"Ah, that sounds interesting. What kind of favor might that be, Matthew Turner?"

"I would like to ask for my old job back," Matt said, tucking his shoulders a bit as if anticipating a blow.

Mr. Sorensen sat back and looked at him for a minute. Then he gave a loud bark of laughter, waking the light sleepers in the room next door. "That's a good one, Matt!" he said, slapping his knees. "I always knew you had a career in comedy bottled up underneath all that Samaritan crap. You doing shows now?"

Matt puckered his lips and sucked up his inner pride. "I know we left things in disagreement and that it was my mistake, and I'm sorry for that. But I want my old job back. I know you could use extra staff, and the center has approval for at least a couple more."

Mr. Sorensen sharpened his eyes.

"Don't make me beg. Please, Mr. Sorensen. I need this. My family needs this," Matt said, hating himself.

"What an excellent idea—making you beg." Mr. Sorensen grinned wolfishly. "You want a job? Fine. You convince me that, deep down in your bones, you know that I'm right and you were wrong. And then, maybe, I'll see if I can find a suitable job for a loudmouth like you."

Mr. Sorensen lifted his chin, tilted his head, and put on a faint, smug smile.

Matt took a deep breath. *Here goes*, he thought. "I was wrong. I was wrong to think I knew more about running this place than you. I was wrong thinking we should break government policy, seeing as we have a valid democratic government of capable politicians. I was wrong thinking there was any way for us to better the future for these people. I'm sorry. I was wrong for … thinking."

Mr. Sorensen put on a more serious face, swung his head from left to right, and waited. Matt clasped his hands underneath the table and ducked his head, avoiding his gaze.

"No."

"No, what?" said Matt.

"I don't believe you."

"But I mean it. I've thought a lot about it, and—" Matt tried to argue.

"No, you haven't. Those were *my* words, *my* phrases—you were just repeating what I said months ago. You need to do better. I want it to come from you. Try again."

Matt pressed his palms against his thighs, channeling all the built-up energy away from an outburst. Inhaled, paused, exhaled. Slumped and then squared his shoulders for round two.

"I shouldn't have distrusted your experience, thinking I would have the answers. It's not for me to decide what's best for these people. I'm sorry, and I was wrong, sir. Please let me show you I've learned my lesson."

"Better. But not enough. Again." Mr. Sorensen sat back, crossing his arms.

"I really need this, sir. I'll do anything. My family is getting evicted. You, of all people, know what that means."

"Again!" Mr. Sorensen hammered a clenched fist onto the table. "With passion!"

Matt felt his calves tighten, his arms squeezing against the sides of his ribcage, holding himself back with every bit of muscle in his body. He closed his eyes, focusing on the outcome, keeping a lid on his simmering pot of cortisol and adrenaline. He opened his eyes and looked up.

"I was wrong not listening to reason," he said, and heard his voice breaking. "For not trusting your guidance, not embracing your infinite wisdom. I was wrong to question researchers, statisticians and scientists far greater and far more knowledgeable than myself, to question the will of the people and the needs of the majority. I was wrong to bring my empathy to a place like this, for not leaving emotion at the door and for thinking of these non-residents, these homeless, these *wasters*, as my equal, for I realize now that they are not."

Matt closed his eyes and kept them shut to stop tears from rolling. There was utter silence in the room. Matt could hear himself swallowing the pool of saliva in his mouth, forcing it down his throat.

"Yes," Mr. Sorensen said. "YES!"

Matt opened his eyes.

"That was exactly what I wanted to hear," Mr. Sorensen said. He started clapping, picking up pace as his hands thundered towards the crescendo of the beat.

Matt felt the ten-ton weights lifted from his shoulders. He straightened up, breathed out as if blowing out a candle. "Thank you, Mr. Sorensen. Thank you! You will not regret it. I will never be out of line, ever again, I promise you. Thank you. I am so grateful—thank you."

Matt looked up at Mr. Sorensen, who wore an expression of surprise on his face.

"I don't think I said anything about you getting your job back, did I?" he said.

"What?"

"I don't think I told you you'd get the job, did I?"

"But you just said—"

"No. I said it was what I wanted to hear," Mr. Sorensen said, waving a finger in the air, "but I didn't say you were even close to convincing. No way was I ever going to believe a word that came out of your mouth. Do you take me for a fool?"

Matt sat squinting at him, shaking his head.

"You see, Matt, you have a problem. Whatever you do, you have an exceptional aversion to authority. And I just can't have that," Mr. Sorensen said.

Something snapped inside Matt's head.

"You are a fucking piece of shit, you know that?" he said through clenched teeth. "They raped that girl, and you blame *me* for wanting to stand up for her? How would you like to see your family raped? How would you like your kids to watch while their mother is being beaten and ravaged, just to make sure she wasn't hiding any drugs from your resident gangs?"

No amount of pressure could keep the lid on his temper now.

"How much are they paying you for not reporting these incidents, you sadistic prick? Are you even bribed, or do you just revel in the misery you think these people brought on themselves? Do you even care for anybody but your own fucking self in this megalomaniac world of yours?"

Mr. Sorensen sat back, a faint smile on his lips. "Are you done?" he said, a smug little smile playing on his lips.

Matt flew off his chair, knocking it backward, and reached out over the table. But Mr. Sorensen was faster: he scooted back in his swivel chair and grabbed a taser from underneath his desk.

"Do you want me to use this?" he said, brandishing it. "Because you know I won't stop when you hit the floor."

Breathing heavily, Matt stopped himself and backed away from the desk. He straightened up, then turned wordlessly and walked to the door. With his hand on the doorknob, he stopped and turned back to Sorensen.

"You have two daughters. How can you do this? I pity you, and I feel so sad for them, having to grow up with a father like you," Matt said.

"Good luck in the actual real world, Matthew Turner," Mr. Sorensen said.

Matt slammed the door behind him and stormed out of the building. Fighting back tears, he made his way to the truck. Matt had always seen himself as a righteous person. Even as a child, he had wanted to stand up, serve the people, be a beacon for his community and be the voice for those who couldn't speak for themselves.

His dad, Jeffrey Turner, had been a contractor. He was successful and well-connected, but still one of the few who cared for every one of his workers. He had always told Matt how he'd cut his own salary when times were tight, and had never fired a worker who was the sole provider for a family. That was just what honest and admirable people did, he had said to Matt: provided the soil for others to grow.

And naturally, Jeffrey's workers had loved him. There had been hundreds of mourners at his funeral, standing in their brown canvas uniforms, holding their J.D. Turner embroidered five-panel caps in front of them as a select few lowered the coffin into the earth. The politicians and management in the front rows had worn their mandatory black suits. But not the workers. They knew better. At the end, when those in the first couple of rows had said their condolences, Matt had noticed the sound of humming from the crowd behind them. They stood as if nailed to the ground, all eyes on the hole in the ground, all humming the same tune. Matt had recognized it from home; he'd heard it before but didn't know the song. That evening he had scoured through his father's old vinyl collection without any luck. The notes were still crystal clear in his memory, but the song's origin was still a mystery.

Now Matt sat in the truck, eyes closed, a flood of tears streaming down his cheeks. He pounded his fists on the steering wheel, screaming at the top of his lungs, his sobs echoing in the old metal chassis. At last, when he could cry no more, he buried his head in his arms, taking long, shaky breaths. He couldn't rid his mind of the image of his little brother in his mother's arms after Jeffrey's funeral, looking so forlorn—and now his responsibility.

Nor could he forget the image of that poor young woman, not a day over twenty, coming up to the front desk of Mr. Sorensen's community center and asking for a room for herself and her children.

Most of all, he couldn't stop hearing himself answering, "Don't worry. We have a nice warm bed for all of you."

08

Matt closed the front door behind him, careful not to make a sound, and leaned against it. After a moment, his legs gave way and he slid down onto his butt on the carpeted hall floor. He sat there, his face buried in his hands, waiting for the swelling around his eyes to diminish, for the redness in his skin to fade.

Five or fifty minutes later, he didn't know which, his mother came through the hallway from the living room, heading towards the kitchen.

"Ah, Matt!" she said, startled. "I didn't hear you come in. Everything all right? Where've you been?"

Matt hadn't told his mother about his plans for the day; he was still not sure how much of the situation she comprehended. He nodded wordlessly, afraid his voice might crack.

Elizabeth continued on to the kitchen. "I'm heating some water for tea," she called. "Would you like a cup? Or maybe coffee?"

Matt cleared his throat. "No, Mom. I'm fine, thanks."

He stood up and went to look in the bathroom mirror. He could still see signs that he'd been crying, but he wasn't sure that

Kevin would notice. He went to his brother's door and knocked. Matt heard the muffled acknowledgment from inside the bedroom and opened the door.

Kevin sat at his desk, back turned, swiping away at their tablet. "How did it go?" he asked, without turning around.

Matt went over and stood behind his brother. The screen showed pictures of a high-end university campus. "You finding something you like?" Matt said.

"Well, some of it is all right, I guess."

"Let me know if you need any help choosing. I would love to sift through courses with you, you know, right?"

"Yeah, I know." Kevin didn't look up.

Matt went over to his brother's bookcase and began glancing over the spines of the books. There were surprisingly few books on the shelves, graphic novels mostly. All of Kevin's schoolbooks were stored on that tablet he was sitting with.

There was a little toy crocodile on the top shelf, only the snout sticking out. Matt had found it in a thrift shop many years ago, buried in a bunch of cheap plastic animals. All of them had been brightly colored, but not this one. This one had been different, he remembered, which was why the little croc had stood out. Painted in muted, non-glossy hues, it had looked like the real thing. He could still feel its sturdiness in his empty hands; it was solid, not hollow like the rest of the toy animals. The little crocodile had had weight. Gravitas. A small text imprint on the belly had indicated it was produced and hand-painted in Germany. Matt had bought it for Kevin for his birthday. He'd turned three that year, Matt recalled—just a toddler. His brother had been thrilled. The little crocodile had instantly become his absolute favorite, and over time it had stayed in his collection, withstanding "shiny new toys syndrome," the tendency to be misplaced under furniture, and playground sandbox accidents. Not a lot of Kevin's toys had survived these episodes over the years, but the little crocodile had persisted. Kevin had even selected it for his first show and tell at school. But now it sat on his shelf, collecting cobwebs and dust.

"So, are you gonna tell me how it went?" Kevin said.

Matt turned around. His brother hadn't moved an inch, still sifting through course material, not looking up from his desk.

"It didn't go well," Matt said.

Kevin still didn't move. Matt didn't know how to proceed.

"So, what now?" Kevin said after a minute of silence.

"I don't know. Guess we might have to pack."

"So we're gonna leave?"

"I don't know. I can't see a way around it."

"I can."

"What do you mean? I don't think we have much choice here."

"You do."

Kevin still hadn't looked at him. Matt went over and stood beside him, trying and failing to catch his brother's eye.

"How?"

"Didn't you talk about some government work? A way for me and Mom to stay? I could take care of Mom, and in a year or so, you would come back," Kevin said.

"Oh, that. Yes, I checked up on that…" The phrase had been remolded many times in his head in the truck at the parking lot, on the drive back, at the curbside before he got out. "…and it turns out it's not an option anymore. They pulled the offer. Something about me not being eligible anymore." No matter what, Matt couldn't let his brother bear the burden that had been bestowed upon him, Matt, as the eldest. It would shatter any hope of a bright future for Kevin.

"It's *you*, isn't it?" Kevin said. "*You* don't wanna take that job, so Mom and I just have to follow whatever you decide, huh? Is that it?" His voice was hard.

"No, Kev, it's not like that. I told you I'm not eligible, so… Mom's sick, and I need to take her to the Central Grid Hospital so she can get better. And then, when she gets treatment, I'll find a job and a place for us to stay. So you can focus on your education."

"Yeah, whatever," Kevin said sulkily.

"It's not what I want, okay? It's what's best for us, for our family. Dad would have wanted me to take care of you two."

"Yeah, fine, Matt. Whatever you say."

Matt could feel his temper rising. "Are you even gonna look at me?"

Kevin sat with his head down, swiping, ignoring him.

"Fine. Well, you'd better pack, 'cause I want us out before dark," Matt said. Shaking his head, he went out of the room and closed the door behind him.

Elizabeth was still in the kitchen, standing and looking out the window. The last remnants of steam from the kettle had fogged up the glass. The little indicator read "full." There was an open box of tea bags on the counter, and a few tea bags lay next to it.

"What are you doing, Mom?" Matt said.

Elizabeth looked up, startled. "Matt? I—I was about to make tea," she said.

"Well, that was five minutes ago. Let me help. Which one do you want?"

"I—I don't know." She looked at the tea bags, flustered, lifting them one by one between her fingers and examining them. "I'm not sure I even like any of these."

"You like them all, Mom. You picked them, so don't sweat it. Just take one. How about peach?"

"Okay, sure. I guess I like that one."

Matt reboiled the water, made his mother a cup of tea, and handed it to her.

"Mom, we're gonna have to pack up. Move for a little while," he said.

"Where to?"

"I don't know yet. I'm hoping Stephanie will take us in for the night. I don't want another run-in with the police. And then we'll head for 0-1."

"Okay, Matt, if you think it's for the best."

"I think it is. Can you pack yourself? I'll come check on you once in a while and help if you need it."

"I think so."

"Thanks, Mom. For making it easy. I'm…" He swallowed. "I'm really sorry we can't hang on to the apartment, but I—"

"It's fine, Matt. You do what you think is best. Follow your gut. And I trust you. Dad did too. We all do."

Matt smiled.

"I like this tea. Is it a new flavor?" Elizabeth asked.

Matt stroked her back and guided her to her room, where he made sure she started packing. Then he went through the apartment and picked up the things he knew meant a lot to her, stashing them in his own bag so she would not forget them herself. Next, he packed the framed pictures, some old ceramics from his grandmother, and his mother's favorite reading lamp, padding them with his clothes so they wouldn't break. He filled bags and boxes with what he could—what he thought they might need and what he loved the most. It would have to do.

He went to check on Kevin and found him sitting in front of a duffle bag filled with clothes. Kevin looked up at him with disappointment in his eyes. The look seemed to encapsulate everything Matt hated about himself, his deepest fears of inadequacy.

"I'm sorry, Kev. I tried."

"Yeah, I know."

He stood in the doorway for a moment. Kevin's face was tilted down almost level with the floor, but Matt could make out a few tears on his cheeks.

"Hey, would you mind helping me with a thing?" Matt said.

There was a soft sniffing as Kevin dried his eyes. His brother looked up and nodded.

"I wanna bring Dad's old armchair, and I can't get it onto the bed of the pickup myself. I would love it if you could lend me a hand."

"Why do you want to take that? It's almost falling apart in the living room as it is," Kevin said.

"Yeah, I know. But it's the only thing I have left from him."

"Sure, then. Let's do it."

They hauled the dusty old chair out the door, bumping walls and doorframes on the way. It was one heavy beast. It contained a sturdy walnut frame, upon which the dark green upholstered cushions rested, and those spongy kinds of springs that made it complicated to get up from once you fell for its ragged charms. The brothers struggled to get it to the curb, but once there, the last lift and tilt went easily. They stood and stared up at it in awe as if they had just fought a three-hundred-pound sloth.

"So we're just gonna drive round, with this thing blocking the mirror, till we find somewhere permanent to stay?" Kevin said.

"Guess so. To be honest, I haven't thought it through. But I just know I don't wanna leave it behind," Matt said.

"It'll soak up a small bathtub's worth of water if it rains. Hey, it could double as our shower till we find a place. Splash about in it, and all's good." Kevin grinned.

Matt shook his head and grinned back. "I'll try to find a tarp," he said.

Kevin patted his back, laughed and went back to the apartment. Matt opened the door of the truck and began to search behind and under the seats. He had collected odd pieces of auto and outdoor equipment for years. You never knew when a time of need might come around. But, time being the enemy of order and the purveyor of chaos, the backseat was now a veritable scrapyard of bits and pieces. Matt gamely rummaged through it and, sure enough, there was a tarp. He stretched it out; there were only a few holes. It would have to do. He secured it over the massive armchair and then went back inside the apartment.

Next, Matt opened all the cabinets in the kitchen and pulled out all the cans and dry goods; he looked sadly at the little mound. It wasn't much of a supply. Their meals over the weekend had made a large dent in the bags of groceries he'd brought back from the supermarket.

■ ■ ■

When Matt finally turned the key in the old truck's ignition a few hours later, the sun was setting, its last rays beaming through the windshield. Kevin was in the passenger seat beside him, and Elizabeth in a space Matt had made for her in the crowded back seat. She hadn't seemed too distant when they'd packed, so Matt hoped Kevin wouldn't notice anything different.

"So, where're we going?" Kevin said after they'd been driving for a couple of minutes.

"Stephanie's. I hope she'll take us in for the night."

"What—Stephanie Mills? Hmm." He was quiet for a moment. "Don't you think her husband will mind?"

"I hope not, but to be honest, I don't know. I haven't seen her for a year or so."

"At your high school reunion?"

"You remember that?"

"I remember she stayed the night."

"Nothing happened," Matt said.

"Didn't say anything did. But didn't you say she got an earful for that little stunt?"

"Yeah, she wrote me an email about what her husband said. He was none too pleased."

A minute went by.

"So do they know we're coming?"

"No. I kind of hope it will be harder to turn us down if we just show up at her doorstep."

"I sure hope you're right," Kevin said.

09

Let it be her. Please, let it be her.

Matt stood on the doorstep, his heart in his throat, pressing the buzzer. Stephanie Mills had been his high school sweetheart. They had stuck through senior year together, but then she had started college, and he'd begun taking care of his mother and little brother, and they had drifted apart.

She'd found herself a nice, educated husband and lived in a three-bedroom house on a calm street on the other side of town. They had a daughter, he knew. Stephanie was a stay-at-home mom, but he couldn't remember what the husband did for work. Something in pharmaceuticals, perhaps, or energy. They certainly had lots of money, by the look of it.

Kevin had been correct; Matt had last seen Stephanie at the reunion about a year ago. They'd fooled around a bit, kissing in the hallways like old times, but when Stephanie had pressed him to go further, Matt had held back, not wanting her to do something she'd regret. She had been very drunk, and he didn't want to take advantage of that. She had been sad, angry too, so he had agreed to let her spend the night. They'd cuddled up in his bed together, spooning until they were both asleep. The next morning, she had seemed ashamed and had left quickly with little talk.

He pressed the buzzer once again and looked back at the parked truck where his mother and brother sat waiting. The door opened, and Stephanie stood there with a baby on her arm.

"Hi, Steph," he said, and tried on a smile.

"What are *you* doing here?" She didn't return the expression.

He looked at the baby. "Wow, congratulations! I didn't know you guys were in for one more."

"Yeah, well, that's what happens in a marriage, you know," she snapped at him.

"Sorry." He looked at his feet and then back up at her.

She stared at him. "So?"

"Oh, I—we lost the apartment. And my mom's sick."

She looked past him, out at the truck. "How bad is it?" she said.

"We'll make it," Matt said with a bravery he did not feel. "We've been to the doctor, but my mom can't work now. That's why they kicked us out."

"Because you went to the doctor?"

"No, because she lost her job."

"So go to the community centers. That's what other homeless people do."

"Mommy, who is it?" Matt heard a young child call from inside the house.

"Nobody. Just some salesperson," Stephanie yelled back.

"We can't—won't," said Matt, returning to Stephanie's question. "She might have a seizure. It's not a place for her. And I don't want Kevin to know how bad it is. He's off to college after summer, so I don't want him to worry."

"You brought him too?" Stephanie said incredulously, peering over his shoulder once more.

"Yeah—didn't you hear me? We lost our home." Matt tried to keep his voice polite, but he could feel his blood pressure rising. Was she completely stupid?

"Mm-hmm," she said, distracted. "Well, I guess you can stay the night. Robert's away on a seminar; shouldn't be back till tomorrow. I'm about to tuck Cindy in, so I need you to pull up to the garage. I'll open it and you can go inside and wait." She leaned closer and lowered her voice. "Do you understand? I don't want Cindy to find out, so just stay there till I come to get you. And be quick—I don't want *them* to notice." She glanced uneasily around at the neighboring houses.

"Thank you, Steph. We... I didn't know where else to go."

Without another word, she closed the door in his face.

He hurried back to the truck and pulled into the driveway of the huge house. The garage door opened, and he pulled in and shut off the engine. The door trundled closed again behind them.

Everything was quiet for about half an hour, and then Stephanie opened the door leading into the house.

"You must be quiet," she told them as they filed in. "Cindy's sleeping now, and the little one too," she said. "Please, come in."

"Hey, thanks again, Steph," Matt said.

Ignoring him, she pointed towards the living room. "You can all sleep in here," she said. "I'll lay out some mattresses and bring you some blankets. You might have to squeeze in a bit. There's room on the couch if one of you wants to curl up there."

It was a while since Matt had been in someone else's living

room. It was like another world. Well kept, no torn wallpaper, no spots on the floor. Pictures of family, he guessed, on a make-believe mantelpiece. He walked over and glanced at the one from Stephanie's wedding. Robert, her husband, was broad and muscular, a whole head taller than Stephanie. He sported a well-kept mustache. Matt couldn't muster a mustache. He'd tried for a beard once, but it had quickly become ragged. Now, he settled for stubble.

"You have a minute?" Stephanie said to him, nodding to the kitchen.

"Yeah, sure. I was just—he looks nice, your husband," Matt said, following her. "Have I mentioned this means the world to me?"

She drew the thick curtains before she snapped her fingers and flicked on the light. Then she turned towards Matt.

"Multiple times. Do you have any idea of the risk I'm taking?" Stephanie said.

"I'm sorry. I thought he was out of town…?"

"No, not him. I can handle him—that's not my point. I mean the government. You're classified as non-residents, right? They threw you out of your house?"

"Yeah, I know, but so what?"

"Non-re-si-dents," she said, as though speaking to a dimwit. "Don't you know what that means? It's illegal to house or feed you. They call it 'unregistered charity.'"

"What? Why? I didn't think it was downright illegal for citizens to help each other. Friends and family…" He trailed off unhappily.

"Yeah, but it is. A guest speaker told us all about it at a fundraiser I attended with Rob once."

"Fuck."

"You can stay the night, but I want you out at dawn. I just … can't run the risk. They might scan for spikes in the electricity and water usage, so don't spend any. Do you understand me? And stay away from the windows. Neighbors around these parts would do anything for a rise in status—including reporting one of their own."

Jesus, Matt thought. "No, it's fine. I understand. We need to head off to 0-1 tomorrow, so we'll leave bright and early. I just didn't want to be on the road in the dark."

Stephanie nodded. "Still having trouble with that?"

Matt nodded.

"Well, for now, you're safe. There's a beer in the fridge if you want one," Stephanie said. She yawned. "I need to get some sleep; the little guy'll need me in a few hours. I'll wake you in the morning."

"Not much rest for the milk lady, huh?" Matt smiled.

Stephanie shook her head and left him in the kitchen.

⁜ ⁜ ⁜

Matt didn't notice Stephanie returning to the kitchen. He'd lost track of time but knew he was on his third beer. After the first one he'd tried to sleep, but had ended up tossing and turning. So he'd tiptoed back to the kitchen, leaving Kevin and Elizabeth sound asleep.

"Don't you think you should get some rest?" Stephanie said.

Matt glanced over his shoulder at her. "Oh, I didn't hear you. Have you been there long?" he said. His eyes felt bloodshot; he knew she'd notice.

She was bouncing the baby on one arm, patting its back with the other.

"Only for a moment or two." She looked at the bottles on the table. "Three beers, eh? I meant to grab *one* on me, but sure. Help yourself."

"Sorry. I can pay you if it's a problem."

"Don't—Ah, there it is," she said, as the baby burped.

Stephanie was smiling now. It was the first time he'd seen her smile since they got there. She sat down next to him, nestled the baby, and started rocking him back and forth. Matt studied the small slivers of his eyes. They were still dark, with no hint of color yet.

"Boy or girl?"

"Boy."

Matt waved a finger in front of the tiny face and watched as the baby followed.

"How old is he?" he said. Hypnotized by his effort, he gave the baby a gentle tickle.

"Only a couple of months," Stephanie said. "We haven't decided on a name yet, but I'm considering Jeffrey."

Matt looked up at her. "That was my father's name," he said.

"I know, but I really like it, and Rob is almost on board. So, unless it's awkward for you or something…?"

"No, no. Why would it be? It's your boy; you should decide. And besides, I'm proud of my father."

They sat there and watched the little hand trying to grab hold of Matt's finger.

"Two months…" he said. *Oh no.* By his on-the-fly math, the baby would have been conceived around the time of the reunion. He looked in panic at Stephanie.

She smiled and shook her head. "Don't worry. I didn't jump you while you slept." She laughed. "Besides, we had help with this one," she said.

"Sorry, I just—had to know."

"You had your chance, and you blew it." Her voice was suddenly hard.

"What do you mean?"

"You left me hanging, Matt. I was ready to marry you after college, to start a family. I waited years for you, and when I came back, you didn't even fucking call me. Not once. That's on you," she said. She gave him a weak, quirky smile, the same one he'd fallen for so many years ago.

"I thought that—you know, you'd moved on," he said.

She laughed. "I sure have now."

They sat looking at the baby again. This time, she broke the silence.

"So are you gonna tell me what's wrong, why you're still awake?"

"My mom is dying, Stephanie. Alzheimer's, or so the doctor thinks. She has a month at most, he said."

"But isn't Alzheimer's slow to progress?"

"Yes, but she has some progressive form of it. I don't know. The doctor said there's treatment available for her at the Central Grid Hospital in 0-1. That's why we have to go. Kevin doesn't know she's dying," Matt added.

"He's not a kid anymore, Matt. Don't you think he can handle it?"

"He's not much older than I was when our dad died."

"I know, but still?"

"I never told anybody. You remember that final exam? The one I ran from?"

"Sure. Remember we begged the supervisors to let the papers you left behind be submitted for evaluation. I think that might be the reason that you even got to graduate at all, after that stunt." Stephanie laughed a bit nervously.

Matt looked down. "There was a question about the streetlights being shut off. Something about the date, I think. And I just kept seeing him."

Stephanie was silent now.

"I was responsible," Matt continued. "It was me. I made him stop at that traffic light. It was pitch black. They never saw us. If I had just—"

"No Matt, stop!" Stephanie raised her voice. "Don't go there. Don't do this to yourself. It was an accident, and you know it. Don't blame yourself. You were just a kid."

"I'm just so scared that if Mom dies, it'll stick with him forever. Force him to quit. Force him to buckle. I just want him to get the education he deserves. I owe our father that, at least. He fought so hard for us to get somewhere, and then I failed him."

"Hey, your life's not over," Stephanie said. "There's still plenty of future left for you."

"And now this…" Matthew trailed off. "Like I said, we lost the apartment. And yesterday I went to get groceries and they refused to let me shop. Not till I get a job or otherwise start contributing. And then we can apply for subsidized housing again," he said.

"Isn't there any way that you could get your own home?"

"Most non-experienced, let alone non-educated, people can't hope to make that kind of money," Matt reminded her. "So it's up to Kevin to help us shed this legacy after he finishes college. That's why his education is so important: with an education, he can get a decent job and break the cycle we're all stuck in. And then, who knows? With any luck, he might get a place for all of us." He leaned on the table and put his head in his hands.

Stephanie tried to catch Matt's eye. "Hey, you," she said, lifting his chin. "You will be fine. I know. You persevere. That's just who you are, Matt. Always have been." She smiled at him.

He lifted the corner of his mouth. "I just hope my mom will make it," he said.

"I'm sure she will. She's a strong woman."

"She has to. *I* have to."

They were quiet again for a few moments.

"You want to hold him?" Stephanie nodded down at the baby.

"Well, I…Sure. If it's okay?" Matt said.

"I want you to."

She handed the cloth-wrapped bundle over.

He cradled the dozing baby in his arms and looked down at the tiny face.

"So peaceful," he said.

"For now." Grinning, Stephanie stretched her arms, straightening her back. "I had become reconciled to having just one child, our Cindy, so you can imagine the surprise."

"Didn't you say you got help … uh… conceiving him?"

"We did, for years. Just didn't seem to help. But I guess a miracle came along," she said, beaming. "And I'm pretty glad he did."

"I remember sitting with Kevin like this, the night my father died. My mom and I both wept like crazy, but the little guy stayed fast asleep. So quiet. So peaceful."

Stephanie looked at him as he studied the little boy. A single tear ran down his cheek, and she reached over and wiped it away with her hand.

"Go sleep. You're gonna need it," Stephanie said.

Matt nodded and handed the sleeping baby back to her. They both stood up. He hugged her, and she did the best she could with her one free arm.

"Let me know how it goes." She tightened her grip on him for a second before letting go, then went quietly out of the kitchen.

Matt went into the living room and settled on the couch. His mother and Kevin were both asleep on the floor, rolled up in blankets on the mattresses.

As exhaustion claimed him, Matt looked over at his little brother. Sound asleep. Peaceful.

■ ■ ■

Matt's eyes flew open. Stephanie was shaking him.

"Get up, get up!" she hissed frantically. "You've got to get out of here! Rob's coming home!"

"What? Why?" Matt mumbled, rubbing his eyes.

"He got an early flight. I saw the text on our tablet when I got up to feed Jeff. He'll kill me if he finds out you're here," she said, panic radiating from her eyes.

Matt jumped up and quickly dressed. "Didn't you say you could handle him?" he whispered.

"Not if he finds it's *you*! Do you have any idea how much he hates you? He knows about the reunion—he still even suspects you're Jeffrey's father, despite the DNA tests and all."

"Shit. I'm sorry—"

"No time for that. Help the other two get packed and go. Please."

Matt hastily woke Kevin and Elizabeth and waited impatiently as they threw their clothes on. Still drowsy, Matt herded them out to the pickup and cranked the engine. Stephanie curled open the garage door, and Matt drove out onto the pitch-black street. Before they'd gone two hundred yards down the road, an oncoming car drove past them. It was the only car they saw as they headed out of town.

10

At last, they were on the interstate, and Matt felt himself relax a little. Most of the other cars and trucks sped by him, all automated and driverless. They could go much faster, since their positioning systems helped them avoid accidents. Now speed limits were fluid, set on a car-to-car basis. The government scientists programmed all new cars to go at speeds where their engines were most cost-efficient, keeping energy consumption to a minimum. Cars with outdated systems, and the few still driven by actual human beings, had to go much slower, and they couldn't use all the lanes available. The statistics showed reliability in programs and algorithms, and so the government trusted in those.

Matt looked at his watch. They should be in WDC-0-1 by sunrise. He was always on edge, driving in the dark. Kevin, by his side, was making peanut butter and jelly sandwiches from the last of their bread. He handed Matt the first.

"Thanks," Matt said, taking a big bite.

"Breakfast of champions," Kevin said. "I remember you making them when I was little, and then teaching me how to do it when

I got older. Guess you grew tired of me dragging you out of bed on the weekends to make me a sandwich."

"Yeah, that was a fucking pain. Also, Dad taught me, so it only seemed fitting to pass down the recipe."

Kevin laughed. "Family secret. I'm honored."

Matt smiled but kept his eyes on the road. Once in a while, headlights appeared in the rear-view and quickly passed them, leaving red dots on the horizon. Driverless upon driverless, effortlessly moving at top speed in the pitch-black darkness, more aware of their surroundings than humans could ever be. All locked onto the same grid, the same tracking system, the same network of information. Saving lives.

The car industry had run aggressive marketing campaigns promoting driverless vehicles after surveys had demonstrated their exceptional safety. Within a year, the roads had changed. There were only a few true drivers left, like Matt, and most of them stayed clear of the pitch-black roads during nighttime.

Matt wanted a driverless car for the family, but the prices were too high. And he'd never come close to a job that included one as a benefit.

"One more?" Kevin said, his knife poised over the peanut butter jar.

"Sure. But go easy on the jelly this time."

"Will do."

Kevin spread the jam thinly and handed over the sandwich to his brother. "Do you miss him?"

"Who, Dad?"

"Mmm," Kevin mumbled over a bite of sandwich.

"Haven't been thinking about him that much lately."

"Not with Mom getting ill and everything?"

"What do you mean? It's not like she's dying."

Kevin glanced at him, but Matt kept his eyes front and center.

"I don't recall him at all," Kevin said after a moment. "I kind of hoped I would."

"Of course not. You were only a couple of months old when he died."

"Yeah, I know, but I hoped for something in here." Kevin tapped his temple. "A hazy image or something. But it's only you."

Matt gave him a thin-lipped smile. "Sorry about that."

"Don't be. Nothing you can do about it."

"No. I know," Matt said.

There was a long pause. Matt was holding his breath, hoping his brother wouldn't press the topic any further. His mouth felt dry.

"What happened that night?" Kevin said.

"Could you hand me the water?" Matt said, stalling for time.

"The car accident. You were there. Mom won't tell me anything. She says it's for you to share, in your own time."

Matt took a gulp from the bottle and kept looking straight out the windshield.

"I'm your brother," Kevin said. "You can tell me stuff, you know."

Matt busily checked his mirrors, looking for something to distract him.

"I'm worried, Matt. About you, about Mom. About us."

"Listen." Matt took a deep breath. "Dad died in a car accident. It happened at night, just after they shut the streetlights off. We were driving home from a movie theater, through the woods—you know, to avoid the highway. Cinemas were about to go bankrupt, and I remember begging him to go before they vanished for good. I can't even remember what we saw, though. Not sure it was age appropriate either, since it was late evening."

Matt looked over at his brother, who was watching him, spellbound. He turned his head forward again.

"And I had to pee," Matt said.

The breaks between the sentences were getting longer.

"So we stopped. At an intersection."

A car passed them, leaving them only taillights.

"One day prior, the lights would have been on. Guess they never saw our truck." He cleared his throat, willing his voice not to break.

"It's okay. You don't have to," Kevin said. "I'm sorry."

Matt took a shaky breath, what felt like the first in minutes. The two brothers sat in silence for a long while, each lost in thought.

Finally, Kevin stopped his questioning, and so Matt loosened up. "Please don't worry about Mom, okay?" He reached over and quickly squeezed Kevin's hand. "She might be sick, but she will be fine. I promise. I'll make sure. So don't worry about that, okay?"

"If you say so. But thanks for telling me, Matt. About that, and about … Dad. It means a lot, you know? To me."

"You're welcome, Kev. It's hard for me to talk about it. And I didn't want to put, well, those awful images in your head. Of the accident, I mean."

"Don't worry. You didn't. It's better for me to know. And Matt?"

"Hm?" Matt looked at Kevin out of the corner of his eye.

"All my images of a dad are of you."

Matt reached over and ruffled Kevin's hair. The brothers sat together in the dark, only the lights from the dashboard illuminating their silent faces.

"We need something to lighten the mood," Matt said. "Hey, you know what?"

Kevin shook his head.

"When we were at Stephanie's and I saw that baby, I thought for a moment that I'd become a father myself."

"You shitting me?"

"Nope. He wasn't mine, of course. But the timing was right – with the reunion and all. I didn't recall having sex with her that night, but you know…" Matt lowered his voice and leaned in so Elizabeth, still asleep behind them, wouldn't hear it by chance. "She was so fucking horny I was afraid she'd done something when I slept." He laughed softly.

"She was, huh?"

"Yeah, and the timeline seemed to fit, so I thought, 'Shit, what if?'"

"Crazy." Kevin looked out the window.

"Yeah, I know, right?" Matt said. "Anyway, have you figured out which college you want to apply for?"

"Huh? Oh, no. Not yet. I mean, they all seem great. It's just—I don't know."

"So have you thought about what courses you want to focus on? What you want to become?"

Kevin straightened up in his seat and kept looking out the window. "Well, I don't know."

"I remember I wanted to study somewhere with a strong program in political sciences, or maybe social sciences. It's so fascinating to me. How about you, Kev? You like biology, don't you?"

"Yeah, maybe."

"I might even pick up some community classes when all this is over. When Mom's better and you're off on your own," Matt said.

"What made you decide not to go in the first place?" Kevin said.

"Well, in my time, you had to apply before the school year ended. And so I did," Matt said, keeping the age-old fabrication alive. "But you know I couldn't leave my family. So I decided to postpone it."

"But weren't you afraid Mom would get upset? That you didn't pursue an education?"

"Yes, of course. I spent days agonizing over how to tell her. In the end, I just blurted it out, I think. And she was fine. It was my choice, she said. And, of course, we both had you in mind."

"What do you mean? Mom could have taken care of me. I wasn't that much of a hassle," Kevin said, grinning.

"No, no, but you know, it's good for a kid to have a father, and with ours gone, I wanted to help. Be there for you."

"How did it feel?"

"I dunno. It felt good, I guess."

"No, how did it feel to put your dreams aside?"

"Oh, I didn't do that at all," Matt said. "I can still pick up my dreams where I left off."

Kevin looked down at his lap, rubbing his hands.

"You shouldn't. Ever. Let go of a dream, I mean," Matt continued.

"But what if you're afraid of not living up to others' expectations?"

"Don't worry about them. If *you* feel some road is calling to you, it's your obligation to yourself to pursue it. And besides, I don't think Mom cares what courses you end up taking. I'm sure she's just proud to see her son off to college. We both are."

Kevin glanced out the passenger side window again, then turned towards Matt. "Thanks," he said.

"You're welcome, Kev. Anytime. And let me know if you want help sorting through all that college information. I love looking at course descriptions," Matt said. That part was true, and he also loved having his little brother ask him for guidance. That was, after all, one reason he stayed.

Behind them, Elizabeth started grunting a bit.

Kevin grabbed a water bottle. Matt held out his hand and Kevin passed it to him.

"You awake, Mom? You want some water?" Matt said, holding the bottle in the gap between the seats.

There was no answer aside from muffled sounds of discomfort.

Matt took a peek back at Elizabeth through the rear-view mirror. "Mom, are you okay?"

"She's drooling," Kevin said, turning to the backseat, having a closer look. "Looks like she's still sleeping, too."

"Can you crawl back there, check if she's okay?"

Kevin unbuckled himself and edged between the seats. He patted her shoulder and looked at her eyes. Then he shook her by the shoulders.

Suddenly, Elizabeth vomited all over the back of the passenger seat in front of her. Kevin jerked aside to avoid being sprayed.

Matt swerved but kept a firm grip on the steering wheel; nearby driverless cars, sensing the erratic motion of his vehicle, honked for attention.

"What the fuck!" Kevin shouted, wiping a speck of vomit off his sleeve.

Elizabeth threw up once more, this time down the front of her jacket.

"What's happening?" Matt squinted at them in the rear-view mirror, keeping his head facing forward.

"What do you think?" Kevin yelled.

"I'm pulling over, just—hold on a bit. Is she awake?"

"I'm not sure. Her eyes are closed."

"Keep her steady! Here, grab a bag!" Matt reached into the glove compartment, yanked out a plastic bag and handed it back to his brother.

"She keeps on coughing and drooling," Kevin said.

"I can't go any slower, Kev. It's the interstate. Just hold the bag under her mouth," Matt said.

"She's gone very pale, Matt. I'm not sure about this."

"So did you, last time you puked. I can't stop here—it's the fucking interstate! It's probably motion sickness. Can you get her steady and lay her down? There's an exit coming up," Matt said.

He pulled the truck into the exit lane, left the interstate and turned at a roundabout.

The secondary roads were in terrible shape, lumpy with cracks and potholes.

Kevin held Elizabeth upright, with her head down and the plastic bag between her legs, but the steady progression of potholes made it a challenge. "Pull over!"

"I can't. Not yet—I just need to get down this hill. The parking brake's all fucked, and I don't know where my metal rod is."

Finally, Matt pulled onto a broad shoulder at the lower end of a long slope and engaged the flashers. Checking for bypassing cars, he jumped out and yanked open the rear passenger door. Elizabeth toppled partway out onto him.

"I can't hold her like this," Kevin said from the middle seat, clutching at their mother's torso.

"Let me get a grip," Matt said, reaching around her. "Got her."

Kevin got out the other side and helped lower Elizabeth down to the ground. Once she was lying on her side, she seemed to settle down.

Matt looked around him. They were in energy country now. Solar panels covered the fields bordering the highway. Row after row, stretching their black, semi-reflective leaves, pivoting towards the sun, conducting billions of watts into the gigantic power plants; each one measuring, analyzing and redistributing its precious load of electricity, depending on changes in the weather, so that the vital government and grid functions across the country always got priority.

After the big oil scandal, the government's first move had not been towards renewables. The promises and potential of nuclear energy had been too great to pass up. But after the first terrorist attacks against two facilities in Texas, which had laid waste to the entire southern region and killed millions of people, it had become clear that nuclear energy was, literally, a ticking time bomb. It took only one lone wolf to set the world aflame. Public pressure had forced plants to close all over the nation. Despite the scientists' best efforts to promote nuclear energy as a renewable alternative, a series of deadly accidents and attacks had resulted in a complete ban on atomic energy and cemented the victory for green power.

After Matt's father had died and energy farming had become the number one industry, J.D. Turner, Ltd. had expanded into windmills, reinventing itself as JDT Energy. It had been like another gold rush at first, but it soon became clear that businesses had underestimated the unpredictability of Mother Nature. With no way to compete, small companies had been outpaced by huge tech conglomerates with powerful algorithms and intricate machine learning based on thousands of data models; bit by bit, these behemoths had swallowed market shares. Most of the smaller operations, including JDT Energy, had succumbed to bankruptcy.

And for Matt, Kevin and Elizabeth Turner, all assets and shares left to them by Jeffrey had evaporated into the wind that had been meant to save them.

Matt leaned into the backseat and tried to clean it as best he could with a dried-out pack of baby wipes.

On the ground behind him, Elizabeth started mumbling. He turned as she opened her eyes and started coughing a bit. A few rivulets of saliva ran out her mouth.

"You there, Mom?" Kevin said. "Here, have some water." He leaned over her with the bottle.

Elizabeth tried to get some words out, but they all seemed to meld together.

"Just drink, Mom," Matt said.

She sat up and took a sip. Then she took a large mouthful, gargled it a bit, and spat it onto the dirt shoulder.

"I'm dizzy. I'm sorry," she tried again.

"Don't be," Matt said. "How are you holding up?"

She didn't answer him.

"I saw a sign. There should be a diner up ahead," Kevin said to Matt.

"No, we have to get going. You up for that, Mom?" Matt gently shook her shoulder. "You can drink a bit more water if you need to, but we have to get moving."

"All right," she said, coughing into a tissue.

"Can't we wait? See if she gets worse?" Kevin said.

"No, I'll take it as easy as I can. Just nausea or something. She'll be fine. Won't you, Mom?" Matt said.

"It's better now, I guess," Elizabeth said weakly.

"There, see? It's gonna be just fine. Let's get you back in the truck."

Matt helped Elizabeth back onto her feet, and then he froze. There was a blotch of dark crimson blood on the tissue in her hand. He snatched it from her and tossed it under the truck, then ushered her into the backseat.

He and Kevin climbed into the front seats, and Matt started the engine again. Checking once more for oncoming cars, he turned the truck around and got back on the interstate.

"Isn't it getting brighter outside?" Kevin said.

Matt ducked his head a bit and looked out up at the cloud cover.

"Yeah. I think it is," he said.

11

As they motored along on the bypass, WDC-0-1 was waking up. Traffic was beginning to get heavy. The huge number of driverless vehicles made the roads buzz like beehives, with the workers and drones of the collective 'hive mind' all heading in to the offices and factories.

The Central Grid Hospital was on the other side of town, out near 1-11, alongside a large row of medical companies. There was a vast car park in front, and Matt pulled in and parked the truck in a vacant spot. The little family opened their doors sleepily, stepped out and stretched. It had been a long journey.

A steady trickle of people was making its way through gates in multiple layers of fences and barbed wire surrounding the compound. The principal building was a ten-story slab of pure white concrete, with vast swaths of glass at regular intervals like deep slashes from a knife. Corridors of enforced steel mesh extended out to nearby buildings like spiders' legs; the compound was a maze of interconnected annexes. As the Turners walked closer, the pathway opened up and they could see that rows of people had already formed. They joined one of the lines.

"What do you reckon? Fifty yards, maybe?" Kevin said.

"Why is it we're here?" Elizabeth said, looking around uncertainly.

Matt, taller than most, glanced over the crowd. "Maybe more like a hundred. And there is still, what? Half an hour before they start taking patients?" he said to Kevin, then turned to Elizabeth. "You need to see a doctor, Mom."

"Why do I need to see another one? I saw Dr. Aldridge days ago; he told me everything was fine."

Kevin looked at Matt. Matt shook his head.

"Mom, you have difficulty with your memory. That's why we need to get in. Don't worry. Kevin and I will come along."

Elizabeth looked around, perplexed, at the others waiting. Most were standing in small groups, probably patients and their relatives. Only a few stood by themselves. Painted stripes on the concrete made distancing easier; Matt listened uneasily to the coughs and groans all around him. Some of the standees wore face masks; some of the masks bore expanding splotches of blood on the clinical white fabric. Close to the Turners, near the end of the line, people were standing; but Matt could see that some were sitting closer to the entrance. Some appeared to have given up altogether and were lying on the ground.

■ ■ ■

"How long do we need to wait?" Elizabeth said.

"I don't know. It's five minutes till they open, but I don't know how fast these lines will move," Matt said.

"I've heard that some stay in line all night because they don't make it inside on the first day," a voice said.

Matt and Kevin turned their heads. A young woman from the line next to them looked back. She was standing with an older man who was crouched over a cane, holding a scarf to his mouth.

"But I don't know," she said, shrugging. "Haven't been here before."

"Well, I guess we should have no trouble since we're here now, before they open," Matt said, in part to reassure his mother and brother.

"Your mom?" said the woman, looking at Elizabeth. "I'm here with my dad. Lung cancer. At least that's what our doctor suspects."

"I'm sorry to hear that," Matt said. "Our mom's not too bad. It's just something with her memory, that's all," Matt said.

"Alzheimer's?"

"No, just some minor thing," he lied. "Nothing too serious. But we have to get an assessment, nonetheless. Will your father be okay?" Matt nodded towards the older man.

"Hopefully, it's in an early stage, so they'll treat him." The young woman raised her eyebrows; she sounded optimistic.

"It's dependent on stage? Oh, I see. I didn't know that."

"Yep, I think it is. Oh, something's happening now," she said, squinting along the lines. Matt followed her eyes.

Guards armed with automatic rifles were accompanying nurses in scrubs out the doors of the hospital, where they took their places at a series of turnstiles. Matt craned his neck; it was hard to see at this distance. There was a commotion around him and people started getting to their feet. Up near the turnstiles, a large digital marquee lit up, and text began to scroll across it. A large speaker system crackled to life, looping soundbites of the same sentences.

DO NOT RUSH GATES.

Matt looked at the queue behind them. Hundreds, if not thousands of people, had lined up while they'd been waiting. He couldn't make out the end anymore.

KEEP YOUR DISTANCE.

People were clumping up, beginning to push and shove, ignoring the separation lines.

FOLLOW INSTRUCTIONS FROM STAFF AND SECURITY PERSONEL.

Matt took his mother's hand and patted it.

A man in a white lab coat took a step up onto a small raised podium. In his right hand he held a megaphone; it made a small *blip* as he turned it on.

"May I have your attention, please," he said. "We are running at full capacity, but we cannot guarantee everybody an assessment today. Please remain calm. If you do not get selected for assessment today, there will be an opportunity for you to try again tomorrow. May we remind you that we are authorized to use force to keep order. Thank you for your cooperation."

Blip.

"Whatever happens, Mom, don't let go of my hand!" Matt said. He turned to Kevin and held out the keys to the truck. "If we get separated, I want you to wait for us in the truck." He had to raise his voice to be heard over the growing shouts from the crowd.

"Sure." Kevin reached for the keys.

Suddenly Matt was shoved hard from behind as the crowd surged forward like a tsunami. He grabbed tight to his mother's hand as he was pushed to the ground. He heard a jangling sound as the keys fell to the ground, and gave a yelp as his free arm was twisted by the crush of bodies. There was a roar of screams and cries as the weaker ones were lifted bodily from the ground and carried forward by sheer force.

"Kevin!" Elizabeth yelled, looking wildly over her shoulder.

Matt staggered to his feet in time to see Kevin's head bobbing away helplessly. A man tried to cut between Matt and his mother, and Matt shoved his elbow into the man's face. He heard a shriek, then hauled Elizabeth close, got an arm around her and began plowing towards the entrance. As he shouldered forward, he stumbled over an elderly man. He kept moving; there was nothing he could do. A moment later, a woman, holding an infant in her arms, was pushed into him. She and Matt locked eyes for a moment; her face was filled with dread. With his free arm, he cleared some space for her to regain her footing. *Not too far now.*

Suddenly everyone froze as the sound of gunshots rang out. Matt felt a slight dip in pressure from behind him, and then a jolt flung him into the people in front. He slammed into a man in front of him, who was holding a young boy. The force ripped the man's mask off, and Matt watched, paralyzed as he coughed and spattered the child with blood.

"Dad!" the boy screamed.

Matt swiveled, turning his back to protect his mother from the possible contagion, and hurried on, still dragging Elizabeth by the arm. He could see people pressed up against the turnstiles now, their sweating bodies doubling as barricades. The guards let only a few of them through at a time.

Matt felt something soft under his foot. He looked down to see a hand under his shoe. Its fingernails were painted a delicate pink. Horrified, he lifted his foot and crouched down, trying to jostle people away, but only freed part of the arm, which was covered in footprints. It was still moving. He bulldozed away at the bodies on top, yelling for people to move away, struggling to be heard amidst the flurry of shots and screams. At last, he saw the bruised face of a young girl, distorted in pain; she looked to be just a teenager perhaps. She was trying to cover her face with her other arm. She looked Matt in the eye; she seemed to be weeping tears mixed with blood.

Matt looked up at his mother. Elizabeth was thrashing bravely around in the stream of torn clothes and flesh, her free arm flailing to push people back, away from Matt and the girl. Matt spread his legs, bent his knees and planted his feet. He let go of his mother and bent towards the girl again, and heaved her to her feet.

She clasped her arms around his chest. Matt moved his mouth close to the girl's ear.

"You with anyone?" he yelled over the roar.

The girl shook her head frantically.

Matt turned to his mother, who had managed to cling to the hem of his jacket.

"Mom, grab onto my arm!" Elizabeth forced her arm in at his elbow joint, and Matt began to push forward again, dragging his mother and the girl along with him.

It was only three yards to the gates now, but it might as well have been a marathon. Some of the guards were standing on a platform, pulling people over; others were preventing people from flooding the gates, their automatic rifles keeping the most obnoxious at bay.

"Matt!" called a familiar voice. *Kevin.*

Matt turned, letting go of the two women, and caught sight of Kevin's face, a few rows back in the crowd. He reached out a hand, but before he could grasp his brother, he felt a savage pull on his shirt collar as a guard hauled him through the turnstile.

The soldier released his grip and stood in front of Matt. "I saw you save that girl, sir," he said, pointing to the teenager. "And is that your mother?"

Matt could see his mother and the girl staring at him wildly through the wall of guards.

He nodded. "Yes. But my brother is still out there." Matt tried to wrestle past the guard, who blocked him.

"Point to him."

Matt did the best he could.

"We need that one," the guard called to one of his colleagues, who stood on an elevated platform with his rifle hovering over the crowd.

The other guard nodded. "GET BACK!" he thundered at the masses, pointing his rifle into the crowd shoving at the turnstiles. "I SAID, GET BACK!"

A small corridor opened between the guards and Kevin, who moved forward under the spiteful eyes of those he passed. An obese man stepped in front of Kevin, holding him back with one arm, and turned to the guard.

"It's my fucking turn," he said angrily.

"Move away." The guard adjusted his rifle in the direction of the protester.

"No."

The crowd was now completely still.

"I don't want to repeat myself," the guard said.

The obese man looked at the faces of the people around him, smiled and turned towards the guard again.

"What are you gonna do, shoot me?" he said.

"Move away." The guard lowered the barrel of his rifle and took aim.

"Thought so," the man said insolently, and took a step forward.

The shot cracked the still air; the man's scream echoed off the walls of the hospital, turning to a high-pitched, continuous tone inside Matt's head.

He watched as dozens of guards jumped to the barricades now, firing shots above the masses now fighting in panic to disperse. He saw the white-coated official yell into his bullhorn. He saw two guards escorting Kevin through. He saw the guards move in formation against the crowd, pressing them back. He saw people running from the one place that was meant to be their last hope, and saw one dissident after another fall lifeless to the ground, riddled with bullets.

■ ■ ■

As Kevin embraced him, he dropped to the ground, exhausted, engulfed in tears. Hospital personnel assisted the four of them through the broad panoramic doors. The teenage girl he'd rescued vanished down a corridor with a doctor before he could get her name or say goodbye. Kevin, Matt and Elizabeth were taken into separate cubicles.

Matt's fingerprints were scanned, his temperature measured, his clothes stripped and his body checked for exterior wounds— a routine inspection, he was told.

Clothes back on, he was given letters to read, affirm, and sign—a legal necessity, he was told.

Inch-wide aluminum wristbands was affixed to his arm—a security measure, he was told.

The brothers said goodbye to their mother as she was whisked away for further examination. They were guided to wait in a large room with rows of chairs, a few tables and a cart with a water jug and cups. There were already many other relatives waiting; some slumped in chairs, some sleeping on the floor.

Kevin grabbed a cup from the cart, filled it with water and sat down in a chair.

Matt picked up a flyer from a nearby table. In big, bold letters, it said *Information for relatives regarding the health assessment procedure.*

He flipped the cover open and began to read.

Welcome to the WDC Central Grid Hospital.

12

Hours turned into minutes, minutes split into seconds, and seconds froze in time. Watching the big clock, Matt noticed the hands had stopped moving. Maybe it had run out of battery, he thought. Maybe *he* had.

Kevin sagged in the chair next to Matt, head on his shoulder and mouth open as he slept. Saliva dripped out of the corner of his mouth, leaving a dark wet spot on his shirt.

Although he was exhausted, Matt couldn't find any rest. His mind spun wildly with worry. About his mom, about Kevin, about the hundreds of people who hadn't made it inside. He could still see their faces. He imagined their loved ones. He felt their fear. When he closed his eyes, it only got worse. So he didn't. The pamphlet lay on the table before him. He hadn't been able to finish it. The letters had scrambled into names, and names had become faces. So he'd put it down.

But the Turners had made it inside. Elizabeth was now being attended to by people with expertise; she was one of the lucky few. And that was what mattered. Focus on your family, Matt told himself. On what mattered most: Kevin.

"Matthew Turner?"

He looked up. A man in a white suit with the government-issue indigo shirt underneath stood in the doorway. His bleached hair was combed to the side, slicked down with enough gel to keep it in place for days.

"Elizabeth Turner? Next of kin?" the man said, eyebrows raised.

Matt emerged slowly from his daze and sat up straighter. "Sorry. Yes, that's me," he said.

"Follow me, please." The man turned around and headed back out into the corridor.

Matt stood up. Kevin woke, startled, as his headrest withdrew, looking around in confusion. "I'll be right back," Matt told him, and hurried off after the official. Up ahead, he could hear the man's black polished shoes clacking away on the tiled floor.

"What about my brother?" Matt said as he caught up to him.

"He is underage, so he will have to wait there," the man said.

They went down a corridor, up a flight of stairs and around a corner, the man stopped. He opened a door for Matt.

"If you would like to take a seat, Mr. Turner," he said, gesturing.

Matt walked in, hesitating between each step. The door opened onto a room with white-tiled walls; a yard-high ribbon of white glass, halfway up each wall, enveloped the room. A broad white halo in the ceiling cast a uniform soft light into the corners of the room. In the center of the floor stood a small, white high-gloss table with four white steel chairs tucked under it. There was not a speck of dust, not a smudge of grease; everything gleamed.

Matt sat down, and the gentleman walked around the table and sat opposite. He pulled out a small tablet screen with a white cover and placed it in a slim groove on the table's surface to his left. He tapped the screen several times, but the angle was too steep for Matt to make out the words. The gentleman looked up at Matt and folded his hands.

"Interview of Matthew Turner, son of Elizabeth Turner, referring to case U G dash W D C dash seven eight four dash nine three dash five seven eight two," the man said, with his head tilted upwards. Then he turned his attention to Matt. "Hello, Matthew. Have you read about the assessment procedure?" he said.

Matt shook his head.

"Then I guess you are probably wondering what you are doing here; many people do, so don't worry. Let me introduce myself. My name is Mr. White; I will be your mother's assessment officer," he said. His sentences were fast-paced, but his pauses were elongated.

Matt looked at Mr. White, around the room and over his shoulder.

"Is this a joke?" Matt said.

"No, Matthew. Why would it be?"

Matt looked around the room again.

"Your name is Mr. White?" Matt said, widening his eyes and gesturing around at the walls.

"To me, that is called a coincidence. You might find it funny, yes, but we consider nothing we do here a joke. Do you consider medical treatment a joke, Matthew?"

"Uh, no. That wasn't what I meant."

Mr. White tilted his head and scanned Matt's face. "Good. Then let's get started, shall we?" he said.

"Uh, yes, but... With what exactly?"

"First, I must inform you that this conversation is being recorded, both in audio and video. For security measures, of course. Do you understand?"

"Yes—"

"Second, I need your consent to measure and monitor your heart rate, blood pressure, pupil dilation, respiratory changes and perspiration. This is to spot attempts at manipulation of the algorithm, and thereby misuse of government resources."

"Wh—"

"It is your legal right to decline this type of measurement, but I have to inform you that declining these measures will reflect on your evaluation and affect the overall assessment of your mother. Do you understand, Matthew?"

"Well, yes," Matt said.

"You need to say *I consent* in a loud and clear voice," Mr. White said, pointing up.

Matt hesitated. "I consent," he said.

"Excellent. Let me just get this up and running, then." Mr. White tapped on the screen again, then swiped and finished with a tap. He looked from the screen to Matt's wrist. "There we go," he said, squinting at Matt's hand.

Matt looked down at the wristband they had given him upon entry to the hospital. A bright green light, the size of a pinhead, emanated from beneath the brushed metal surface. Matt rubbed it. There was no bevel, no outline, but the bracelet itself was thick, maybe a quarter-inch all way round. Not much weight to it, though; maybe it was hollow.

"Now, let's see here," Mr. White said.

Matt raised a finger. "I have a question," he said.

"Go ahead, Matthew."

"What is this? I mean, why is all this necessary?"

"As part of your mother's assessment, we need to consider all potential outcomes, and their impact going forward. You can be of great help in that regard. Would you like to help your mother, Matthew?"

"Yes, of course, but I don't see how talking to me can change anything about my mother's illness. I mean, she's dying, isn't she?"

Mr. White regarded him for a moment.

"I'm not at liberty to share details of an ongoing assessment, but simply put, it would appear so, yes. But let's not get ahead of ourselves, shall we? That is, after all, what we are here to prevent." Mr. White looked down at his screen. "I can see here that your mother has no higher education, is that correct?"

"Yes, she always took care of me when I was little. My father wanted her to stay at home."

"And *you* do not have any education beyond high school. Is that correct, Matthew?"

"Yes, but what's that got to do with her illness?"

"Let's agree that I ask the questions, and you stick to answering them, shall we? Would you care to elaborate on your lack of education, Matthew?"

"My father died, so I felt it was my duty to stay home, to take care of my family, you know. My brother needed help with school, so I thought that once he got off to college, I could look at community classes."

"But it says here you failed to graduate. Would you care to comment on that?" Mr. White looked at the screen and tapped it several times.

Matt shifted in his chair. The slim cushions on the seat and backrest had decompressed, so it felt like he was sitting on bare metal now. "Uh, yes. I failed the last test, but besides that, I was a perfect student," he said.

"Interesting. I can see here that your mother lost her job recently," Mr. White said.

"That was because of her illness. She couldn't do the work. So, I guess they had no other option."

"In the event of your mother recovering, what future endeavor will she spend the remainder of her life on?"

"What do you mean? If she gets her memory back, and her confusion dissipates?"

"Yes, let's say that."

"I guess she'll work as secretary again; she's always been good at that." Matt shrugged.

"And does she have anything lined up?"

"Lined up? She can't fucking remember which day it is. What do you think?"

"Easy now, Matthew. We need these answers for a full assessment."

"No, she hasn't got anything lined up. But I'll help her get a job. It's not gonna be a problem."

"In the event of her death, what future do you see for yourself and your brother?"

"What do you mean, if she dies? Isn't that what you're gonna prevent?"

"Yes, if we decide to admit her as a patient. But as I told you, we have to consider all feasible options. Now, please answer my question, Matthew."

"I don't know. I guess I—*we*—would have to get on with our lives."

"Doing what, Matthew?"

"Well, I'd have to send my brother off to college and find a place to live. Then I'd need to pick up work somewhere—

construction, perhaps. I'd continue my education on the side, when time permits," Matt said. He sat straight up and leaned towards Mr. White. "Are we done with this, or what?" he said.

"Do you want us to be, Matthew?"

"You fucking tell me! I don't see the point of this, and how *any* of these shit questions has anything to do with my mom's health!"

"I'm not here on false pretenses. Rest assured, Matthew, that these questions are essential in order to assess your mother's situation thoroughly. Let's shift perspective for a moment. Did you know that you and your brother were conceived through the help of a fertility clinic?"

"What?" Matt stared at him, dumbfounded. "No, that's wrong. I know that my mom and dad had help with my little brother, that's all. But not with me."

"I'm sorry if this comes as a surprise to you, but we need clarification. Do you know if either you or your brother have a complete genetic history or genome from your mother?"

"I don't understand." Matt narrowed his eyes, but Mr. White didn't move a muscle.

"Do you know for a fact whether your mother's eggs were used in the reproductive process at the clinic, for either you or your brother?"

"No, I don't know." Matt sat back in the chair, deflated.

"Well, we are about to wrap up here, Matthew. Do you have anything else you think might be of value to us, anything further that you would like to add?"

"Um, I don't know. I wasn't prepared for this, so you've caught me a bit off guard."

"Don't worry, Matthew. That's a good thing. The machine

learning algorithms have a preference for the genuine, and that should be evident in your body readings. Any further questions before we conclude this interview?"

"What is all this being used for?"

"All of your answers will be added to the general data input. We collect information through interviews and your personal data history, along with means from your mother's demographic standard, statistical data models, and economic resource estimates from medical professionals on the most viable successful treatment. We will use all gathered information for an algorithmic assessment, calculation of your family's net worth, the probability of profitability, et cetera. A single recommendation number will then be turned over to a board of auditors, who, using a subset of interim calculations and your mother's bullet-point journal, will proceed to approve or reject the number and thus give a verdict."

Mr. White was all fired up. The artery in his neck was throbbing and his pupils were dilated. He exhaled after the flow of incomprehensible nonsense. His forehead shone slightly with perspiration, reflecting the pale light from the surrounding walls.

"So, you have nothing to do with my mother's treatment?" Matt said?

"No—and that's the beauty of it." Mr. White beamed with joy. "I just gather the data."

"This is sick."

"Thank you, Matthew. That will be all. Don't risk your mother's life by doing anything stupid, now. We will let you know once we're ready for the final evaluation screening," Mr. White said. He looked up at the ceiling. "Close interview file."

Matt sat looking blankly down at the glossy surface of the

table, watching the reflection of Mr. White as he slid the tablet back into his jacket pocket. The tiny green glow on his wristband faded and went out.

13

Matt walked back to the waiting room, followed by Mr. White. Whenever he stopped to look around or took a wrong turn, Mr. White pointed or corrected him. At the door to the waiting room, Mr. White veered off as Matt went inside.

"What did they want?" Kevin said, standing up from his chair.

Matt slumped into the one beside him. "I'm not sure," he said. He started scanning around the waiting room.

"What do you mean? What happened?"

Matt ignored him. Sitting straight up, he peered at lamps, tables, chairs, walls, the little trolley with its carafe and cups. He looked at the enormous screen at the end of the room, playing slides of infomercials. He focused on the little green dot under the screen. There were no sounds from the screen itself, but he could hear a faint, unmistakable white noise.

"Hey? Matt?"

"Shh."

Kevin stuck his head in front of his brother. "Are you listening?" he said.

Matt shook his head and pulled his attention away from the little green dot, leaving a purple dot dancing on his retina for several seconds.

"What did they want?" Kevin repeated impatiently.

"It was an interview, of sorts. They asked about Mom," Matt said. He started looking around the room again, tilting his head. Listening. But not to Kevin. He shifted his head around, trying to locate the source of the noise.

"You seem distracted." Long pause. No response. "Are you okay, Matt?"

"What? Yes," Matt snapped. He glanced around at the others sitting in the room. They were all minding their own business, it seemed. Then he raised his voice a bit. "Yes, I'm perfectly fine. They were all routine, relevant questions. I thought it was very professional."

Nobody in the room turned their heads at the sound of his voice. Every one of them sat still, reading pamphlets and looking at brochures. Picture perfect.

"Who are you talking to?" Kevin tried to follow his eyes.

"I'm gonna go to take a piss," Matt said, lowering his voice again. "I suggest you do the same in a minute," he added.

"What?"

Matt stood up, looked around for reactions, and then followed the signs to a bathroom. Inside, there was a long row of stalls and a large mirror above the row of sinks on the opposite wall. He ambled down the row of stalls, tapping at each door. All empty. He went into the last stall, shut the door and locked it. He closed the lid of the toilet, sat down and listened. He could hear a dim buzzing sound, just loud enough to be noticeable if you knew to keep quiet.

The door to the washroom opened, and someone came inside.

"Matt?"

It was Kevin's voice.

"Down here," Matt said. He heard footsteps nearing, coming to a halt outside his door.

"Would you mind telling me what the fuck you're doing?"

"Grab a stall. Next to me," Matt whispered.

He could hear Kevin going in and closing his door.

"Lock it."

He heard the lock slide over.

Matt flushed the toilet. "I think they're watching us. And probably listening too," he said, squeezing the words in before the water stopped gushing.

"Aren't you being just a little paranoid?" Kevin said.

"Keep it down."

"Why would you think that we're being watched?"

"They asked me a bunch of questions," Matt said. "It just seemed odd; it made no sense. It seems like they are looking for reasons not to treat Mom."

"Why would they do that? We've been paying our taxes; we have doctors' appointments and prescription medicine all the time. Isn't surveillance by insurance companies a thing of the past? Besides, we don't even have insurance, so who the fuck would bother?"

Silence.

Matt opened the door and walked to the sink in front of the mirror.

Kevin flushed and came out of his stall, zipping up his pants. Matt turned on a tap and cranked it as high as would go.

"I'm not sure, but I think they are trying to estimate her value in gold or something like that. To find out how much she's worth."

Kevin took a spot at the adjoining sink and began soaping his hands. "Are you kidding me? Have you any idea how ridiculous that sounds?" he said, turning off first his running water and then Matt's.

Matt looked at him, annoyed, and turned the tap back on. "You weren't there, Kev. You didn't have your whole body monitored. I'm telling you—this Mr. White guy? He almost seemed to enjoy belittling me," he said.

"Have you considered that you might have come off as uncooperative in the first place?" Kevin smirked.

Matt grabbed him by the collar and slammed him backward into a stall door. "This is not a fucking joke," he said, stepping back and squaring off with his brother.

"Easy, man. Relax. Calm down." Kevin straightened up, brushing Matt's hands aside. "Have you any idea what you're suggesting?"

Matt looked at him quizzically. Why wasn't Kevin listening to him? He dropped his gaze and began to pull at his wristband, trying to squeeze his fingers between metal and skin. The damn thing was too tight.

"Look," Kevin said, walking to the bathroom door. He flung it open and pointed into the corridor. "Look at them."

Matt peeked out. Nurses and doctors were passing, carrying tablets, various medical supplies, bags of blood. A porter pushed a bed on which a patient lay sleeping, hooked to an IV. It looked like a regular day at a hospital. Matt watched for a minute, scrutinizing anybody who dared to look his way. No one paid him the slightest bit of attention.

Kevin let the door close itself.

"If what you're suggesting is true, then these people, all those people—" he swung his arm over his head in a rotating motion, "—should be in on it. Have you thought about that?"

Matt stood motionless, refusing to shake his head, refusing to give his acknowledgment.

"They would all be working for a fraudulent hospital system. Or maybe—wait, do you think they are actors?" Kevin laughed. "Don't you think someone—just a single decent man or woman— would have noticed this by now? That someone would have come forward to tell? For fuck's sake, Matt, I thought you, of all people, possessed a higher regard for your fellow human beings."

Matt stared at Kevin, who stared back at him. It was hard to wrap his brain around the contradictions in his head. "But what if they don't know?" he ventured. "What if someone, some senior manager, is having them all monitored? So that they can crack down on the employees who don't fall in line?"

Kevin didn't bite.

Matt turned and looked at the big mirror over the sinks. It was spotless. Not a smudge, not a remnant of calcium from water splashing near the faucets. He stepped up close to it, peering into his own eyes, shifting his focus, looking past his face. He really was getting pale. He could smell fresh detergent, a hint of alcoholic sanitizer in the air. "They're watching us," he said.

Kevin adjusted his jacket sleeve and looked at the long, wide mirror. Then he raised his elbow and smashed it. There was a loud crash as shards of glass and the aluminum backing splintered and bounced off the ceramic sinks, then shattered on the floor. All the way down the wall, pieces of mirror hung from their mounts, revealing the bare wall underneath. There wasn't a single camera, not a single microphone, not a single hole in that wall.

A nurse poked her head inside. "What's happening?" she said, sounding frightened.

"I slipped. I'm sorry—I'm so sorry," Kevin blurted, brushing his jacket.

"Are you all right?" she asked.

"Yes, thanks, I'm fine."

"I'll send for the janitor. He'll take care of it. Don't worry." She smiled reassuringly at him.

"Thank you very much," Kevin said.

Matt stood looking at the glass shards, the bare wall, the nurse on her way out, and then at Kevin.

"I'm sorry, Matt. I just don't believe that you are even remotely right," Kevin said.

Matt shook his head. He felt the blood rushing back into his brain, the buzzing in his legs subsiding. "Thanks, Kev. I think I needed that." He gave his brother a hug.

They walked back to the waiting room, where a doctor greeted them at the entrance.

"The Turners?" he said.

"Yes." They both nodded.

"We've finished your mother's tests. Follow me."

He led the way into a small room with a hospital bed. Elizabeth lay under a blanket, eyes closed, breathing heavily. There were many monitors on the wall, but none of them was connected or turned on.

"We've given her a bit of sedative so that she could relax while we conducted some tests. So she's sleeping now. She needs the rest. Your assessment officer will be back once they're ready," the doctor said, and left the room.

Kevin sat down beside Elizabeth in the only chair. He took her hand and stroked it.

Matt jogged out of the room after the doctor.

"I'm sorry, Doctor. Can I ask you something?" Matt said once they were farther down the hallway.

"Sure."

"What is wrong with her?"

"I'm sorry, I'm not allowed to comment on a patient's status or illness until we admit them for treatment."

"But can't you tell me something, anything at all?"

The doctor looked around, waiting for some coworkers to pass.

"Your mother is very sick. And she has a complicated procedure ahead of her." He looked Matt in the eye, waiting. "Are you looking for honesty or hope?"

"Both," Matt said.

The doctor stood, shifting his weight. "Let me say it like this. If your mother doesn't get admitted, don't give up the fight. She *can* be cured. But maybe it won't be by us."

Then he turned on his heel and walked briskly away, leaving Matt dumbfounded.

Matt returned to the little room and stood behind Kevin's chair, laying a hand on his shoulder. Elizabeth was still out cold.

"I'm scared," Kevin said. "What if they don't take her in?"

"Don't be. You said it yourself: Why wouldn't they? And besides, if this somehow fails, Dr. Aldridge told me about a group of practitioners he called rogue doctors, or something like that. I won't stop looking until she's in care. Don't worry. I'll find a way."

"But where do we go?"

"I'll have to figure it out, I guess."

Hours went by. Nurses came by once in a while to check up on their mother. One of them put a clip on her finger to measure the amount of oxygen in her blood, ensuring she was recovering from the anesthesia. Matt, reluctant to make small talk, was lost in his thoughts. The hours passed slowly as the brothers waited in anticipation.

Finally, Elizabeth woke, and they helped her to sit up. Curious, Matt and Kevin asked about the tests and her talks with the doctors, but she couldn't remember much. She felt lightheaded, but as the drugs released their grip, she at least regained her appetite. Matt went out and asked a nurse for some food, and she returned a few minutes later with a tray, treating all three Turners to a cling-wrapped hospital meal. As none of them had had any food all day, the mashed potatoes, soggy fried chicken lying in a pool of murky sauce and lifeless boiled green beans all amounted to a feast. They sat with their trays on Elizabeth's bed, laughing, reminiscing, pushing back any thoughts of the outside world while requesting refills of diluted soft drinks.

Hours later, as they sat chatting together, two armed guards in regulation indigo-blue government uniforms stepped through the door.

14

The entourage comprised the two armed guards, a porter with a wheelchair, and Mr. White.

"Matthew," he said, shaking hands, and turned to Kevin. "You must be Kevin. I'm Mr. White, your mother's assessment officer."

"Hello," Kevin said.

"Elizabeth." Mr. White nodded to her and signaled the porter, who assisted her into the wheelchair. "Gentlemen, if you would please follow me."

They followed behind Mr. White and the porter with the wheelchair. The guards brought up the rear. The little procession marched through another set of hospital corridors and set off through the mazes teeming with doctors, nurses and more porters.

"Here we are." Mr. White opened the door to the room where he had interviewed Matt. An extra chair had been put in place. The porter rolled Elizabeth over to sit at the table.

Matt sat down beside her and patted her hand. "Don't worry, Mom."

Kevin sat on the other side of her and whispered to Matt across their mother. "Mr. White... Really?" He grinned.

"I know—don't mention it."

The guards took up stances in the two corners behind the Turners.

Mr. White sat down in his chair, put his little tablet in the groove and started tapping away.

"Evaluation screening of Elizabeth Turner, case U G dash W D C dash seven eight four dash nine three dash five seven eight two. Also present are Matthew Turner and Kevin Turner, both sons of Ms. Turner."

Mr. White looked from one to the other, his smile plastered from ear to ear.

"Let me say we record evaluations in both video and audio, for security reasons. I'll start by telling you about this evaluation and what to expect. I'm going to read the key points of our medical findings and tell you about their impact on the assessment, and then I'm going to put us on hold for a board of auditors. Once they are online, Elizabeth's recommendation number will be disclosed, and the auditors will ask questions as they see fit. Immediately afterward, all auditors will assess the validity. If the number clears our margins, we will either admit Elizabeth for immediate treatment on the premises, or transfer her to a more suitable, available hospital. If not, we assume you as good citizens will respect the board's decision and leave the premises in an orderly fashion." Mr. White looked at Matt. "Are we clear on that?" The wide smile was gone now; Mr. White's eyes bored into him.

Matt looked from his mother to his brother, as Mr. White continued to stare at him, and then nodded. "Yes, we understand," he said.

Mr. White turned to Elizabeth. "Are you with us, Ms. Turner?"

She looked at Matt, then at Kevin. "Who is this? What are we doing here?" she said.

"It's okay, Mom," Matt said. On her other side, Kevin didn't move a muscle.

"Matthew, I have to go on with this evaluation. We cannot wait for your mother to be mentally present. Do you understand? I trust you to explain the details to her at a later time, yes?" Mr. White said.

"Yes, I will." Matt took Elizabeth's hand.

Mr. White sighed and leaned back, glancing at his screen.

"Your mother has signs of progressive Alzheimer's, but with complications—"

"What?" Matt tried to look surprised.

"—which are not familiar to us at this point in time. Under normal circumstances, advances in medical science would provide us with a viable treatment. Through the use of genetic therapy, we could expect a full recovery. This is a very demanding treatment, though, requiring large numbers of staff, hospitalization, analysis and medicinal application. But unfortunately, your mother does not reside within the standards of regular Alzheimer's. We are witnessing irregularities, and thus would need to do extensive research into the exact origins of her disease."

Mr. White paused to glance from one Turner to the next. Matt followed his eyes; Elizabeth gave a slight smile; Kevin remained silent. He looked petrified.

"Now, I will say, this does not necessarily mean that your mother will be disqualified from treatment," Mr. White said. "But I am bound by law to give you this information in order to keep the process and decision making as transparent as possible without revealing any confidential government information. I will now put us on hold to allow the auditors to join the evaluation, and while we're waiting, I'll take a moment to explain this part in further detail."

The portion of the large white glass ribbon situated behind the assessment officer lit up now, creating a wide screen that covered half the wall. Five squares outlined with black borders appeared on the screen, and within a couple of seconds, the first headshot appeared in one of them. It was blurred beyond recognition, but Matt detected a large beard. Besides that, however, it was hard to make out features.

"Auditors will join us from all across the country," Mr. White intoned. "These are important members of society who hold key positions, such as scientists, doctors, politicians, judges, et cetera. They are anonymous, and we will scramble their voices in order to avoid repercussions, should you be able to recognize any of them. But it is important you understand that the auditor board is not here to evaluate your mother's illness or decide whether we should admit her for treatment. Unfortunately, many patients and especially relatives believe that. Rather, the auditors are here only to audit the algorithm. Their sole purpose is to screen for errors in the algorithm's calculations and verdict. If just one of them suspects the algorithm could be wrong, or that an error or bug may have occurred, they can nullify the algorithm's decision, and Elizabeth's case will then be up for human peer review."

More washed-out faces turned up at the screen.

"The auditors will have access to interim computations to properly assess the validity of each subcategory's partial results. And speaking of end results, I see we have a board ready," Mr. White finished.

"Now what?" Matt said, raising his shoulders. Five blurry heads bobbed around in their respective squares.

"Now, we'll get the number," Mr. White said, pressing on his screen. "Zero point three one two," he read, as the digits appeared beneath the middle portrait.

"Is that good?" Matt said.

"I'm afraid not. Right now, the requirement is two point five. But let's see what the board has to say," Mr. White added hastily, countering Matt's outburst before he got riled up.

Mr. White turned his head to look at the screen.

Matt's attention carried him to the edge of his seat.

Everything in the room stood still except time. None of the blobs moved in their frames.

"What are they doing?" Matt whispered across the table, eyes fixed on the screen.

"They are going over the individual numbers. Searching for inconsistencies." Mr. White motioned for patience.

Three of the heads disappeared, each replaced by a thick black oversized check-mark in their box. Before Matt could separate his dry tongue from his palate, the fourth tuned out as well, leaving the mark of approval.

"What? What happened?" Matt blurted.

Mr. White swiveled back towards the Turners. "They have validated the number and confirmed the algorithmic outcome."

"But they haven't even heard what we had to say! Didn't you say there would be questions?"

"*Could* be. Only if the board deems it necessary. And it seems there is one who has a question." Mr. White pointed at the screen behind him. "Go ahead, auditor."

It was the bearded one. Muffled, distorted to a low pitch, a voice came from speakers in the ceiling.

"Do you know where you are, Madam?" the auditor asked, apparently addressing Elizabeth.

"Of course she does," Matt cried, jumping to his feet. "She's a kind woman! And a mother! Save her! This is wrong!"

"Matthew, please sit down," Mr. White said, signaling with one hand for Matt to sit and raising the other for the guards to keep back. Matt noticed they had taken a step closer, guns raised slightly.

"I would like the lady to answer for herself," the auditor said. "Do you know where you are, Madam?" the voice said again.

Matt sat down, taking his mother's hand. "It's okay, Mom. Go ahead."

Elizabeth turned to him, her eyes apologetic, shaking her head. "But, Matt, I *don't* know where I am," she said. "I'm so sorry."

"Thank you. That will be all," the auditor said, and then vanished, leaving the last frame with a tick of confirmation.

Matt slumped back in his chair, deflated. He looked up at the screens, hoping for the heads to appear again. Something. Anything. Mr. White turned off the screen, and the white glass reappeared, reflecting the guards in their corners.

"So is that it? Wait, wait—let me get this right," Matt said. He pointed his index finger at Mr. White and gave him a piercing stare. "So, what you're saying is that you *can* treat her, but you won't? Is that about right?" His upper lip was trembling.

"I'm sorry that you see it this way, Matthew."

"What other way is there?"

"Well, I see several," Mr. White said, dodging the issue.

"What other way is there, Mr. White?"

"One could say that we—the hospital, the WDC, the United Grids—have a very limited number of resources, of which you are well aware. And that we need to prioritize said resources in order to thrive as a society, as a grid and as a country."

"She's dying?" Kevin muttered, but nobody replied.

"And Mom's not pitching in, is that it?" Matt said, his voice rising. "Is that why you asked those fucking questions?"

"Easy now, Matthew. Every possible future scenario has all been calculated and weighed, by the very best in algorithms and machine learning, including eventual ramifications for you and your brother, so that nothing slips through the cracks. This is all standard procedure, in accordance with the *Energy Efficiency Act*. This is not *my* decision. It is *the system's* decision. It's for the good of society, not the individual. We cannot let emotion and irrationality tilt our hands when allocating the sparse number of resources left at our disposal. Don't you see? We must let math, science, technology and research be our guides, or we cannot thrive into the future."

There was a pause. Matt tried and failed to find words. His mother had been reduced to a single, floating decimal number.

"Would it help you if I told you she might not even *be* your mother?" Mr. White added.

Matt flew up from the chair and thrust himself across the table, reaching for Mr. White.

"Fuck you, you arrogant fucking streetlit bastard!" Matt yelled into the haughty face of Mr. White. Froth flew from his mouth as the guards rushed forward and dragged him away, slamming him to the floor.

As Matt thrashed and wrestled, the guards twisted his arms behind his back and pressed his face into the tile floor. "You don't know what it's like, do you, you rich, privileged fuck?" Matt spat, his voice muffled. "Being rated second like this?"

He felt a sharp sting in his wrist underneath his hospital bracelet. His muscles loosened, and his rage dissipated like air from a punctured balloon. The guards let go of their hold.

"What are you doing?" His words came out thick and slow. He began to salivate heavily and rolled with difficulty onto his back on the slippery floor. Instructions from his brain halted, stuck in rush hour, before reaching the muscles.

Mr. White stood up. He walked around the table and looked down at Matt.

"Relax. We've given you a neurotoxin. It's designed to make you more manageable. Make you listen," Mr. White said. He turned to Kevin. "Your brother will be fine. He will regain complex muscular activity in a couple of hours. Don't worry. Within ten minutes, he will regain basic muscle control. Legs, arms, et cetera. It will be some time before his neural pathways get back up to speed, though."

Presenting his hand like a gentleman, Mr. White helped Elizabeth to her feet and motioned the guards to lift Matthew into the wheelchair. Then he unlocked the Turners' bracelets one by one. That done, Mr. White turned to Matt once again.

"You see, Matthew? This situation is exactly why we have *the system*: so that we don't let our emotions take control. That way, no one throws away limited resources on endeavors with no future beneficial outcome. Now, you will go home—or… somewhere, I guess—and you will let my words settle in your head. Within a couple of days, you will realize that this is for the best. This decision is also for the good of *your* future children. If you have any, that is. And now, gentlemen, we will escort you out of the building. I trust you, Kevin, not to make any sudden outbursts of emotion. The next one won't be mitigated with neurotoxin, but with something far more impactful and longer-lasting. Have I made myself clear?"

Kevin nodded.

They followed Mr. White out of the building, the guards walking close behind.

15

Dr. Christopher Henke Waldhaven sat back in his office chair and ran a hand through his well-groomed beard. He had just finished his duty as a government-appointed auditor. He had been on a call with a Grid Hospital, though he didn't know which one. The identity and location of patients were kept hidden, even to him.

He had wanted to press the error button, rejecting the result, but knew he couldn't. It would have been too suspicious. The woman's rating had been low; the algorithm had calculated no future value in her life. The fact that the other auditors had approved the algorithm so fast had forced him to follow suit. He had tried a question to see if she would reveal a location—the name of the hospital, a sector, or a grid even. But to his chagrin, she hadn't.

He had, however, recognized her face. Elizabeth Turner. Could this be right? Was this her? That would make the young men Matthew and Kevin. It had been years since he had stopped his search, but seeing them through the video feed had rekindled a flame within him. If the father hadn't died and the family hadn't had to move, he would still be monitoring the family closely.

Most of his audits were straightforward. This would have been as well, if not for the otherwise thorough algorithm's one simple flaw: it couldn't see behind the numbers. And Henke knew Elizabeth Turner was far more than just a number. But now, she was being left to die, and all their research would go down the drain.

He picked up a framed picture from his desktop and inspected it in the light from the window. It showed two girls wearing identical red dresses. He put it back down.

He had to convene the council. There was no way to flag these cases in the algorithms, but their subjects shouldn't be allowed to slip through the system like this. He pulled a voice recorder from a drawer. It was the only safe way; record, encrypt, copy to the system. A closed loop. The only way to keep council communication safe.

"Message to the Council of the Judicious," he began. "Request to amend functionality in algorithm two four six, in current use in government health care approval systems."

16

Kevin wiped the last of the tears from his eyes. As they had trudged through the hospital corridors, the tears had trickled slowly and steadily, dropping from his chin to his brother's head. Now he stood, his back turned to the hospital, out on the plaza. The square was empty; the crowds had gone. There was no one in sight, except for a man scrubbing the ground with a broom and soapy water.

Matt was lying on the ground, and Elizabeth was tending to him. The guards had thrown him from the wheelchair as soon as they'd cleared the sliding doors. He still wasn't able to walk.

"Mom, stay with him, okay?" Kevin said. He walked towards the man with the broom. "Hey, excuse me? Have you seen any car keys lying around?" The last time Kevin had seen them, a boot had kicked them into a torrent of legs and feet.

"No, sir, I don't think so. Been here a couple of hours now, round most of the square, but found no lost property so far. I'm sorry. The wasters get here before us, though. Whenever somethin' like this happens."

"You mean this happens a lot?"

"Not uncommon, I'd say. Someone loses their temper, messes

with a guard or somethin'. Been a while since I cleaned this many, though." The man pointed around at the dark patches on the asphalt.

"Okay. Thanks anyway." Kevin went back to Matt and Elizabeth. "Let's check the parking area. Help me get him up, Mom." He lent a shoulder to Matt, who was slightly more able to keep his balance now.

Even before they got to the parking lot, Kevin could see that their pickup was gone. There were only a few cars left on the lot.

"Fuck." He looked at the other two. Neither one responded.

This was a first for Kevin. Matt had never relinquished responsibility or granted him any say in family matters. For as long as Kevin could remember, it had always been Matt commanding, acting like the man of the house. It pissed Kevin off. But now, with Matt out of commission, all decisions fell on him. Now was the time to prove himself. Prove *he* could be a father, too.

Kevin couldn't count the times he dreamed of taking charge, taking the reins from his brother, but the very same thoughts had always constricted his throat and frozen his blood in his veins. But now things had changed. Their mother was sick, and it was on him to do something about it.

Or he could wait. A couple of hours seemed an eternity, and Matt had been hit hard by whatever they put in those wristbands. By that time, it would be dark out, Kevin guessed. Act or abstain: now was the time.

Kevin unloaded Matt on a boulder, leaving Elizabeth next to him for support. The worker from before was walking towards a tiny utility car, carrying his bucket and broom.

"Hey, sorry to bother you again!" Kevin called, running over to him. The man stopped as he opened the car door and turned to him.

"Is there a problem, sir?"

"Do you know where the nearest community center is located? Someone has stolen our truck."

"Damn wasters," the man griped. "Ain't got nothin' to do but steal and plunder decent folks' property. Anyway, I think you can go to Brentwood. I know there's one in the old postal building. Red Line goes all the way."

"Sorry? I'm not from around here."

"The Red Line, just up there, from Med Center." The man pointed with his finger. "Goes all the way to Rhode Island Avenue and Brentwood. Should be signs from there, I imagine. Don't think you'll find anythin' out here. Might not be the closest one, but it's the fastest for sure."

"Thanks again. Really appreciate it."

"I would have taken you myself if this damn thing would fit anythin' but me." The man chuckled.

"It's fine; don't worry about it. Thanks."

"No problem, sir. You guys take care."

Kevin returned to his mother and brother. Matt was regaining muscle control in his legs and arms, so with a bit of help from Kevin, he was able to walk along. Elizabeth seemed catatonic as she shuffled along behind them. Matt tried to mumble something, but dribble just ran from the corner of his mouth.

"Come on. This way, Matt. I've got you," Kevin said encouragingly.

When they got to the tube station, the escalators leading underground weren't running. Beneath the glass- and steel-framed arc, the lighting was sparse, and so the deeper they went, the gloomier it got. The platform was empty; only a few bulbs were still working. A bluish glow came from an electrical screen displaying the timetable. They had ten minutes to wait until the next train. The government had drastically reduced public transportation after the energy crisis exploded; a ten-minute wait wasn't long compared to some other schedules, Kevin knew. The first minute was the hardest, as Kevin waited for his nose to adjust to the stench of piss and vomit emanating from the long, harsh shadows. When the train finally pulled in, they were still the only people on the platform.

Inside the car, however, the space was packed with people standing shoulder to shoulder. The doors opened, but nobody got off. Passengers shuffled back, trying to make room.

"Med Center! Make room for disease," someone cried.

The Turners pushed their way into the train car; passengers standing nearby kept watchful eyes on them.

"She's got Alzheimer's," Kevin explained to no one in particular.

"That's what they told you."

It was impossible for Kevin to make out who the speaker was. He remembered the discussions on the talk shows when he was younger. Each epidemic following the energy crisis had spurred debates about whom to save, given the ever-declining number of resources. Most of the panelists agreed that you couldn't save everybody, so the discussions had revolved around the *who*. Kevin had been more interested in *how* you could save more people; even as a small child, he'd believed that everybody was born equal. He had never thought the animosity from the fearmongers on-screen would reverberate out into the public. He realized he'd been wrong.

Elizabeth coughed.

"Get away from me!" a woman screamed, pushing and shoving to get away from the Turners.

"Get the fuck off this train!" A man tried to push Elizabeth into the doors, but Kevin threw himself in front.

"Wasters, wasters!"

"She's not sick!" Kevin shouted. "It's not infectious."

"How do we know?" Another woman joined in.

Kevin took his jacket off and held it up in front of Elizabeth's mouth, holding his other arm around her.

"There. Now calm down!" Kevin said.

There were a few more murmurs and then the crowd settled. Many of them were staring uneasily at Matt. Even though he was swaying from side to side, he was still bigger and broader than anyone close to them. Kevin pulled him closer to deter confrontation.

Two stations later, the Turners claimed a corner where they could stand in peace, their backs against a glass shield separating a small seating area.

"Where are we going?" Matt managed. His tongue was still getting in the way of his words.

Kevin looked at him and hesitated. "Somewhere safe. Somewhere we can get help." He knew Matt hated the community centers, but Kevin saw no other option.

Finally, the train pulled into Brentwood Station. Getting out of the train car felt like a blessed relief, in part because the station was above ground with plenty of fresh air. On the platform, Kevin was looking at a map as a tall young man approached them. Matt held his hand out to stop him.

"Looking for medical services?" the young man said. Well-worn clothes hung loosely on his skimpy body. "I heard some harassing comments back there."

"No," Matt said.

"I know a place that could help, you know? I'm guessing you got rejected from Med Center." He looked furtively around. "You're not the only ones, you know."

"No," Matt repeated.

"Hey, didn't you say that we needed to—" Kevin started.

"We're fine," Matt cut in over him.

"Suit yourself. But looking at her, I'd reconsider," the guy said, nodding towards Elizabeth.

Kevin spun around. His mother was undressing in the center of the platform, coat already at her feet. He sprinted over to her. "Mom?" He grasped Elizabeth's hands and tried to hold them down by her side. "Mom, don't take off your clothes. We're out in public," he said.

"I feel so warm. So humid," she said.

"No, Mom, you can't do this. We're close now to a bed, where you can get some sleep. I'm sure it's gonna pass," Kevin said.

"Where is it?" Matt said as he stumbled over. "Where are we going?"

"It's not far… It's a—community center," Kevin said.

"What? We can't—"

"We *have* to, okay? I don't know why you resent those places, but we don't have a lot of options, so this time I'm calling the shots. And I say we go!"

"No!" Matt said.

Elizabeth groaned and collapsed into Kevin, who caught her as her legs buckled.

"Help, Matt!" Kevin said, trying to keep both himself and Elizabeth upright.

"Let go of me. LET GO OF ME!" Elizabeth screamed into Kevin's face as Matt tried to get a good grip around her body.

"Mom, you can't—" Kevin tried, but Elizabeth's arms were flailing at his face as she wrestled to get free.

"RAPE! RAPE!" She began clawing and scratching at Kevin's face. Her cheeks were fiery red, her eyes dilated and wild.

"No, Mom!" Kevin tried to keep her hands down.

Elizabeth screamed at the top of her lungs, and then, like a siren switching its tune, she burst into tears, crying, grasping at Kevin like he was being torn away.

"You weren't supposed to see. You weren't supposed to witness," she wailed between sobs.

Then, quick as lightning, she was back on her feet, suddenly perplexed.

Kevin put an arm firmly around his mother, supporting her once more, and turned to Matt with a frown on his face. "I say we fucking go, and then you just follow, all right?"

■ ■ ■

It wasn't a long walk to the old postal building. Matt had regained much of his muscle movement and was now able to walk by himself. Both he and Kevin tried to initiate conversations with Elizabeth, but with no luck. She said nothing, refusing to acknowledge Matt and Kevin's attempts at communication.

The building's red brick walls were lit up in the early evening light. Parking spaces ran along one side of the extensive building, most of them empty, now occupied by barrels and benches. Under some trees, a young couple sat sharing a needle. At the front of the building, Kevin could see a big glass entrance, now all covered in graffiti. One window had been broken; duct tape had kept it from shattering.

"This is why we should've stayed away," Matt said.

That was it. He'd had enough. Kevin turned around, squared off with his brother, and leaned into his face. "Shut the fuck up. Do you have anywhere else to go in that magic bag of tricks of yours?" he snapped, leaving a slight pause for Matt to respond, then continuing in his brother's silence. "Didn't fucking think so. So please, let me handle this for a change so that Mom can get some rest at least."

Kevin turned around and started walking again. Then he stopped. His brother had known all along. He turned back around to face Matt, narrowing his eyes.

"You didn't seem too surprised when the doctor started talking about Alzheimer's, did you?" Kevin said.

"He wasn't a doctor, Kev," Matt said.

"That wasn't the fucking question!" Kevin took a couple of steps towards Matt. "You knew this whole fucking time, didn't you?"

"Relax."

"How long have you known?" Kevin's heart started cranking up the beats.

Matt didn't reply.

"How long have you fucking known?" Kevin reached out and pushed his brother. Matt took a step back.

"Calm down, will you?"

"Why are you fucking lying to me all the time?" Kevin was getting loud now.

"I'm not."

"Fuck you." Kevin pushed him even harder this time. His brother was a big guy, though, and not easily moved.

"Stop it," Matt said.

"Tell me you knew. Tell me you fucking knew!" Kevin paused, waiting for a response.

Matt looked at the ground. "I knew."

Kevin jumped at his brother, punching at him, missing his face and hitting his shoulder instead. Matt was caught off-balance and they both tumbled to the ground.

"Fight!" someone yelled from over near the entrance.

Kevin, the scrawnier of the two, let punches fly as best he could. There was the dull smack of knuckles pounding into hands and arms as Matt tried to fend him off. Finally, like a bear swatting a squirrel, Matt brushed Kevin aside. Kevin landed heavily on his back on the rocky ground. Pain shot up his left side. Matt pinned him down against the gravel pathway and wiped away some blood from the side of his mouth.

"Are you done?"

"She's dying!" Kevin thrashed and fought under the weight of his brother.

"Are you done?" Matt said again in a lower tone of voice.

Kevin suddenly went limp and felt the tears rising. "She's dying, and you won't let me help."

"I'm so sorry, Kevin." Matt loosened his grip and sat back on the path. "I should have, but—well, she's *not* dying. I can still figure out a way to help her."

"But what if you can't?"

"Don't say that."

A small crowd of people had gathered around them now, hoping the fight would go on. Elizabeth stood among them, watching as Matt and Kevin got slowly to their feet.

"What are you gonna do?" Kevin said to Matt. "We've got nothing left. Nothing. And you scared away the only person willing to help," he said, meaning the scruffy young man at the train station.

"He didn't want to help; he was ready to rip the last pieces of clothes off our backs." Matt looked around. "Come on, let's get inside. I'll figure something out. Mom, come on." He grabbed Elizabeth by the arm, parted the crowd, and strode off towards the entrance.

Kevin watched them for a moment and then set off grimly after them. So that was it, then, he thought sourly. Back to the status quo. Back to Kevin being shoved to the side, waiting for his big brother's magnificent plan to unfold. He stepped through the door to the community center and suddenly realized that *he* had led them to this place; *he* had taken this particular decision, *he* had carried that burden. He allowed himself a small smile. He had proven to *himself*, at least, that he could be a father.

17

Rubbing his aching jaw, Matt tipped his head back and gaped around the immense entrance hall. It was two floors high, and warm evening sunlight flowed through the graffitied panoramic windows, creating a myriad of colors, even more vibrant than they had seemed on the outside. Like the stained glass in the church down the street from the house where Matt had grown up, they cast their colors onto the floor, lighting up the bare white marble slabs like a mosaic. Matt almost gasped in wonder; it was an artwork, much like the ones he'd seen in that church.

Here, the image of a woman, big fluffy round afro, stood with her arms out receiving, wrapped in an orange shawl, backlit with pale yellow beams of light. The glow of the rays holding off an enclosing deep blue creeping around the edges. Outlines of faces in the dark, but hard to make out.

At one side of the entrance hall was a long oak desk, worn and dented along the edges. Its surface was in dire need of grinding and lacquering; the previous layers were cracked and flaking. An older woman stood behind it. She had a large mop of frizzy hair, curling more to the sides than up, and parted down the middle. She wore an orange pullover, half-rimmed glasses, and bright crimson lipstick.

"You the boys that were fighting out front?" she said without looking up from a stack of papers. She continued scribbling, dotting, crossing items out with a worn-down pencil. An old eraser sat to the side.

Matt looked at Kevin and back to her. "Yes," he said in a tiny voice that he seldom put to use.

"Ma'am," she insisted.

"Yes, ma'am," he said, with a bit more power.

"Can't do none of that here. Understand? Or I'll kick you out before you're back on ya feet."

"Sorry—ma'am. It was a one-time deal." Matt looked at Kevin again. Kevin kept quiet.

"So?" the woman said. She looked up and adjusted her glasses on her nose.

Matt didn't catch her cue.

"So, are you gonna tell me why you here, or should I just venture a guess?" she repeated.

"Uh, we—kind of lost our apartment, and then we had to go to the Central Grid Hospital. But they couldn't help us, so…"

"Who's sick?"

"Nobody. It's—"

"So why'd ya go to the hospital?"

"Uh—"

"Don't be hiding from me, kid."

"It's our mom. She has some sort of Alzheimer's."

The woman looked at Elizabeth. Sized her up.

"My second husband died of that shit. What d'ya need?" she said.

"Somewhere to sleep. And maybe some food. Our truck got stolen, so we have nothing." Matt said.

"All right. I'll get you settled in. Ruby!"

A tall young girl with cornrows gathered into a bun appeared from a room in the back. She wore a thin, drooping tank top and high-rise denim shorts.

"Take the desk, sweetie."

"Sure, Momma," Ruby said.

"Follow me, boys. I'm Grace, by the way." She took a key with a wooden stick attached from a corkboard covered with hooks and trotted out from behind the desk.

She led them along corridors painted in artichoke green, the paint blending with swathes of mold smeared along the edges. Bare fluorescent tubes hung from the ceiling, adding a cold blue hue to the stale air. One of them blinked to an irregular but persistent beat. Matt passed an open door. A stench of sweat poured out and found crevices in his nostrils, where it lingered.

"I have male and female dorms," Grace said. "I don't care what nobody says, but I'm not sure you want ya mother on her own, so I'm gonna give you boys a family room. Ordinarily, they're for parents with small children, but one's vacant, so be on ya best behavior, and I'll make an exception."

"Thank you," Matt said.

"That way the dealers won't bother you too much." She kicked at a needle lying in the middle of the corridor, sliding it off to one side. "You boys do drugs?" She turned around and stared Matt straight in the eyes. She wasn't blinking, so he did.

"Uh, no, ma'am," he said.

"Good. Now listen." Grace stopped at a door, inserted the key, turned it and opened the door. "This here," she said, motioning inside, "is my place. I don't care about the people taking drugs. That'd be impossible. But for ya own sake, and especially hers, you boys stay off that shit, all right?" She went inside.

Matt followed. There were bunk beds on both sides and a little table in between. Grace turned on the light.

"It's not much, but it should fit you fine. Communal bathrooms are further down the hall. Hit the showers, if you like."

Kevin went to one of the beds and helped Elizabeth to lie down. "Get some rest, Mom."

Grace stood in the doorway. "So, a couple of rules."

Matt nodded, looking at her.

"As I told you, I don't care about drugs. Should but can't. But *I do* care about my girls—both staff and residents. Touch them, you're dead. And not in that 'Let's call the police' kind of way. Here, I deal with shit myself."

Matt and Kevin both nodded in unison.

"All the women in here? Those are my daughters. All those fucked-up junkies and deadbeats? Those are my sons. So take a moment and imagine what Momma here's gonna do if you cross one of her daughters. Yes, that's right: she gonna tell all her sons to go fuck you up, in ways I couldn't even imagine myself."

Grace looked from Matt to Kevin.

"Which brings me to my second point. While you're here, *she* is ya mom." Grace pointed at Elizabeth. "Me?" Pointing back at herself. "I'm ya momma. Get it?"

Again, a frantic bobbing of heads.

"And here," she continued, "you do whatever the fuck Momma tells you. And then Momma takes care. Any questions?"

Dumbstruck, Matt looked at Kevin, who was just as speechless.

"Yes, ma'am. Just one question," Matt said humbly. "Uh, do you serve food here?" He stared at the floor. "Government froze our bank accounts."

"Yep. Minty cooks up a communal supper. We get donations from local stores, so it depends day to day. You grab a bowl for ya mom if she needs it, bring it back here. Should be ready in half an hour. Dining hall is to the left of the front desk."

"Thank you so much," Kevin said. He looked like he was on the verge of tears.

"No problem. Y'all drop by the front desk in the morning, and I'll get you sorted out with an allowance on ya funds. Need to go through government systems, and I hate that computer, so it's gonna have to wait till morning."

"Thanks again," Matt said. "For the room and all."

Grace looked past him at Elizabeth. She had already dozed off.

"Seems like she needs it," Grace said. She nodded a last time and went back out into the hallway, shutting the door behind her.

Kevin and Matt sat down on the lower bunk opposite their mom. They watched her in silence for a couple of minutes, neither of them willing to speak. Matt was waiting for his brother to apologize, since he'd clearly been the asshole. Matt only did what he did, after all, in order to protect them. Besides, this was all just as much Kevin's fault for losing the car keys.

"Hey man, I'm sorry for what happened out there," Kevin said at last.

"Don't worry, Kev. I get it. I didn't tell you the truth, and maybe I should have. But I needed to protect you—protect you both. You need to understand that."

Kevin didn't reply.

Matt sat quietly again, letting his little brother feel the pressure and intensity of the silence weighing on his shoulders, giving him time to realize that Matt was right.

"Okay," Kevin said grudgingly after a few moments. "But how long have you known?"

"Just a couple of days. Since we saw Dr. Aldridge."

"And what did *he* say?"

"That she might not have long."

Kevin squeezed his lips together. Matt could hear him swallow. He put his arm around his little brother.

"Easy, Kev. No need for tears. Be strong. I won't let it come to that, okay?" Matt said. He squeezed Kevin's shoulders, holding him tightly for a minute. "We know there is a working treatment—gene therapy, they said, right? I just have to figure out how to get it," Matt went on.

Kevin nodded and wiped a tear away. "If we *can* get it."

"I *will* get it! Okay? Trust me on this. I won't stop until we succeed. You with me?"

"Yes," Kevin said in a faint voice.

"You with me, Kev?"

Kevin straightened his back. "Yes."

"That's more like it. So, do you think we can trust Grace?"

"Sure, why not? She seems pretty straightforward."

"Yeah, but you know... This is a community center, after all. Underground hospitals and doctors are illegal. And she *does* work for the government."

"Yeah, well, I don't know. She doesn't strike me as the bureaucratic type, you know?"

"You might be right," Matt said. "I'll ask around at supper. You want something? I'll get some food for Mom anyway."

"No, thanks. I'm not hungry. Well, maybe some bread for later. That'd be nice."

"I'll get you a plate, too, for later. But you'll have to settle for cold. This isn't room service, you know." He ruffled his brother's hair. "You have to eat something, cold or not. Same with her. Okay?"

Kevin nodded and looked down, away from his brother.

Matt stood up. "Now's not the time to be pouty, you know," he said, and left the room.

18

A long line extended past the front desk and out the entrance. Matt found his way to the end and joined the queue. As it inched closer, he caught a savory whiff from the dining hall. Once he was inside, he could see steam rising from an enormous pot towards a nicotine-yellow ceiling. The room was huge, stuffed haphazardly with tables and chairs; every available inch was taken up with seating.

Most people in line were on their own. Many scratched at their tangled hair or placed their hands in the hollows of their crooked backs. Some coughed into their sleeves; others looked down at the floor. Most avoided eye contact. A large battered chandelier high overhead cast a bleak light on the room from bulbs missing their lampshades.

At the front of the line, Grace stood handling the plates. Next to her was Ruby, and at the end was a big broad man who swung a ladle.

"Evening," Grace said, handing Matt a bowl. "You're in for a treat. Gumbo. One of my own recipes."

"Are all these people staying here?" he said.

"No, a lot of locals come for the supper. Their one meal a day. Need one for your mother? And where's your brother, by the way? Here, get some rice." She waved him along to Ruby, who had large trays filled with rice in front of her.

"Both resting," Matt said to Grace over his shoulder. "I'll take some for them on the way out, if that's okay with you."

Grace nodded. Matt turned to see a scoop of sticky rice land on his plate, and then a spoonful of something hot and fragrant from Minty, as his nametag revealed.

Matt inhaled with pleasure as the spices rose to his nostrils. Holding his tray in front of him, he turned and looked over the crowded room. The guy next in line bumped into him and grumbled a bit.

"Sorry, man," Matt said, and took a step away from the swell of people coming off the line. Many of the tables were already filled, though the people eating at them seemed to keep to themselves. He recognized a couple of people from the crowd that had gathered to watch him fight with Kevin. They, at least, seemed to be talking to each other. He went over.

"Is this seat taken?" he said, pointing to one of the chairs.

There was a collective pause as the little group put down their spoons and looked at Matt.

"You can take it," a young man at the end of the table said. He was tall and broad, a bit like Matt himself. One side of his head was covered with ruffled, mangy spots of dark hair; the other was shaved clean. A large scar ran from the edge of his eyebrow to the top of his ear, then traveled all way round his skull. "If your brother didn't split your ass in two, that is."

The rest of the group broke into laughter.

Matt didn't respond.

"Where's your mom?" the man went on. "I'd pin her to the wall any day of the week." This earned him another huge laugh, and so he knuckled the guy next to him, not taking his eyes off Matt.

Matt sat down, avoiding the two men's eyes, and turned to his food. His first mouthful was equal parts gumbo and pride. The group went back to talking, leaving Matt to himself. It was difficult to eavesdrop; conversation was drowned out by the sound of spoons clanking on bowls, munching, and burping. Straining to hear, Matt leaned his shoulder towards the conversation.

"You catching that, Splitter?" It was the young guy at the end of the table again.

Matt looked up, paused, and withdrew his gaze to his bowl. "No," he said.

"Why you here, Splitter?"

Matt stopped his spoon on the way to his mouth and then lowered it again. He looked up and around the group.

"I'm looking for medical help. Serious doctors."

"You sick?" The people closest to him scooted their chairs back a bit.

"No, but my mom is. Do you know anyone that could help me? I can pay."

"That fine piece of meat? What she got? Ripped anus, from the pounding I gave her last night?"

There was another burst of laughter. Matt sighed and swallowed another mouthful of pride.

"It's none of your business. If you don't mind," Matt said.

"Sure. It's fine. We're just having some fun here," the guy said. "I might know someone. How much you got?"

"Whatever he charges."

"Well, I don't know how much he charges, but I reckon a fair referral price is—let's say two grand?"

"Shit, guys, you won't believe what I got my hands on this morning!" Another young guy with bleached hair slammed his bowl on the table and sat down next to Matt.

"So, I went to Med Center, you know, to hawk a bit," the guy continued.

"Hey, Skinny, you know better than barging in."

"Let me just tell my story, Rawls," Skinny said, but he held off, waiting.

Rawls nodded.

"So, people come running from the hospital," Skinny continued, "all yelling they're shooting and shit. So, I had to look, right?" He took a huge mouthful of food but kept talking. "So, I go against the stream of people to see what's up. Everyone's screaming. Some have bullet wounds and shit." Sauce ran out through his blabbering lips. "Bleeding all over." Skinny wiped his mouth with his sleeve. "So, I get to the plaza, and it's empty. Bodies spread out on the ground. Some guards apparently went crazy. And the kicker? There were dropped bags and valuables all over the place. So, I search. A wallet here, a purse there. Bit of cash, you know. Then I see keys."

Skinny took another huge spoonful. The others around the table looked at him with anticipation. He glared back at them, chewed a bit faster, and then swallowed.

"Car key," Skinny said.

Matt turned towards him and focused his attention to cut the noise.

"A fucking car key! So, I go to the parking lot, and there it is. My new pickup. Well, not new, but you know."

"Fuck off. No way!"

"For real! I'll show you. Just parked it out here."

"You can't get it to drive, man. It's voice controlled."

"Nope, not this one. It's one of the old ones—you know, all simple and shit."

"That's mine," Matt said, raising his voice to catch their attention.

Skinny turned and looked at him. The rest of the table did too.

"That's my truck," Matt repeated. He kept his head down, fixating on his bowl.

"Who the fuck are you?" Skinny shifted from all jolly to menacing in an instant.

"I'm Matt. It's my truck you stole."

"The fuck it is."

"Hey, Matt," Rawls said. "It's not your truck anymore. Skinny *found* it. You heard. Finders keepers and shit."

"Then I would like it back," Matt said.

"And I would like to have my dick tickling the back of your mom's throat, but when I look under the table, that ain't happening, now, is it?"

Matt paused and willed himself to breathe calmly. This time, there was no laughter. He raised his eyes slightly and saw only glares around the table as the group waited for the outsider to speak.

"No." Matt thought it best to keep his words simple and calm.

"Good."

Skinny, Rawls and the rest of the table turned back to their meals.

"How much do you want for it?" Matt said.

They all turned their heads again.

"So you want to buy it?" Rawls said. "Not sure Skinny wants to sell."

"Nah, man. I never had a truck before," Skinny said.

"What's your price?" Matt said.

"Uh, I don't know. Like ten, maybe?" Skinny laughed, and the rest of the table joined in.

"I can get that."

Skinny's laughter died down. He looked around the table, then back at Matt.

"You got that kind of money? Who the fuck are you?"

"Do we have a deal?"

"Fuck, yeah, we have a deal."

"Eh, Matt? What about my two grand?" Rawls said.

"Sure, that too, if you take me to a legit doctor," Matt said.

"So hand it over," Skinny said.

"I need to see the truck. See that you didn't wreck it."

"Of course I didn't. Who do you think I am? I know my driving."

"Eh, Skins. Show the man the merchandise," Rawls said.

Skinny stood up, leaned over, and looked down at Matt.

"So follow me, why don't ya?"

Matt stood up and walked after Skinny. The rest of the table followed along, with Rawls leading.

Matt's heart was pounding. What the fuck had he been thinking? He didn't have the money, but if he got the truck back, his mother could get out of this dump. So, if everything looked fine, he would figure something out.

Skinny strolled out the main entrance, swinging the truck key on his index finger, and started walking along the side of the building.

"You better not be fucking with us," Rawls whispered as he passed Matt, catching up to Skinny.

Matt's heart accelerated its pace, thundering to get out of his chest. He forced it back down. His brain cells were working double-time to produce an exit strategy.

"Is that it?" Rawls said from up front.

"Yeah, that's my new fucking ride," Skinny said.

The pickup was parked beside a couple of burn barrels, the moth-eaten armchair still on the bed. Matt couldn't see any scratches on the paint, though it was hard to tell in the twilight. He peered through the windows, walked around the truck, and tried to make out all their bags. Everything seemed to be there.

"So, everything in order?" Rawls said. "Quite the living room you got there."

"Yeah, seems like it," Matt said.

"So—show me the dough," Skinny said.

He'd been working on the answer for minutes, but came up empty-handed. "I don't have it right here."

"What?" Skinny said.

"I need to have my account unlocked. I can have it by tomorrow."

"No way. Fuck you. Where's my money?" Skinny started pacing behind Rawls, his arms jittering, fidgeting with the key.

"You see, Matt," Rawls said, "what Skinny is saying is that he kept his end of the bargain, and now it's time you keep yours. And then there's our little arrangement as well."

"I have the money; trust me. I just can't get it until morning."

Rawls held an arm out, blocking Skinny as he took a step forward.

"That wasn't the deal, now, was it? And you see, me, Skinny and all the others, we kind of feel you wasted our time. Isn't that right, boys?"

"Fuck, yeah!" Skinny was almost bouncing now.

"But I have the money," Matt protested. "I can get it. All of it."

Matt saw Skinny pull out a little plastic bag from his pocket and take a sniff of its contents.

"See, the problem is," Rawls went on, "that the more you keep talking, the more you're lying to my face. And I can't have that, you see."

He turned and took the little zip bag from Skinny. "So I'll ask you one last time. Do you have the money?" he said. He stuck his face in the bag and snorted the rest of its contents. When he'd finished, there was a film of white powder around his nose. He stretched his back, cracking his neck.

"No, bu—"

Rawls' fist hit the left side of Matt's jaw. Matt felt bones crunching. He dropped like a stone, asphalt scraping his chin. Matt lifted his body off the ground with one arm, extending the other towards Rawls. He tried to push the words through his lips, but excruciating pain stopped him from opening his mouth.

"Plea—"

Skinny's foot caught him in the armpit, twisting his shoulder and flinging Matt onto his back. Sounds became muffled. His eyes closed. He felt something cold tapping lightly at his right cheek. He opened one eye. Skinny squatted beside him, dangling the key in front of his eyes.

"HEY!" Grace screamed.

Pain shot up Matt's left side. Twice. He gasped for air.

As the gang fled, Skinny was bumped from behind, knocking the keys out of his hand. He crouched and scrabbled on the ground for them, then looked back at Grace running towards them, thought better of it and sprinted away into the darkness.

Matt coughed; his mouth filled with viscous iron. He reached out and clutched the keys, then touched his left side. Blood streamed between his fingers.

19

Glowing orange specks danced across Matt's eyelids. His abdomen was being squashed inwards; bandages were wrapped tight around his upper body, constricting his breathing. With every breath, he felt a dragging convulsion in his left ribs. As he tried to lift his right arm, the joint locked and pain pounded away underneath his shoulder blade.

The bright light disappeared as he opened his eyes. The woman standing over him moved her little pencil-sized flashlight. Her chestnut hair was pinned in a messy bun to the back of her head, keeping it away from her deep almond eyes. She wore a worried look; her lips were puckered and skewed to the side. She held his gaze, still dashing the light back and forth over Matt's face.

"Good. Fine reactions. No signs of concussion," she said. Then she smiled at Matt. "And you're awake." He smiled back.

Matt raised his head to look around. Agony radiated from his torso, forcing him back onto the metallic surface of the large prep table; his feet dangled over the edge. He was in a kitchen, with Kevin standing on one side and the woman on the other.

"He'll be fine, but he needs to rest," the woman said to Kevin.

"Thank you, Doctor. How can I pay you for your troubles?" Kevin said.

"Don't worry about it. Hospitals don't treat gang-related crimes anymore, so give your thanks to Grace for calling us."

Matt felt down the side of his chest; the gauze's light fibers stuck to his sweaty palm. His upper body was swaddled in the fabric; he was shirtless, and it kept the cold from creeping through. His bare arms trembled at the touch of the cold steel table, while fever kept his forehead bathed in sweat.

"Isn't there any way to repay the favor?" Kevin said to the woman.

A man stepped out of the shadows, into the light from a bulb dangling over the table. Matt hadn't noticed him before. He wore a black baseball cap that was frayed at the edges and a dark dusty-green trench coat. His chin was clean-shaven; the rest of his face was shadowed by the brim of the hat.

"Grace took care of that," the man said. "Again, you must thank her."

"Who are you?" Matt asked the woman in a muffled voice through his swollen jaw.

"I'm a doctor, Matt. My name is Ems," the woman said. "Listen, you got stabbed. Twice. It almost punctured your lung. You need to rest up, but I'll leave you some pills to keep infections out and reduce the fever, and some painkillers too."

"How about Mom? Can you help Mom?"

"Your mom?"

"She's got some form of Alzheimer's. We don't know what's happening to her," Kevin said, cutting off his brother.

"We don't really treat complicated things like that. You need to rest, too, Kevin," Ems said.

"But can you? Treat my mother, I mean," Matt mumbled.

Ems turned to the man in the trench coat, awaiting his answer.

"Just like everybody else, we don't have infinite resources," he said to Ems, then turning to Matt. "I'm afraid that your mother wouldn't be within our limitations."

"But *could* you?"

The man tightened his lips. His eyes were still hidden by the baseball cap.

"Maybe we could," he said, and paused. "But we won't." The man turned and walked to the door.

Ems looked back at Matt, her sparkle fading. "Get some rest, Matt. I'm sorry."

Matt tried to sit up, but the pain sent him tumbling off the side of the table. Kevin, trying to put his thin frame in the way of physics, gave way under the full dead weight of his bigger brother. The two of them tumbled to the floor with a thud.

Kevin helped Matt stand and gave him a shoulder for support as Matt tried to turn and face the two people leaving.

"Why did you save me, then?" Matt screamed.

The man in the trench coat stopped in the doorway. Ems passed him and hurried out into the hallway.

"Why did you save me?" Matt repeated, panting with the little breath he had left.

"You deserved a second chance," the man said.

"And my mom doesn't?"

"It's not that simple."

"Fuck you! You saved me because you could, and now you don't want to save her because it's hard? Who gives you the right to judge?"

The man turned back towards them, stepped up close to Matt

and his brother, and took off his cap. His eyes were a sharp, arctic blue. He stared at the two trembling brothers for a moment.

"You have no clue what's going on, do you?"

Matt glowered back at him.

"Do you really want to know why saving your mother isn't simple? Why saving your mother could cost the lives of millions? Why nobody, *nobody*," he hissed, "is willing to sacrifice anything for the benefit of others?"

"Yes."

The man straightened and pulled his cap back on, tucking it down and covering his face again.

"Fine. Go rest, and then meet me at eight o'clock tomorrow evening at Union Station." He looked at his wristwatch. It was gold, or golden at least, as far as Matt could see under the dim light. "Let's say forty hours. That gives you more time to recover. And please, bring an appetite so that you don't embarrass me." He turned on his heel and went out the door. Ems, who had been waiting outside, followed behind him.

Kevin shut the door, hooked a chair with his foot, scooted it over beside Matt, and sat him down. "What happened?" he asked.

"A fight. For our truck."

"So that's why you had the key?"

"Do you have it?"

"Grace gave it to me."

Matt sighed in relief.

"You can't do that, you know," Kevin said.

"Do what?"

"Get into shit like that. Ems said that guy's knife came inches from puncturing your lung. Didn't you listen? Pure luck, she said."

Matt was silent.

"What did you think would happen, Matt? You don't know how to fight. You're not a drug dealer or a fucking gang member," Kevin continued.

"But we needed the truck."

"We need *you*! I need you. Mom needs you."

Matt was silent again.

Kevin looked around the kitchen.

"It'll be morning soon. I promised Grace I'd clean this place up before they come in to cook breakfast." He held out an arm to Matt. "Come on. Let me help you get to our room."

The two brothers staggered down the corridor. Kevin had wrapped a dish rag around Matt's bloody bandage so that it wouldn't drip along the way. Back in their room, he put Matt to bed and tucked the blanket around him.

"We need water, food. I need to—" Matt started.

"You don't need to *anything*. You are going to rest, and I will get whatever stuff we need."

"No, I'll do it tomorrow." Matt winced in agony as he adjusted his pillow.

"Are you kidding me? You need to listen. And for once, trust *me*. Does it hurt?"

Matt nodded.

"Good, so use your fucking brain and stay in bed! My god, you're an idiot. You just got twelve stitches. Give yourself a fucking break." Kevin shook his head.

"Sorry, Kev."

"Ems gave me these." Kevin tossed a blister pack of white, unlabeled pills onto the table beside Matt's pillow. "For all that stuff she told you about. Take two every couple of hours. Three if you need to," he said.

"Thanks."

"You're welcome. And now, if you'll excuse me, I have a kitchen to clean."

Matt took a couple of pills and closed his eyes.

■ ■ ■

After hours of sleep, Matt woke. Beside the other bed, Kevin was helping Elizabeth get up, occasionally bumping into Matt's bed. If he lay still, the wound was bearable, but even the tiniest twist of his back sent flutters of stabbing pain underneath his ribs. Seeing he was awake, Kevin told him to go back to sleep, told him he needed rest and told him everything was being taken care of. Matt tried to let the discomfort from his sweat-drenched pillow take his mind off the agony in his jaw. Carefully, he reached for the packet of pills. Two wouldn't do it this time. Three—no, four. He swallowed them without water and went back to sleep.

The next time he awoke, Kevin was sitting at his bedside, helping him get upright so he could eat a sandwich. Kevin had stocked up on supplies. He told Matt that Grace had helped unlock their account, but other than a newly imposed spending limit, everything worked as it used to. He'd even bought Matt some Reese's Peanut Butter Cups for dessert.

Chewing was easier now; Matt managed half the sandwich and a couple of the candies before his jaw demanded rest. Then Kevin left him to check on their mother, who was playing cards with Grace. Matt dozed off once more.

It was the middle of the night before he woke again. He lay watching Elizabeth sleep for a bit. He heard Kevin outside their door talking to somebody for almost ten minutes, but the voices were too muffled for Matt to make out the words. Finally, Kevin tiptoed into the room; Matt pretended to be asleep.

The next morning, Kevin helped Matt out of bed and down to the showers. Elizabeth was helping Grace prepare breakfast, Kevin said. He had bought fresh bandages for Matt and wrapping to protect his stitches in the shower. There was also a fresh new set of clothes, all thanks to Matt's little brother. Clean and dressed, Matt popped into the kitchen, chatted with Elizabeth and Grace, who were both cheerful, and then the Turners all ate breakfast together. Afterward, Matt and Kevin went for a walk, though the soreness in Matt's chest made it more of a stroll. Taking the pills helped, so he kept at it.

He had an afternoon nap, and when he woke from that, he felt better. It was almost dinner time, and he remembered that he had a meeting with the man in the green trench coat.

"Do you really need to go?" Kevin said, worried.

"What do you mean? Of course I need to go. They might be able to help Mom and get us out of here."

"But you said to be wary of these people…"

"Yes, but they also fixed me up, never asked for a penny. Don't you think they might be legit?"

"I guess. Maybe. But Mom seems to like it here. She's been having a great time, chatting up staff and helping Grace. What if this place is what's best for her?"

"She's dying, Kevin. And I can't stand and watch as that happens. Can you?"

Kevin frowned. "I guess not."

"Exactly! So I'm gonna do whatever I can. Trust me. You don't have to be scared. I'll fix this," Matt said. "You wait and see. I think this guy with the cap, and especially the doctor, could be Mom's saviors."

Matt left for the metro station. It was still early, but since his speed wasn't up to par, he wanted to be sure that he wouldn't be late.

20

Coming up from the metro, Matt spotted the man in the green trench coat and baseball cap. He was standing under the vaults and arches of the station, looking over the top of a large unfolded subway map. As Matt approached, the man curled the map into one hand and began walking towards the exit. Matt paced himself to keep up, closing the distance as the man stopped outside to throw the map into a trash can.

"We're not alone in there. How's your wound, Matt?" the man said.

"Better. The pills are helping a lot."

"Good. But you wanna be careful with those. Ems didn't give you over-the-counter stuff."

"Sure. I'll go easy. Where are we headed? And do you have a name?"

"You hungry?"

Matt nodded.

"Good. I'm Zee. Follow me."

Zee slowed down but kept a step or two in front of Matt. If Matt caught up, Zee looked away, acting like a stranger. Matt kept quiet, panting, holding a hand over his wound whenever he felt like the stitches were stretched to their limit.

They were somewhere downtown, Matt reckoned, though having never been to 0-1 before, he recognized only glimpses of the dome and the needle. They were headed towards high-rises with double-digit floor numbers and sharp geometric steel and glass constructions. Now that the sun was far under the horizon, most were black and dark, offering faint mirrored reflections of their surroundings. Matt could see an occasional office, apartment or even a full floor with lights still on. It was still gloomy but, combined with the ambient light from the surrounding cityscape, not the deep darkness Matt knew back home.

"Almost there," Zee said, letting Matt get alongside him now.

They turned a corner, and on the other side of the street Matt saw a line of people snaking away from a tiny door leading inside a towering office building. There was a neon sign hanging above the door that read *Yamada's* in a curvy bright-red script. Matt couldn't remember the last time he'd seen a neon sign that was not sterile indigo blue. Neon signs were restricted to infrastructure, emergency hospitals, police stations and such.

They continued down the street, opposite the line, passing close to fifty people. Then Zee stopped at the next corner and turned around. He looked at Matt and nodded towards the gathering.

"Did you notice anything—odd, let's say?" he said.

Matt looked back at the line. "Besides the neon sign? No."

"Exotic, isn't it? But no—look at the people waiting in line."

Matt squinted and peered back at the queue. It was hard to make out faces, and the glow from the sign only stretched so far.

"That line includes people from all walks of society, from high and low," Zee said. "Those two men there, in suits? Politicians from the hill. One of them is on the Board of Electricity. Meanwhile, the other's having an affair with his wife, but of course, he doesn't know that. Guy over near the end, that's Oleg. He's a Russian ex-military scientist, except that he hit the bottle hard once he got fired, so now he's living out of a cardboard box, down near the overpass."

People came out of the building every once in a while, letting the next duck inside.

"And that is Rosie." Zee nodded at a little old woman whose bent shape resembled the arches at Union Station. She carried a large plastic bag of Styrofoam containers. "Comes here every Tuesday to pick up for her five grandkids. Her daughter works the late shift at Central Grid Hospital. You know, where they rejected your mother. Rosie can't cook anymore, because of her back. So she goes to Yamada's."

Rosie looked across the street at them and lifted one hand to give Zee a quick wave, then reached back down to steady the plastic bag. Zee gave her a nod.

"Oh, and if you ever say hello, she'll give you shit if you don't call her 'madam.' Just so you know."

They stood for a minute watching the line as it edged along the sidewalk.

"How do you know all this?" Matt said.

"I look. And I listen. Amazing the number of people looking for a willing ear these days. And there are surprisingly few who think you remember what they say."

"So, why are *we* here?" he said.

"Same as everybody else: to get the best Japanese in two hundred miles. I'm fucking starving, aren't you?"

"Well, sure, but—"

"Come on. I have a table; we don't have to wait in line."

Zee led him around the building, and they scooted down a ramp to a garage in the basement. Through boom barriers, Zee nodded at the man in the booth. On the far wall, opposite the entrance, past rows of fancy driverless cars, there was a cargo lift. Zee and Matt walked over and stepped in, and Zee pressed a button. When the door opened again, they stepped out into a small storage room and through a pair of revolving doors, and suddenly Matt found himself in the middle of a bustling kitchen.

Steam sizzled from pans; there was the clank of cast-iron pots tossed between metal shelves, the rhythmic sound of a cleaver chopping scallions, all while a flurry of Japanese chatter floated above the noises, from chef to chef.

"*Konbanwa*, Mr. Zee," one of the chefs said. He had streaks of gray in his pitch-black hair. He wiped his hands in his apron and shook both their hands with both of his. Then he ushered them towards a door, away from the constant flow of servers. Matt followed Zee and entered a small break room with an old TV screen and a table with four chairs around it. The chef yelled something at two younger chefs who were sitting and watching baseball. Flinging down the last of their rice, they hurried back to the kitchen.

"What do you want?" Zee asked Matt, taking a seat. He hung his coat over the back and set his cap on the table.

"I don't know. Do they have a menu?"

"Ha. Not for us. That would be rude." Zee winked at him. "Never had Japanese?"

Matt shook his head.

Zee spoke to the old man waiting in the corner. They both

laughed, and then the chef walked out. He came back thirty seconds later with two frosted mugs, beer splashing at the brim and frothy foam overflowing.

"Don't you just love baseball?" Zee's eyes were fixed on the television.

"I haven't seen much, to be honest," Matt said.

"That's a shame. It's the ultimate conversational spectator sport. Not much going on, so you can sit with your friends, get some dogs or a Big Gulp or whatever. But then there's the anticipation." He took a big sip of his beer without taking his eyes away from the screen. "Everybody goes silent. The whole crowd locked in for that one pitch," he said, and paused. "SWING AND A MISS!" Zee yelled at the screen and gave a laugh. "And then it's back to your popcorn," he said, and looked at Matt. He raised his glass. "Sorry—how rude of me. *Kanpai!*"

Matt raised his glass, feeling a bit insecure, and took a mouthful, trying not to spill. Tiny hairs on his forearms rose as he wiped the foam from his upper lip.

"That was Mr. Yamada, by the way. He always greets me. I like that—tending to a patron," Zee said. "So Matt, why are we here?"

"I don't know. To eat, I guess?"

"Oh, yes. That's a given. But why? Think I dragged you all the way down here to tell you that Mr. Yamada's noodles cure all illnesses? Though they might do that. Any illness that matters, anyway."

"No, I guess not. I don't know, to be honest."

"Then I guess it's time I told you. You see, Yamada here is doing something exceptional. He feeds both the poor and the rich with very limited resources. He doesn't care about your status. He believes in the good in every human being, and therefore, takes honor and pride in serving the best ramen, for *everyone*."

"They let him do that? I mean, the neon sign, the non-segregation. He gets to do all that? How?"

Matt sat back, perplexed, holding his beer in his hands. Zee took another sip from his mug, gazing right back.

"He grabbed our government by the balls and squeezed till they yelped, I guess. I think we need more people like Mr. Yamada, don't you?" Zee said.

Pushing the door open with his back, Mr. Yamada walked in again, two steaming bowls in hand. Zee and Yamada exchanged words, nods and bows, and then the old man disappeared again.

"Ah, tonkatsu. My favorite." Zee sniffed above the bowl. "Get a whiff of that. Did you know that you can tell by the color how thoroughly the chef cleaned the pork bones of coagulated blood?"

Matt shook his head and lifted the wooden ladle sticking up from the bowl. The powerful pork broth hit his nose like a sledgehammer, steaming open all the pores in his face. Zee grabbed a pair of chopsticks from a cup on the table, then took a paper napkin, tucked it into his shirt, and lifted the whole bowl up under his chin. He flung noodles into his mouth, almost faster than he could swallow them. Many of them splashed back down into the bowl.

"Slurping helps the aromas and the flavors unfold," he said.

Matt tried to get a hold of his noodles, but with a spoon and a stick, he couldn't make ends meet. He settled for some spoonfuls of the broth first.

"I love these eggs," Zee said cheerfully. "They soak in soy sauce for twelve hours. Can you believe it? The amount of effort baffles me every time."

Before Matt had even gotten halfway through his food, Zee put down his empty bowl, gulped down half his mug of beer, and sat back in his chair. He studied Matt as he tried to stick noodles on the spoon. Matt noticed he held back a grin.

"Don't worry; it takes practice. You'll get it after a few more times," Zee said. "Did you like it?"

"Yes, it was—I don't know. Very… rich, flavor-wise."

"Yes, exactly! Rich. That's what care and attention get you. Oh, look—here come the gyozas."

Yamada came in once again with two plates of half-moon-shaped dumplings.

"They come steamed as well, but I like pan-fried the best." Zee took a few small bottles from a tray and mixed himself a sauce in a small bowl. "We can share if you don't want to make your own. I don't mind."

Matt tried to pick one of the little crescents up with his chopsticks, and to his surprise, succeeded.

"You're getting the hang of it. So how does it feel to be rated second-hand human?"

The words sliced Matt's eardrums and exploded inside his head. He coughed, half a dumpling still in his mouth. He looked at Zee.

"What do you mean?" Matt already knew what he meant.

"At the hospital. Getting told there's no help for you or your kind. I know the drill; I know how it works. How did it make you feel?"

Matt put down his chopsticks.

"Angry, I guess."

"Yes. That's right. Angry. And do you know why it made you feel angry?"

"Because my mom couldn't get the treatment?"

"No. That hurt, sure, but what made you angry was the stamp they mashed onto your forehead. They said that your lives—your life, your mother's life, your brother's life—are not worth our *investment*," Zee said.

Matt, taken aback, slumped almost a full foot down in his seat.

Zee dipped a gyoza and then bit it in half. Turning the remainder between his sticks, studying the insides, he chewed and continued. "*We* don't think you will ever repay what it costs. So *we're* cutting the slack. Trimming the weeds. *That's* what they said." Zee put the other half of the gyoza down on the plate, leaned forward, and peered into Matt's eyes; his own were gleaming with contempt.

"That's government for you. Right there. Assessments. Not to see if something is possible or plausible, but to make sure that *everything* is a positive return on investment. It's how we flourish, how we keep the growth potential, they say."

Matt's shoulders sank, and he pulled his knees together. He looked around at the table, from his plate to his glass, to the mug of disposable chopsticks, to the little tray of soy sauce, oils and vinegar, trying to avoid that piercing stare.

Zee sat back, giving him a break to recuperate. "Do you think Oleg out there pays the same as the two politicians to eat here?"

Matt shrugged.

"He doesn't. Mr. Yamada charges the man, not the item. Some have more to spare, and so they pay for those who don't. It might seem like an idea from socialism or communism, but that's not what Mr. Yamada believes. His simple thought is that we are all human, and we all deserve to eat well."

Matt didn't know how to enter the conversation, let alone figure out what his mother had to do with the price of noodles.

"And that's why we all come here at the end of a long day," Zee said. He emptied his beer. "The food is the best you can get, no doubt about that, but that plays second in our visits to Yamada's. He makes us feel human amidst all that is going on. He shows us there's a better place. He makes us believe. He shows hope. *'All men are created equal'*—do you know who wrote that? Thomas Jefferson, in the *Declaration of Independence*, back in 1776. And no, I don't believe in gender inequality, and I don't think Jefferson did, either. But all people being created equal—don't you think our government forgot that phrase?"

Matt didn't know what to say. So again, he kept quiet.

"I know it's a lot to process. So take your time. Meanwhile, we are gonna finish up with some yakitori. Skewers over charcoal. Ah, here he is."

Mr. Yamada walked in the door.

"Do you need one more?" Zee asked Matt, and pointed at his beer.

"I'm good."

"Just for me, then." He waved his mug, and Mr. Yamada exchanged it for a new freezing-cold lager right away.

Zee looked at the plate of yakitori. "It's chicken liver and chicken skins. Just feel the contrast in texture. If there were a God in Heaven, this would be his recipe."

Matt watched Zee pincer the slivers of meat between his teeth, pulling the thin wooden sticks through. His own appetite had depleted.

"How's this going to help my mom?"

"You've come to a fork in the road, Matt, and you need to

decide. Would you sacrifice thousands of people to hunt for a cure, potentially saving your mother? Or would you help thousands of people to *not* end up in a similar situation to hers, potentially sacrificing your mother?"

Matt was silent.

"You asked if I could save her."

"Yes."

"I believe I can, though, of course, nothing in this world is certain. I can, however, promise you that if you walk down the road I suggest, you'll get to save the millions suffering under this segregation. But I need to trust that you're on my team and ready to make the necessary sacrifices.

"So, tell me, Matt. Are you ready to get to work and change this system?"

21

"She started drooling half an hour ago. I haven't been able to get a response," Kevin said as Matt walked into their room at the community center. Elizabeth lay on her side in bed; Kevin was sitting on the floor next to her head. He was holding a tissue to her lips, dabbing at a near-constant trickle of saliva flowing from the corner of her mouth. Tissues were strewn all over the floor.

"What?" Matt rushed over and kneeled down next to her, joggling her. No response.

"She also cramps sometimes. See, like this. The arm."

Elizabeth's left arm trembled; her eyes flickered under her half-closed eyelids.

"Why haven't you done anything? Help me get her up. I have a place we can go," Matt said. He'd left his brother alone for barely two hours, and this was the result.

"What, should I have left her? A place where?"

"Yes, a place. Grab her."

The two brothers carried their mother through the hallways. The tremors had spread through her body to all her limbs. They passed the front desk, where Grace stood talking to Ruby.

"Hey, Kev?" Ruby called out.

Kevin looked over his shoulder.

"We'll pray for her. Let me know, yeah?"

Kevin nodded.

Matt could see his brother's eyes were welling with tears. "Let's go," he said.

They carried her out through the entrance. Zee stood under a tree, lighting a cigarette.

"This way." Matt nodded towards the truck. "She's gotten worse."

They hurried down the rows of cars and burn barrels. Matt was in front, walking backward, supporting his mother's body. Flickers of light cast Elizabeth's shadow like a stretcher up against the bricks.

"That your truck?" Zee asked.

Kevin stopped suddenly, and Matt struggled not to lose his grip.

"Kevin!"

His brother looked past him, frozen solid, his hands still holding on to their mother.

Matt turned and looked over his shoulder. Someone had trashed the pickup. The side windows were broken, the front and tail lights bashed to pieces. Glass shards lay all around the truck. Graffiti had been sprayed onto the sides, spelling out *WASTERS*.

Matt sighed. "Can you open the door, please?" he urged Zee.

Zee reached in through the broken window to unpin the lock. He opened the door and brushed glass fragments off the backseat. They slid Elizabeth inside. Kevin climbed in the other door and rested her head on his lap, and Zee got into the front passenger seat.

Matt walked around the truck and smelled something burnt. He looked up and saw the smudges of smoke on the upholstery of his father's armchair. He jumped up on the truck bed. The bastards had slashed the bottom cushion of the chair; springs were sticking out. He ran his hand across the fibers of the back rest. Wet. The drizzle from the day before had probably prevented the fire from fully consuming the chair. The once-smooth velvet felt rough under his hands as he found the hotbed down near the seams.

Matt shook his head in disbelief. It was the last physical remnant of his father, and he only himself to blame. How could he have been so reckless, leaving it here in the truck like that? He could see his father's disappointed face in the patches of charring. With a sigh, he heaved and pushed, and at last the chair tumbled off the bed, hitting the ground with a dense thump. He jumped down, shoved it out of the way and got into the driver's seat.

"Where to?" he said, his voice cracking. He brushed away a tear, forestalling an onslaught.

"Just follow my instructions," Zee said.

They drove through downtown, past dark buildings illuminated by the streaks of headlights weaving through the pitch-black streets. Here and there, Matt could see the glimmers of lighted windows. Like the tiny sparkles of stars above an infinite, deep blue sky, the shimmers of bulbs glittered along the buildings in the dark, endless abyss of glass, steel and stone.

Gradually, as they worked their way out of the populated inner city, the blackness thickened and the embers of streetlit neighborhoods became visible on the horizon.

Matt stopped outside a fence in front of a large low-rise warehouse, per Zee's request. There were no lights anywhere in sight. Matt had lost his sense of direction; bigger cities were not his area of expertise, and keeping his inner bearings became impossible once all the colors and shapes had melted into shadow and gray.

"Is she still trembling?" Zee said, turning to speak to Kevin.

"Yeah, but no vomit or blood," Kevin said.

"Okay. See that gate over there?"

"Yes," Matt said.

"Driver over to it, and I'll make sure it opens." Zee jumped out of the truck and ducked through a small tear in the fence, vanishing into the dark grounds.

Matt steered the pickup over towards the gate.

"You trust this guy?" Kevin said.

"He's an alternative. And he might save Mom," Matt said.

"Alternative to what?"

"The hospital. Government."

The gates slid apart, barbed wire rustling atop it. Matt continued inside at walking speed. He couldn't see any people and didn't know where to go. Zee stepped into the beam from the only working headlight and pointed Matt towards a stack of shipping containers in the farthest corner of the lot. Matt parked, killed the engine, turned off the lights, and jumped out of the truck.

"Can't we park near the entrance? She's quite heavy," Matt said, walking towards Zee.

Zee stood at the end of the container. He pulled the big lever down and dragged at the large metal door. "This *is* the entrance." Walking inside the pitch-black enclosure, Zee pulled a cord attached to a lightbulb, revealing a large metal cage. Pulleys and gears were attached above it; wires ran through a rough-cut hole in the ceiling up into the container above. All around, acoustic foam covered the walls, serving as impromptu sound-proofing.

Matt and Kevin carried Elizabeth into the cage, and then Matt went back outside and parked the truck, as Zee instructed, inside the warehouse. Twenty or thirty other cars were already in the vast hall, all of them, Matt noticed, older, discontinued models.

The steel-framed freight elevator hummed as the two brothers stood with Elizabeth in their arms. Over them, a single bulb lit the bare walls as a jolt sent the platform lowering down into the underground. Slow and steady. Zee stood, one finger pressing a green-lit button.

For a few minutes, they stood inside the rattling cage, listening to the sounds of steel bars and wires screeching, and then the slight hints of motor oil were replaced by a repugnant odor of rot. A sliver of dim light flooded the lift from the floor up. As the sliver grew to fill half the elevator, Matt looked out at a massive ceiling with what seemed like endless rows of rigid pipes and bent tubes winding in, out and around each other. Further down, a hall stretched out into the distance, with bare lights swaying from the rusty maze above. Here and there, bulbs were blinking, crying for replacement. Sheets of drywall, erected at floor level, turned the vast room into cubicles and offices. Enormous fans were swishing at both ends, providing a gentle breeze in the not-so-fresh air.

Matt clenched his jaw, blocking his nose.

"It gets better further down," Zee said.

"What is this place?" Kevin muttered.

"Home. For the future of humanity, as I like to call it."

The elevator came to a halt. They stepped out on to the rock and dirt floor, flattened to be functional, and greeted Ems, who wore a white coat, and a man in oily rags.

"We need a medical check on Elizabeth here," Zee said. "Symptoms of Alzheimer's, but I doubt that's it. Something doesn't add up."

"I'll find a room and get to it right away," Ems said. She turned towards Matt, sizing him up. She lifted his shirt a bit and ran a finger gently over the edges of the bandages. "You doing better, Matt?"

"Yeah. The pills helped a lot. Thank you."

Ems smiled. "Don't mention it."

"And Ems?" Zee said.

Ems pulled her gaze away from Matt's.

"Get Faulk to pull up her medical records," Zee continued. "It might prove useful."

"Will do." Ems helped the other man heave Elizabeth onto a ragged hospital bed.

"Give her ten mills of synaptic fluid for starters," she said. The man hooked up an IV bag, and Ems proceeded to insert a Venflon catheter into the back of Elizabeth's hand. Matt noticed her hands were clean, as opposed to those of the man in rags. Then she turned to the brothers, who stood watching the commotion without getting in the way.

"Would you like to see where she's going to stay?"

They looked at each other, flabbergasted.

"Uh, yes. That'd be nice," Matt said.

They followed Ems. The man pushed their mother's bed along the bumpy floor, down a corridor and into a small, square room. There were no decorations, but it had an abundance of electrical outlets.

"This will be her room," Ems said. "If needed, we can hook up all necessary devices here and operate as well, so at times, we might restrict access. But you're always welcome to come and check up on her. You can look through the little window in the door if it's closed."

"Uh, thank you," Matt said.

"What happens now?" Kevin said.

"The synaptic fluid should stabilize the trembling, and then we'll hopefully get to the bottom of all this." She smiled at them. More at Matt, he reckoned. "I'm sure Zee will show you the rest of this place. I'll see you later, I'm sure, but now I should get to work."

Matt and Kevin went back outside the room, where Zee waited in the corridor.

"Let's get you some bunks so you can get some sleep, guys. And we'll see how she's doing in the morning," he said.

Matt and Kevin followed Zee through the twisting corridors until they came to a room attached to the main hall. It was like a cave dug out of a wall; big dark theater curtains hung over the entrance, shielding what turned out to be a dormitory from the lights of the main hall.

"You can grab a bed in there, but if you need to talk, please, do it out here. There are water coolers all around. And if you're hungry, the mess is straight down there." He pointed down another hallway. "It's not a lot, but we're keeping off-grid."

"Thanks. For everything," Matt said.

"*Off-grid?*" Kevin asked.

"For protection. From the government. Many people's futures depend on us, so we depend on them and their electricity. If we plugged ourselves into the regular grid, it would be easy for the government to monitor power surges. Their crawlers would easily spot excessive use in an abandoned warehouse. All of this?" Zee motioned around the hall. "We're skimming off the existing grid, from established low-risk endpoints, a few watts here and there. Ever heard the expression 'Many a mickle makes a muckle'? This way, it's almost impossible for the government to notice us without auditing all endpoints simultaneously."

Matt put a hand on his little brother's arm and cut him off. "We're just happy that you'll take us in. We'll help with anything. You name it," he said.

"Sure. But first, get some rest. Your wounds still need it. Then let's look at it in the morning, shall we? I have some business that needs my attention. Goodnight, guys."

22

It was still early morning, Kevin's wristwatch told him. Matt was still sleeping. Kevin decided to vacate the hard mattress and take a gander at the complex.

There was already a faint buzz of activity. By the looks of their pasty skin complexion and sunken eyes, the people here were running on independent biological clocks. He wasn't hungry, so he skipped the mess and found himself lost in the intricacies of the drywall maze.

Moisture hung in the air; the huge fans were not powerful enough to keep a coherent flow. Mold grew from corners, spread through entire corridors, and crept its way from room to room. Running his hands along the walls, he found a particularly soggy spot and prodded his finger through. He felt a drop of water trickling its way down his spine and glanced up at the ceiling. There was a leaky pipe above him, dripping enough to make a puddle on the floor. Kevin held out his hand, caught a drop, and put his nose to his palm. Acidic in smell, opaque brown, though viscous like water. He dodged the next drop and trotted along the corridor.

Some rooms were empty; some were like his mother's—outlets all around, hospital bed in the center. A few were locked and had no windows to look through. Some had pieces of Scotch tape and residue from felt pens on them, but it was impossible to make out the writing. A door stood open, letting blue-tinted light flood into the corridor along with a faint buzzing noise. Kevin walked closer and peeked inside. A man sat in front of a multitude of various sized screens, crammed like puzzle pieces sticking against the wall, showing various text outputs and graphs. Below the monitors, a desk ran along the entire wall; old computer keyboards were strewn across it. Kevin hadn't seen those since computer basics in fourth grade. He gave a slight involuntary cough; the guy turned in his swivel chair, then got up and walked over to Kevin, excused himself, and shut the door to the corridor. No window for Kevin to look through.

He wandered on and turned up at the entrance, retraced his steps from the day before, and found his mother's room. Elizabeth lay in bed, eyes closed, wrapped in hospital rags with holes and tears at the seams. Now tubes were protruding from her nose, taped to her cheeks, running down to an apparatus pumping air through the clear plastic. Kevin scratched at the surface of one of them, removing some grime near the nozzle entrance. He stood and inspected the bandage wrapping Elizabeth's Venflon. There was a dark crimson blotch of dried blood underneath the top layer.

Grabbing a skimpy metal stool, he sat beside her and held her free hand. He looked at the display on her heart rate monitor and sighed. The beat was steady and rhythmic; a tiny dot made its elastic bounces on a thin green line. He adjusted a volume knob, closed his eyes, and fell into sync with her heartbeat. Running his fingers across the back of her hand, he could feel how prominent her bones were. He caressed her forearm; the skin was loose. He sat for minutes in silence and then leaned towards her ear.

"I'm sorry, Mom. I can't do this anymore. I tried; I really did. But I have a place to be. Someone waiting. I'll check in with Matt, just to see… You know… But if not…"

The last two sentences he wasn't able to put into words. Kevin wiped away his tears with his sleeve, leaving dark spots on his light gray shirt. He took a last look at his mother, so peaceful in sleep. He kissed her forehead.

"I love you."

He let his tears fall freely as he left the room.

■ ■ ■

Kevin found Matt on his way to the mess hall, rubbing crust from his eyes.

"Hey, Kev, wanna eat?" Matt said.

Kevin still wasn't hungry but followed his brother into the mess hall. Matt told him how well he'd slept, and how rested he felt, and how, for the first time since the assault, he had managed a night on only the prescribed dose of painkillers.

There was no queue, and only a few people sat around the many tables. There was seating for fifty, Kevin guessed. Three trays stood on a serving table, heating lamps above each. Scrambled eggs, scrambled vegetables and scrambled oatmeal. All the plates were cracked; Kevin sifted through them to find a clean one. Matt piled his plate with food from all three trays; Kevin only sampled the eggs. There was a lump where his appetite should have been.

They sat down at a table by themselves. Matt dug in, shoveling up scramble after scramble. Kevin sat and watched, shifting his eggs back and forth on his plate, listening absently to his brother's constant flow of talk. Everything from the food and his sleep to the friendly people received praise from a cheery Matt, and of course, his own initiative in getting them here didn't go by unmentioned. Eventually, Matt made a passing comment about the positive outlook for their mother. It was the proverbial straw, and Kevin couldn't hold back any longer.

"So you think she's gonna make it?" Kevin said.

"I'm sure. If there is a place that's able to cure her, then I guess we found it." He smiled at his little brother. "Don't you think so?"

Kevin just stared at him.

"Zee is really forthcoming," Matt continued, "and Ems seems like an excellent doctor, so I guess there's not much more that we can do. And Mom's a strong woman, you know. She raised both of us." Then he grinned. "Nothing she can't get through."

"Are you kidding me? Can't you see?"

"See what?" Matt glanced up from his plate, still half full, before scooping up more vegetables.

"See this for what it is? Are you that blind? Is it the all-knowing presence of Zee or Ems's wavy locks? Tell me how this place isn't exactly what you warned me against?"

"It's not. These people are legit, Kev. Ems fixed me out of sheer compassion. Don't you remember?"

"Spoken like a true addict," Kevin spat. "'The first one's free.'" He looked down, shuffling his spoon around the eggs. Matt ducked his head to regain eye contact.

"Hey, Kev?" Matt said. "What's wrong?"

Kevin looked up. "Look around this place. Does it seem clean? Does it seem sanitized to you?"

"Hey, it's the best we can get, so lay off."

"The fuck it is."

"Do you know anywhere better we could be?" Matt raised his voice.

"Yes, and *you* do, too."

Matt looked perplexed.

"Grace told me," Kevin continued. "Everybody gets the offer before being thrown to the streets. If you took part in the labor force, we would get to keep the apartment, and Mom could get treatment at the hospital. But you turned that offer down, didn't you?"

"It's not that simple, Kev."

"Yes, it is. I would have accepted it on the spot. But I can't, 'cause I'm a minor." Kevin kept his gaze locked with his brother's. "But your pride stood in the way, didn't it?" He shook his head. "You would never dream of letting me care for Mom. You don't think I can handle it, do you?"

Matt slammed his spoon down hard on the plate, drawing attention from the other diners.

"No, you're right. I *don't* think you can handle it; I don't think you have any clue what it's like losing a parent, and I *don't* think you have any chance of making it through college without my help. So forgive me for putting your needs before my own."

Kevin sat back in the chair, relaxing his clenched jaw, opening his eyes wide. He looked down at the table, shaking his head back and forth. "So that's it. You want me to succeed in what you couldn't." Putting his hand to his head, Kevin combed his fingers through his hair and looked at his brother. "Haven't you figured it out yet? I'm not going to college, Matt."

"Of course you are. You've got honors. You can pick any place, any school in the country." Matt picked up his spoon and began eating again.

"No, Matt. It's not what *I* want. I thought you'd guessed it by now, with all the questions, plus the fact I never wanted your help to find any fucking courses. Sorry, but I'm not gonna live up to your expectations. You said it yourself: I need to find my own way."

Matt stared at him as though he'd grown another head. "That would be stupid! Not to go to college. Are you out of your fucking mind?"

"I'm not gonna do it. I'm sorry, Matt."

"You're *sorry*? Your way is going through college. Have you any idea what I've gone through to give you this opportunity? Any idea what Dad went through?"

"*My* dad? I never had a dad. You were my dad—don't you know that?"

"Dad always told me that he worked to give his children the possibilities he never had, and so did *I*. Dad and I both made sure *you* got that opportunity. And you're telling me you're not gonna take it?"

"Is Dad still running the show in your brain?" Kevin tilted his head, and Matt's eyes dodged and stared at the table.

"Look at me, Matt!" Kevin kept at it. "I know you're lying. Why do you keep doing this?"

"What do you mean? I'm not lying! I told you about the crash, didn't I?"

"Yes, but I can see you're still hiding something from me! Why do you keep doing it? Is he still talking to you? Why won't you tell me the truth?"

"I told you. Don't you get it? He died in a fucking crash!" Matt shouted across the table.

The mess hall had gone silent. All eyes were on the Turners.

"What are you afraid of? Why won't you tell me?"

"What do you want me to say? I killed him! I was responsible for his death! And so I sacrificed my fucking life for you, you little prick."

Kevin sat back. Matt took a napkin and dabbed his mouth.

"I never asked you to," Kevin said. "I never wanted for you to give up your own dreams. *You* did that. Don't blame that shit on me."

Matt took a deep breath. "Can we please concentrate on Mom's treatment and then talk about this some other time?"

"Wake up, Matt. She is dying. And you're clinging on to some pipe dream that this place can somehow cure a genetic disease. You're delusional. Let go of Dad, and whatever it is he keeps telling you, and start saying your goodbyes."

Matt shook his head in disbelief, squinting at Kevin.

"Do you want to know what I did while you were sleeping after that infinitely stupid brawl you had?" Kevin said. "I took Mom for a walk. I talked with her. I spent time with her. I took her to a park. We sat watching birds. Lay in the grass, looked at the clouds. And you know what? She seemed happier than she has in months. When was the last time you did something like that? Now, I can't take her with me, because I know you wouldn't let me, but fuck if I'm gonna sit around watching while you drain the last bit of soul from her in that crusade of yours. And do you know what I was doing this morning? Saying my goodbyes.

Saying my fucking goodbyes, and she's not even dead yet." Kevin stood up. "If you want to reach me, I'll be at Grace's." He shoved his chair back and left his brother sitting stunned, watching him.

"Kevin!"

He didn't turn around.

He bumped into Zec on his way to the entrance and assured him he wouldn't tell anyone about the warehouse; he just needed to get away from his brother. Zee told him not to waste the elevator and showed him an emergency staircase.

Outside, the air was crisp and abundantly fresh.

23

Matt sat in the cantina, stung, slumped back in his chair. His appetite had gone like someone had clicked a switch. He was in complete disbelief. His brother had lost faith. Kevin had abandoned him in order to be with some people he'd just met? Their mother didn't deserve that. And Matt wasn't about to abandon hope, nor bail on the responsibility entrusted to him.

He lifted one hand inches off the table to greet Zee as he walked towards him, his other still rummaging around the remaining food with his spoon.

"What's with your brother?" Zee said, taking the seat Kevin had left vacant.

"Don't know. Think he just needed some air to get a break from this claustrophobia or something. He's having a hard time believing that our mom will survive, so his fears paralyze him, I guess."

"Do you think we can trust him?"

"What do you mean?"

"Well, we have a lot at stake here, so we can't have him running around telling everybody."

"He wouldn't do that. Besides, Mom is here, so…"

"What about you? You're not paralyzed?"

"Fuck, no. I'm not going anywhere. I'm ready to give it all I've got, grab at every possibility, and then some."

"Good to hear. 'Cause we need to talk."

"Sure. What's up?"

"It's Elizabeth. I think it's best if you follow me. Ems can explain the details."

They got up from the table; Zee waved at the kitchen staff to clean up after them. Matt followed him down the corridors into the little room where Elizabeth lay. Her eyes were closed, a thin blanket covered her body, and her bare arms rested on top. Ems stood beside the bed, reading some brain scans on a tablet.

Matt darted to the hospital bed and ran his fingers across his mother's forehead, touched the tubes in her nose. He observed the screens mounted around the room, displaying cardiograms and other incomprehensible graphs.

"What's happening? Is she all right?" he asked Ems, distraught. "This stuff wasn't here yesterday!"

"Easy, Matt. She's okay, for now. We're just monitoring her to make sure she's not getting worse, so you need to calm down," Ems said. She took her eyes off the tablet. "All this," she pointed around, "is a good thing. Should we wait for Kevin?"

"Don't think so. I'll update him later," Matt said, looking at Zee, who kept quiet. "So, what's new? What's happening to my mom?"

"Let me start by saying you did well taking your mother to a hospital. This isn't something you weather like a storm, so to speak. Sometimes, people think that time will solve their health issues, but unless it's a common cold, it rarely does. I'm impressed by your resolute action. It gave her a fighting chance. Any mother would be proud. All that said, however, I see complex patterns and anomalies here."

"Complex? What do you mean, complex? How?" The words seemed to tumble out of him.

"Well, as you already know, your mother is showing signs of late-stage Alzheimer's. Dementia, memory loss, uncontrollable muscles, those kinds of things. But Alzheimer's is also a disease that causes changes in the brain tissue, particularly the amyloid plaques and neurofibrillary tangles," Ems said.

"What? Ems, I'm sorry. All those words, they—confuse me," Matt said. He took a stool nearby and sat down.

"I'll try to lay it out simply. So, yes. In patients with Alzheimer's, there are—clumps and tangles of fibers. Imagine a ball of yarn. It might seem like it's a mess of threads, but in reality, it's laid out in a meticulous curl so that the strand of yarn comes off easily. Now imagine a two-year-old child unspooling that same yarn and then clumping it back together in a tight coil. Same string, same yarn, but not the same output. That's what we typically see in Alzheimer's, which is why parts of the brain malfunction. The later the stage, the bigger the mess. But your mother's brain scans show none of that."

"So she doesn't have Alzheimer's?" Confused, Matt was clinging to any and every scrap of hope.

"No, she hasn't got Alzheimer's as I know it."

"Well, that's excellent, right?" Perhaps Dr. Aldridge had been wrong all along, he thought, his heart hammering.

"Yes." Ems tried to find a comfortable posture. After shifting her weight and shuffling her feet, she continued. "Well, no. See, the problem becomes…" She paused. "…that we don't know what's causing her illness."

The corners of Matt's mouth dropped as though pulled down by ten-ton boulders.

"But we have clues," Ems added. "And that might help us decide where to look for treatments."

Matt raised his eyebrows again.

"Now, bear with me here. This might get technical, but I'll try my best. She has a high number of dead neurons… uh, nerve cells… in her brain. When we gave her synaptic fluid, which is a sort of lube for the brain, her connections reignited, and her motor functions were restored to normal."

"So, can't she just get a shitload of fluid?" Matt said.

"No. It's not that simple. There are side effects that are best avoided; let's leave it at that." Ems looked a bit nervous.

"Like what?"

"Let's not go there, Matt. Just know that it's a temporary solution." Once again, Matt noticed her nervous hesitation; she was hiding something, forcing it down to keep it from coming to the surface. "But we found the reason behind the increased number of dead neurons," she continued. "She has a genetic mutation, and we are trying to isolate the culprit as we speak. But we need to know if it's somatic or hereditary." She nodded at Zee.

"What difference does it make?" Matt said. Ems ignored him.

"And that's where we need you," Zee said.

"Wait? What does that mean?" Matt said.

"For now, it's not that important," Ems said.

"We pulled your mother's medical records," Zee began, "from a central database, and it shows—"

Matt shook his head. "Wait, how d'you do that?" he said.

"Well, we hacked it. We have been maintaining backdoors for a while so that we can collect data and information from government systems," Zee said.

"Okay. So then, what did it show?"

"I'm getting there, Matt. You see—" Zee gave a deep sigh before he continued. "Your mother has been admitted, on a number of occasions, to a fertility clinic in 0-1. Not a regular clinic, but one specializing in genetic engineering."

Matt looked perplexed. The additional information, along with the medical jargon, had bombarded his concentration. He knew that his parents had visited and gotten help from a fertility clinic, but other than that, he had given the matter little thought.

"'Designer babies' is a more common term," Zee added. Matt kept quiet.

"Yeah, I knew about a clinic. They went there to get help conceiving Kevin," Matt said.

"Do you know exactly why they went there?"

Again, Matt kept quiet, trying to sort through his thoughts.

"There could be several reasons," Zee continued, "but we can only speculate. The clinic and government marked the files from these visits as classified, so for security reasons, they aren't stored in a central database like the rest of your mother's information. Which strikes us as odd."

Now Matt felt *he* was under scrutiny.

"Normally, a visit to a fertility clinic wouldn't receive such a classification." Zee stopped between each sentence, waiting a bit, scanning Matt's reaction, before he continued. "Do you know anything about this?"

"No."

"Do you think Kevin might?"

"I don't think so. He never mentioned anything like that, no. I'm not sure he even knows."

"Your mother and your father visited the same clinic prior to your birth."

"No, that can't be true."

"The data doesn't lie, but what's different is that the files concerning your conception and birth aren't classified. But all of Kevin's are."

It made no sense. No up, no down.

"And another thing that strikes us as a bit odd? The clinic in question is reserved for streetlighters." Again, another pause. "Would you happen to know when your mother and father were given the opportunity to visit such a clinic?"

"Hold on a minute—are you saying that you know why my parents visited the clinic back when I was born?"

"No. No, I didn't say that. All data from the visits concerning you is available, but all data involving Kevin is on a closed-system network, requiring a local access point. Do you know how your family got appointments to this place?"

"No, I promise. I don't understand any of this," Matt said. "Are you questioning me?"

"No, Matt. I believe you." Zee raised his hands defensively. "But if we are to save your mother, we need you to help us and to be as forthcoming as you possibly can."

"I'll do anything to help, whatever I can do."

"Good. You see, we need that classified data about your mother. It will help determine the type of genetic mutation she has. And we need you to help us get that data so that we can treat the right thing."

"Sure. But where do I go? What do I do?"

Matt could feel the tension drain out of both Zee and Ems.

"I knew I could count on you, Matt." Zee reached over and patted him on the back. Matt noticed he poked Ems as well.

"You're doing the right thing, Matt. Your mother would have been proud—" Ems said.

"*Is* proud. She *is* proud," Matt corrected her.

"Ah, sorry. Of course. That's also what I meant. If you somehow see or talk to Kevin, make sure he sticks around. He might be able to help us with our questions as well."

"Come on," Zee said, nudging him towards the door. "Let's go see Faulk."

24

As they walked back along the corridors, Matt peeked inside doors as they passed. He saw no other patients, but ten rooms had been prepped like Elizabeth's, with hospital beds, monitors and equipment. All of them stood empty. Zee stopped as he noticed Matt looking around. He put his arm around Matt's back and ushered him on, attaching himself to Matt's shoulder the rest of the way.

"Here we are," Zee said, opening a door to a room full of screens. Some big, some small, some vertical, some horizontal; computer screens, TV sets and tablets stitched together with cables and wires running rampant in between. Text prompts, code, graphs and tables sparkled on the glossy panels. Pixels in white, green and pink flickered on black backgrounds every few seconds.

Underneath all the screens, multiple old office desks ran around the perimeter of the room, making one enormous horseshoe-shaped desk, though the height varied at their intersections. A slim young man in his late twenties was sitting in a chair, its high backrest tilted, a small keyboard in his lap. He wore a gray loose-fitting t-shirt with sizable armpit stains, black sweatpants and worn-down sneakers. On the desk in front of him stood a fluorescent-red energy drink in a tall cup. He swiveled around and got to his feet.

"Keep the door open, will you?" he grumbled. "It gets so damn hot in here. I just hate when people snoop," he said. "You must be Matt?" he said, extending his arm. "I'm Faulk, but you probably guessed that by now. Haha."

"Sure. Nice to meet you," Matt said, shaking his hand. Faulk's grip was the picture under 'flaccid' in the dictionary. The stench of sweat tickled his nose, but he kept a straight face.

"Faulk is our resident programmer and computer engineer," Zee said.

"So, Matt, pull up a chair. How much do you know about data transferring?" Faulk said, sitting back down and folding his legs underneath him on the chair.

"Not much, I guess. Drag and drop, I don't know. The basics?"

"Haha, yeah, that's basic. No code, no terminal, no shell?"

Matt shook his head.

"Then I might need to remotely guide your fingers. But hey, that's totally fine," Faulk said. He opened a drawer underneath the desk he was sitting at, took out a small piece of hardware and handed it over.

Matt turned it around in his hands. "Flash drive?" he said.

"Haha, yeah, you'd think that, but no, no, not entirely that, no," Faulk said. He gave another one of his stuttering laughs. "It's a *kind* of flash drive, but with a rapid transfer bus and some homemade software to boot. Plug it into any computer, and I'll have access to the system within thirty seconds. That way, I can browse for the files we need while you sip Piña Coladas. Easy peasy, but keep the lemons away. Got it?"

"Lemons away. Got it," Matt said, not getting it.

Faulk gave another weird laugh as he nodded.

"And, of course, it's geolocated, in case you lose it. It has a satellite uplink. And that, you will need to manage. We can't exactly go on the regular wireless networks around here, so we're renting a satellite from a Chinese company. That way, we can bypass most of the regular government monitoring that goes on. But you need to type a couple of lines into a prompt once you insert this into a machine. Tell it to connect, so to speak. And then it's time for the piñas, on your part at least, haha."

It was a bit of a dry laugh, more like a tic than a sign of genuine enjoyment.

"And then you transfer the data back here?"

"We could, in theory, but with the amount of data we're talking, it could take hours if not days to go through the sat link. Chinese and cheap, remember—haha. And then there's a moral issue with personal data going through China. Everything is under surveillance over there. Not a practical solution. Instead, we transfer to the stick, and you bring it back here. And the sticks are not cheap, per se, even though I make 'em myself. Custom design and all, haha," Faulk said, tapping a finger on his skull.

"All right. So I find a tablet, plug that thing in, type a few lines, and then you take care of the rest?" Matt said.

"Yes. Handy dandy, right? Haha. Want a test run?"

Matt pulled up a chair and got a view of the interface, what to expect once he'd popped in the custom drive. The lines were short and easy to remember, so he didn't figure they would become an issue. Faulk was worried, however, and wrote it with a marker on Matt's forearm. He wrote it again on a little scrap of paper and told Matt to put that in his pocket, too.

"So I'm all set, right?"

"Haha, yeah, for the best-case scenario, at least. Worst case, I'm gonna have to remote type through you, so you're getting an earpiece. You know, in case something happens and I need direct access to the tablet. Then you'll be my eyes and fingers." Faulk smiled.

"Well, wouldn't it be easier if you joined me, then?" Matt suggested.

"Haha. Easier for *you* maybe."

Zee interrupted Faulk's nervous chatter. "Faulk can't go. It's too risky," he said. "If he gets caught and scanned, they might trace him to this place, and we can't take the risk. That's why you're essential in this, Matt. Are you good with that? Can I count on you?"

"Yes. Of course, that's not what I meant. I just figured... You know."

"It's all right," Zee said. "Just keep your mother in mind, and she will help you focus on the job at hand. Whatever happens, we'll be back here guiding you through it."

"Okay, so show me where to go." Matt tried to stand, but Zee laid a hand on his shoulder, keeping him in the chair. Then he walked to a cabinet on the back wall and pulled something out, tucking it behind his back so that Matt couldn't get an unobstructed view.

"You're going to want this," Zee said, slamming down a gun on the table. It made a heavy clunk.

Matt looked at it. Black, not a revolver. That summed up his knowledge about guns.

"Do you know how to fire one of these?" Zee asked.

"I've been to a firing range once if that's what you mean."

"That will have to do. But you may need to use it as a deterrent, just in case."

Matt's neck moistened. "In case of what? What do you mean? Where am I going?" he said, picking up the gun and turning it around in his hand.

"The clinic has armed guards—another testament to the fact that this isn't your ordinary fertility clinic. But this," he pointed to the gun, "is not for them. You're not going inside the clinic. There's too much security and surveillance."

"So where, then?"

"We're going to find a doctor that works there. They'll most likely have remote access to the same data, in case they have to work during a lockdown."

"And what if they haven't?"

"We have to put our money on something, and trust me, the odds are infinitely better than you taking on armed guards and government security forces," Zee said.

"Okay. So, do we know where the doctors live?"

"No, we don't. That information isn't public, and given that they all live in the streetlights, their private homes are not part of any accessible registry."

"So what do you want me to do, then? I can't go kidnapping the clinic staff or anything like that."

The room fell silent.

"You'll have to," Zee said.

Matt's jaw nearly hit the table. "Are you fucking *crazy*? There's no way in hell that I'm going to kidnap anyone. Have you lost your mind?"

"No, Matt. I haven't. But you wanted my help, and this is the only way forward. I didn't say it would be easy, but I'm afraid it's necessary. You need to threaten your way back to a doctor's house, where security measures shouldn't be as prominent."

"But you can bet that his private access point will require biometrics," Faulk chimed in. "So whatever doctor you grab, please don't hurt him too badly. You'll need him alive and cooperating."

Matt stood up, shook his head, and started pacing the room. Zee leaned against the gun cabinet, getting out of his way. Matt could now see that the gun on the table was the smallest in the arsenal, and in a weird way, it comforted him. Zee would have given him something bigger if they were expecting the cavalry.

"You're absolutely sure there is no other way around getting this data?" Matt said, after a few rounds back and forth. "I'm not killing anybody!" He pointed at Zee.

"We're not asking you to," Zee said, striking up his arms.

"And there's no way I can get any help on this?"

"I'm afraid not, Matt. All of us here have links and ties that, if exposed, could compromise our entire operation. Your digital trail only leads as far as the community center, so unless you get Kevin to help you out, I'm afraid you're on your own."

"I can't put Kevin into that kind of danger. Are you fucking mad?"

"Just said it was an option. And you might want to remember that it's his mother too, you know? Don't you think he'd want to fight for her?"

"I can't let him," Matt hissed to himself, but loud enough for Zee to pick up on.

"Why? Isn't it worth giving your mother the best chance she can get?" Zee looked at him, trying to penetrate the myriad of thoughts blasting around his brain. "You know that bringing

Kevin along could up your odds. I can see that you know that. But we're on the clock, Matt. When the clinic doctors leave for the day, that's your opening. And remember, this is bigger than you and your family. We all want you to succeed."

"Fuck this. I'm getting my truck," Matt said, and picked up the gun.

25

Kevin relaxed in the grass, leaning back on his elbows and looking out over the reflecting pool. Ruby was sitting next to him, hugging her knees, trying to keep warm in the cool summer breeze. Kevin had put his jacket over her shoulders; her skimpy top was not nearly warm enough. Her thick cornrows hung loose, not budging in the gusts of wind.

"So what ya gonna do?" Ruby turned her head, looking at him over her shoulder.

"I don't know. I just hope he comes to his senses, I guess," Kevin said.

"What if he doesn't?"

"Then I think I'm gonna leave. Find my own place. Dunno. He did all these things, never stopping to ask whether I wanted them. Pushed me through high school. And with him pressuring me to get good grades, I didn't make a single friend. Do you have any idea what it's like being the only student with a college future? They fucking hated me. So now, I want to find my own way, whatever that is. I know college doesn't feel right… At least for me."

"Yeah, I feel ya. When Momma Grace asked me to help, I remember I was hesitant at first. I ran away from home at fourteen, ended up at the center after my first time on the needle. I didn't want to end up like my family, so Grace was the only option besides drugs. Haven't regretted it since."

"Do you know what you want to do now?"

"Hell, no. But at least I'm out of trouble, and then I'll see what happens. I never dreamed of being a good Samaritan, and I still don't. But for now, it seems all right."

Kevin gazed out over the pond. A duck was pushing her tiny ducklings into the rippled water. When they were all in, she jumped in herself and led them off into uncharted territory.

"How about starting your own? Family, I mean." Kevin asked, looking at Ruby.

"You're coming on hard, ain't you?" she said, turning away.

"No, no, that wasn't what I—"

"Did I say I would fuck you? I ain't fucking you. Not yet, anyway."

Kevin could see she was smiling by the dimple in her cheek.

"Keep wooing, though, if that's what you're thinking about," Ruby continued.

"What I meant was, what would you do? If you had a family to care for?"

"I know what I *wouldn't* do. I wouldn't trust the system to help out, that's for sure. Try to claw my way to the top, maybe. Or find somewhere to go off-grid, you know? I heard about these people down south, past the nuclear wastes. Living off the land, making their own electricity and all. Heard there are entire communities like that. But I don't know. Might be too overboard."

There was a long pause. The wind stirred the line of trees, rustling their leaves.

"But didn't you hear what I said?" Ruby turned and looked him straight in the eye. "I ain't letting you knock me up." There was a momentary pause. "Yet," she said, and then she blinked and fell back in the grass beside him, her one arm wrestling him to the ground as well. She rolled on top of him and put her face close to his, locking her eyes with his. She placed her lips close to his, pressing his shoulders down with her hands so he couldn't move an inch. She held his gaze for ten seconds. Kevin counted, for he felt every hesitant heartbeat as if time was about to stop.

Then she pushed herself up, laughing, and threw his jacket over the front of his trousers, saying something about covering something up. Kevin felt like his head was spinning.

They grabbed a bite at a hot dog stand, then jumped on the metro and headed back to the center, having promised Grace to help out with dinner. She was waiting at the front desk, expecting them.

"My lovebirds," she greeted them, giving a hearty laugh.

"He ain't my lover, Momma," Ruby said, already passing on her way to the kitchen.

"Your brother was here," Grace said to Kevin as he turned to follow Ruby.

Kevin stopped.

"Wanted to see you," Grace continued, "but I reckoned you didn't want him to know your whereabouts. He don't know about Ruby either, right?"

"You're right. I don't want to see him. Not for a couple of days, at least. And I'd appreciate it if you wouldn't spill about Ruby. At least for now."

"That's what I reckoned. But he seemed desperate." She slid her finger across the desk; there was a note underneath it. "And so he wrote you this."

Kevin reached for it, but Grace didn't lift her finger.

"Remember, Kevin," she said. "Just like you have only one mom, you also have only one brother." She bobbed her head a bit until he acknowledged with a nod, and then lifted her finger.

I'm sorry.
I need to save Mom and wanted your help. Leaving this afternoon from the warehouse. Hope you get this in time.
If something happens, know I tried for you.
Matt.

Kevin looked up at Grace.
"Go," she said. "I'll let Ruby know."

Kevin turned and ran out the front door, feeling sick to his stomach.

* * *

He caught the next metro and stood against one of the grimy windows as it sped through 0-1 and on out into 1-5. He took the stairs to street level two at a time and reached the warehouse just as his stomach told him supper was overdue.

He pounded at the door and banged against the security cameras. The door buzzed open and he sprinted down the staircase Zee had shown him. Ems stood at the bottom to meet him. The look on her face told him everything he feared had come true, what his gut had already told him. He was too late. Matt was already gone. But where?

She told him Elizabeth was sleeping and then led him down the corridors to the same room Kevin had stumbled upon that morning. The man he'd met earlier introduced himself as Faulk, and Zee was present as well.

"Take a seat, Kevin," Zee said. The look on his face told Kevin not to argue.

For the next few minutes, Zee explained what Matt had been asked to do.

Kevin felt all the air go out of him.

There was nothing more to say. All four of them now sat watching a map, a maze of schematics that seemed to have no connection to his brother.

They waited.

And waited.

Time ticked away as prompts of code ran across the screens. Faulk became more anxious as each minute followed the previous one.

"He should have been online by now," Zee said eventually.

26

Matt waited at the warehouse until afternoon, hoping Kevin would show, but to no avail. He didn't need his help, of course, but rather some reassurance that Kevin understood his motivations. He longed for Kevin to understand this was all for him. Not for their mother. And he knew his written note wouldn't cut it. Finally, after waiting for hours with his eyes surveying the fences and gates, Matt gave up and drove off for a chance at snatching a doctor clocking out.

The clinic lay in a well-kept neighborhood; upscale shops and boutiques dotted vast boulevards lined with trees and trimmed hedges. He located the clinic and parked opposite, at the curb outside a car dealership. His trashed pickup wasn't much good as a stakeout van, but he hoped passersby might mistake him for a buyer browsing for an upgrade.

Two armed guards stood at the clinic entrance. Zee and Faulk had given him a printout with names and photos of the four resident doctors so that he wouldn't end up with an intern. He consulted it every time someone came through the sliding glass doors. So far, none matched.

As he sat there killing time, he marveled at the white brushed concrete, the huge panoramic windows, the silver-top ash cladding on the geometric protrusions cut into organic, flowing waves. A brushed copper plaque near the curb read *Clinique A.D. – Guiding Nature since 1994.*

There was a tap on the backseat window. Matt started, then turned his head to see a suited man glancing at him across the truck's interior. He locked his narrow eyes on Matt's.

"Can I help you, sir?"

"Uh, no. Thanks," Matt said. He didn't want to roll down the window, so he raised his voice.

"I'm sorry, sir, but I'm going to have to ask you to move your vehicle."

Matt shook his head and peeked back at the clinic's front doors. A blonde woman who looked like a secretary was chatting up the guards, looking at her wristwatch. She went into the building.

The man tapped the window again and stepped towards the front passenger door. Matt, annoyed, turned his attention to him again.

"I'm sorry, sir, but you are parked on our property. We have the right to ask you to leave if you're scaring or harassing our clients or staff. And, frankly, this kind of vehicle doesn't belong in this part of town," the man said, sniffing and looking along the side of the pickup. "If you don't leave now, we will notify the police."

"No, no—that's all right." Matt, flustered, fumbled with the keys, dropping them on the floor and bending down to pick them up. The gun sat tucked underneath his seat. Snatching the keys, he placed his right foot in front of it to block it from the man's line of sight. He turned the ignition on and nodded. "Yes, yes. Sorry, I'm going," he said.

"Thank you, sir."

Matt pulled away from the curb. Fuck, that was close, he thought. He drove a couple of blocks away and parked in a large lot at a supermarket. He had to get back. They could all be leaving now, at this very moment. He folded the sheet of headshots, grabbed the gun, and stuffed both into the waistband of his pants, making sure his shirt was covering them. Locking the truck, he stuck the keys deep in his pocket and headed for the clinic on foot, hurrying down the sidewalk as fast as he dared without attracting attention to himself.

Coming up behind the clinic now, he noticed a sign pointing to staff parking and a small driveway leading around the side. There were only five cars there, meaning a lot less clutter for him to monitor, and no guards in sight. The staff entrance was a metal slab of a door. There was ample video surveillance, but all of the cameras were pointing at the entrance and none at the cars themselves.

Matt went and stood at a bus stop across a street, which gave him an unobstructed view of who was leaving. He pulled out the sheet of paper, patted the handle of the gun, and went over the pictures once more. He needed to memorize the faces so he wouldn't be looking back and forth at the paper. All of the doctors were male; one wore a pair of oversized black square glasses, one had long frizzy hair, and one had a very round face and sunken eyes. Finally, there was one with a beard. A huge, full-size, well-kept beard, straightened with a comb and trimmed into shape. Matt prayed none of them had left in the fifteen-minute gap.

It was getting late. The man with the frizzy hairdo left, but he was with the blonde from earlier; he kept grabbing her ass as they went down the stairs. They stood and talked a bit outside, and then he ushered her into his car. So the frizzy-haired guy was out, Matt thought. Too risky to try and snatch two people at once.

Matt's plan was to trail a doctor to the staff parking lot, pull the gun and force himself inside the car with them. He wasn't sure it would work—wouldn't the guy just drive off or run him down? Or both? Could bullets even shoot through modern cars?

The sun was setting. Matt wiped his forehead with the sleeve of his shirt, catching the stench from his armpits. A bus was approaching the stop, signaling to pull over. At the same moment, the side door of the clinic opened and the doctor with the full-size beard came out, briefcase in hand, open coat fluttering in the light breeze. This was his opening. He jumped to his feet and stepped out onto the road. He heard the screech of brakes and the honk of the bus's horn. Matt threw himself out of the way and tumbled to the ground, scraping his forearm. He could feel the stitches in his abdomen protesting. *Fuck, fuck, fuck.* He hoped he hadn't opened the wounds again. Lying on the ground, he waved at the bus to continue and got slowly back to his feet, turning towards the parked cars. The doctor was looking straight at him, his face full of concern. Matt raised one arm, motioning an okay, and lowered the other to keep his shirt in place. The doctor smiled and turned away, continuing on to his car. Matt began to move now; he dashed, half-limping, towards the lot. When he was just a couple of yards away from the doctor, the man turned towards him, startled.

"What the—" he began.

Matt pulled the gun.

"Get in your car," he hissed.

The doctor didn't flinch. He didn't seem scared, or even surprised.

"Get in your fucking car," Matt commanded again, through clenched teeth, clasping the gun between his slippery fingers.

The doctor, meticulous in every movement, sat down in the front seat. Matt yanked open the rear door, still keeping the gun trained on the bearded man, and tumbled into the tiny back seat.

"Drive," Matt said, twisting and turning to face forward and keeping the gun pointed towards the doctor.

"Relax," the doctor said.

"DRIVE NOW!" Matt pressed the gun's muzzle into the back of the doctor's neck.

"Where to?" the doctor said calmly. "I need to tell her a destination."

"Home. Your house."

"Tessie, let's go home."

The car turned on silently. The dashboard lit up, and a screen showed backward-facing cameras as the car backed itself out of the parking space, shifted gears and put itself into drive.

"Don't do anything you will regret," the doctor said.

Matt didn't reply. He was glancing out the windows, trying to spot potential witnesses, but it seemed like they had been the only two around. The bus was long gone.

The car slid out of the driveway, merging effortlessly with the traffic. They passed the supermarket, and Matt saw his banged-up pickup being inspected by a security guard.

"If it's money you're after, we can go to the ATM. We can take a drive-through so you can hide from surveillance. It's not a problem." The doctor spoke in a collected tone of voice.

"No, we're going to your house," Matt said. After a brief pause, he said, "Any chance your family is home?"

"I don't have a family. Not one that lives with me, anyway."

Matt fiddled with the gun, not knowing where to point it. He wanted to be threatening, but was afraid it might go off if an unexpected bump should override the shock absorbers. He placed it on his lap, pointing it toward the driver's seat but aimed at the door, just in case.

"There's a roadblock and heavy traffic on your usual route, Dr. Henke," Tessie said. It was a soft female voice, gentle on the K sounds. To Matt's surprise, it was as fluent as any human he had ever listened to. Its tone was personal, almost intimate, and its pronunciation was impeccable. Somehow, the gentle voice dampened Matt's peaking adrenaline.

Dr. Henke looked back at Matt and raised his eyebrows. Matt raised his right back.

"I think we will go around, Tessie. If you please," Dr. Henke said.

"Oh. Yes," Matt said. "No roadblocks."

Tessie recalibrated. Matt watched as the lines on the map changed. It gave him an overview of the metropolitan area, and now at least he knew which corner of the world they were headed towards.

"Who's your guest, Dr. Henke?" Tessie said.

Shit. He hadn't thought of this. Matt looked uneasily around, trying to spot cameras, shielding his face from anything he thought might be a sensor.

"Will he be driving at any point during our trip?" Tessie continued. "I can start the voice analysis as you converse if you like."

"He's just an associate. I do not think he will be driving anytime soon, no. But thanks for asking, Tessie."

"You're welcome."

The doctor looked back at Matt. "You can relax. There are sensors in the seats, and she filters out your voice, but she collects no data. I always drive in privacy mode, for the needs of my clients, of course."

They rode for a few minutes in silence as the scenery flowed by. It was impossible for Matt to keep track of his whereabouts; he was unsure if they had entered a different grid circle. Well, if it came to that, he figured he could rely on Faulk getting him back to the warehouse.

"Do you mind me asking who you're with, young man?" Dr. Henke said.

"What do you mean?" Matt said.

"W.A.H., C.L.B.G., or maybe even T.I.G.?"

"I don't know what you're talking about."

"You know it's not the first time I've been taken at gunpoint, don't you? I assume you do your research," Dr. Henke said with an almost accusing tone.

"Just shut up."

"As you wish. But please realize you and I both want the same thing."

"What would you know about that?"

"We both want to get out of this rather chance encounter with our lives intact. Am I right?"

Matt nodded, and the doctor continued.

"So, let's promise each other to work towards that very goal, and not do anything sudden or irrational, shall we?"

Matt glanced out the window. "I guess so," he said.

"I'm not much for irrationality, you see."

27

As they drove through the evening traffic, Matt finally began to unwind. Henke hadn't spoken for fifteen minutes, and Tessie weaved through lanes, adjusting her speed and positioning like a philharmonic musician at the will of the conductor's baton. She even adjusted the cabin lights as the sun set, creating a harmonious balance between the ambient light and the dashboard instruments, as the last of the daylight punched out over the rolling suburban hillside.

"Not long now," Henke said. "Would you mind telling me what you hope to find at my private residence?"

"A medical journal," Matt said.

"Whose?"

"My mom's."

"And what makes you think I have it at home?"

"They told me."

"'They'?"

"Yes."

"Who are *they*?"

Matt was silent. Come to think of it, he didn't know. Zee had never introduced his group as anyone or anything tangible.

"Well, do you trust *them*, then?" Henke said.

"More than I trust you, that's for sure." Matt noticed the dashboard lights brightening and looked out the front windscreen. "Wow," he said under his breath.

They were approaching a concrete slab wall, twelve or fifteen feet tall, curving out to both sides so Matt couldn't see an end. In front of the car, the road was leading into an opening with small guard towers on both sides and rolls of barbed wire fence at the bottom of each. Massive cylinders dotted the road to prevent unauthorized access. And shining out through the steel mesh gates between the towers, Matt could see a warm gleam of light permeating the darkening sky, a bright glow emanating from the walled-off streetlights.

Synchronized with the speed of the car, cylinder after cylinder slid down into the ground, creating a smooth surface for Tessie and her company of two. The gates drifted apart. A red laser grid from each tower flickered across the car, measuring, scanning. Matt ducked as red dots pierced the windows and kept pressed to the floor until they passed through the two-lane opening in the wall.

They rolled onto an avenue lined with lamp posts. All bulbs were on and functioning. The glow of the streetlights glistened in the wax on Tessie's bonnet, like specks of stars, plotted in a symmetrical universe. Light pulsated on the skin of Matt's arms, backlighting the tiny hairs that were now standing on end.

"Beautiful, isn't it?" Henke said.

Matt, trying to comprehend the spectacle before his eyes, had a hard time passing sufficient air through his vocal cords. "How is this possible?" he murmured.

They passed vast front yards extending up to magnificent

houses, their facades lit by spotlights tastefully set in ornamental shrubs. He saw couples strolling along sidewalks, kids wheeling their bikes, zigzagging back and forth across the road. Farther on, he saw a gazebo lighted with colorful strings of bulbs, around which milled a gathering of people laughing gaily, clinking champagne glasses together. Off to one side, Matt saw a chef in a hat and white apron, tending a barbecue. The scent of sweet caramelized, slightly charred pork wafted into his nostrils through Tessie's fresh air intake.

"We're nearly there, Dr. Henke," she informed him. "Would you like me to turn on the lights and maybe some music?" she said.

"Thank you, that would be lovely."

"Certainly."

Matt relaxed in his seat, almost hypnotized as he looked out the windows. He had heard stories about how the streetlighters lived, of course—everyone had—but he'd never imagined anything like this. The shows, the clips on the news—they all faded in comparison to the real, live thing. It was hard to fathom how anything like this was possible with the limitations on electricity that the government had imposed. God, it was beautiful.

He yelped as something struck his right wrist.

Henke snatched at the gun. Matt flailed his arms, trying to wrestle it back. But Henke had the advantage of surprise and easily broke Matt's grip. With a flick of his wrist, he turned the gun on Matt. Matt thrust himself deeper into the back of the seat, closing his eyes and raising his arms as if to fend off the incoming bullet. It didn't come. There was only silence as the car purred to a stop.

"We're here," Henke said. "Get out."

Matt opened his eyes, staring down the barrel of the gun.

Henke, facing backward from the front seat, held a steady aim right between his eyes. Tessie's doors slid quietly open and Matt got out and stood on the pavement. Henke followed, keeping his distance and still pointing the gun towards Matt.

They were standing in the driveway of a big white two-story mansion. Bathed in spotlights, it loomed like a hyper-minimalistic castle behind the doctor.

"Now listen," Henke began. "I'm not out to kill you. If I wanted to, you would have been dead already. But I do want some answers. So pay attention, *please*." He gave a forced smile to emphasize his sarcasm.

Matt nodded.

"Who sent you?"

"I don't know, I swear," Matt stuttered, afraid his unambiguous answer would result in a flash and a crack.

"Why are you here?"

"My mom is dying; I need her medical history. The people who sent me—I don't know what they're called, or if they're a group at all—they promised me they could help her."

"What makes you think I have had anything to do with your mother? We don't treat your kind," Henke said.

"They told me. Also, the staff at the Central Grid Hospital confirmed that she had been to a fertility clinic. I don't know why she went to *your* clinic—I swear."

"Who's your mother? What's her name?"

"Elizabeth. Elizabeth Turner."

"Step into the light there."

The doctor gestured, and Matt followed his order. He could make out Henke tilting his head, squinting his eyes, examining him closely.

"Inside. Too many eyes out here." Henke pointed the gun up toward the front door of the mansion.

Matt walked up the long front walkway. The thick oak door opened before he had time to grab the handle. With Henke still holding the gun at his back, he stepped into an immense hall with a broad staircase leading upstairs. He could hear piano music playing, something classical maybe. There was a door leading into a kitchen to one side. Matt stepped into the middle of the foyer, followed by the doctor. The door shut with a thud behind them. Matt turned questioningly towards Henke.

"So, here's how this is going to play out," the doctor said. "We are going to go upstairs to my office, and then we are going to dig out your mother's file and data. Then you will let me explain what it says, in layman's terms, of course, so that you are prepared."

"Prepared for what?"

"For the lies your people inevitably are going to present. As said, I am a rational man, and I can't see why these thugs would need medical records."

"They said her DNA sequence was in the files, that they needed it for treatment."

"And you didn't question why these people couldn't find said sequence themselves?" Henke rolled his eyes. "It's a simple procedure, given today's technology. And so, you've ended up putting your hopes into the hands of these incompetents?"

Matt was silent for a moment. "I had no choice. She's dying. They said she has some strange form of Alzheimer's, so I'm clutching at every straw."

"Hmm," Henke mused, the corners of his mouth turning down. "I'm sorry to hear that. But I'm impressed by your resourcefulness."

Matt didn't know how to respond, so he eyed the gun. Just a glance, assessing distance.

Henke followed his gaze and gave a small smile. "Oh, so you're still trying to figure out whether you can somehow get this firearm back and regain the upper hand in our little soiree?" He looked Matt straight in the eyes.

Matt blinked first.

"I thought as much. Well, it's of no use to me anymore," Henke said, "so you might as well take it." He swiveled the butt of the gun towards Matt with artistic grace, presenting it like a military officer relinquishing his sidearm.

Matt stood frozen in place, dumbfounded.

"Surprised? As I told you, Matt, my sole objective is that you and I both get away with our lives intact. The best chances of that happening derive from you not doing anything foolish. And right now, me having this gun increases the likelihood of idiocy. So here. Please. Take it."

Matt took two halting steps forward and lifted the gun from Henke's hand. He didn't raise it; instead, he let it drop, along with his arm, down along his right side. Pain shot up through his shoulder as he grazed the bandages around his torso, and a muscle in his face twitched. He hadn't been aware of his wound since leaving the warehouse; his adrenaline had taken over, dulling the receptors in his nerves.

"Are you hurt?" Dr. Henke said, his brow creasing with concern. "Let me see."

Reluctantly, Matt pulled up his shirt and looked down at himself. There was a dark red stain expanding through the gauze. His stitches must have burst when he and the doctor were wrestling in the car.

"Let me help you with that, get you fixed up. I'm not letting you bleed to death on my rugs. They're hand woven, you know."

Henke led him into a lavish bathroom. Mirrors lined the walls from top to bottom, and enormous slabs of black marble covered the floor. Henke found some alcoholic sanitizer, swabs and fresh bandages. He grabbed a box of steri-strips and a tiny tube of glue. Matt took off his shirt, leaving his gun on the black marble sink next to the shiny copper faucet.

Slowly and meticulously, Henke removed the old bandages, cleansed the gash, and then squeezed glue into the wound and covered it with sterile strips, adjusting them as Matt bent and stretched according to his orders. While the doctor worked, Matt heard a faint knock on the front door over the distant sound of classical music. He flinched, causing Henke to grunt in annoyance as he readjusted the strips and stuck them back in place.

"The kids all come around when they tumble on their bikes. No need to worry," he said.

Finally, Henke wrapped Matt in fresh, clean bandages, tossed the old ones into a bin, and cleaned his hands with soap and sanitizer.

"Don't forget your gun," he said, exiting the bathroom before Matt got his shirt back on.

28

Dr. Henke's study was on the second floor, the first door at the top of the stairway, and featured a wide, panoramic view of the garden. Trees and bushes lay in shadow; the streetlights did not reach this far back onto the property. There was a huge oak table in the middle of the room, with a tablet stuck in a groove. Sculptures of various sizes and materials, some on floating shelves, others on the floor, depicted strains of DNA, each coiled in a new, peculiar way.

"I commission most of them, but some I have found in my travels. Quite a collection, you might say, but they remind me of the stakes at hand," Henke said. "Isn't it magnificent how the variations in the sculptures resemble the differences in our genetics? What a marvelous world. What was your mother's name again?"

"Huh?" Matt turned and looked at Henke.

"I need it in order to locate the file for you." He sat behind the desk. "As said, I want to help you get what you want."

Matt shook his head to reset himself. He remembered the earpiece he had in his pocket. *Shit.* The people who were with his mother were waiting for him to call. Without bothering to be discreet, he pulled it out, inserted it, turned it on and pointed the gun at Henke.

"I'll take it from here," Matt said.

"As you wish." Henke raised his hands from the tablet and rolled back in the chair.

"You there, Matt?" Faulk said in his ear. "Reply if you can hear me. There's a built-in mic."

"Yes. Yes, I hear you," Matt said.

"Good. Have you located a tablet?"

"Just a second."

Matt walked over to the desk, waved the doctor up and motioned him away from the tablet. He grabbed the chair, sat, and pulled the tablet towards him.

"Yes, it's here," he said.

"Great. Now, plug the stick in. And then the doctor has to authorize access when the prompt comes."

Matt reached into his pocket for the stick, keeping the gun pointed at Henke, and shoved it into the port on the tablet. "I need your access," he said.

The doctor returned to the desk, placed his fingers on the tablet's surface, and adjusted his head straight on to the screen. Then he stepped back.

"I think we're in," Faulk said in the earpiece.

"That's it?" Matt said.

"Sorry?" said the doctor.

"Yes, yes. We're in," Faulk said.

"No, that wasn't for you," Matt said to Henke.

"Take a breather, Matt. It took some time, but you did good. Hard part's over. It's gonna take a little while now," Faulk said.

Matt turned away from the tablet, keeping both it and the doctor in his view.

"So now we wait?" Henke said.

"Yes. Now we wait," Matt replied.

The doctor glanced at the screen. He leaned against the panoramic window and gazed out, then looked back to Matt, sizing him up.

Matt noticed and rolled further back in the desk chair, lifting the gun. "What's on your mind?" he said.

"Nothing," Henke said, and went back to looking out the window.

"I saw you."

"Just wondering."

"Yeah? Wondering what? There's no fucking way you're stopping me from getting this data."

"Oh, I know. No, I was just wondering if you have any clue what your friends are actually downloading right now."

Matt looked at the screen. A progress bar crept along. "They are copying my mother's journal."

"No. They are copying *all* the journals," Henke said, not turning away from the window.

Matt looked at the screen again. He wasn't sure what the progress bar meant, only that it was … progressing. "Faulk, you there?" he said.

"Yes, Matt."

"What's it doing?"

"Copying. The journals, you know."

"But just my mom's, right?"

"Uh… right. Hers will be in there, somewhere."

"What do you mean, *somewhere*?"

"I mean that there are tens of thousands of journals. And hers is one of them. Don't worry. We're getting it."

"Why are we getting them all? I thought we only needed *hers*?"

"You do," Henke intercepted. A faint smile on his face, he was still looking out over the garden.

"Yes, well, we do," Faulk said. "But this is an opportunity to get insights about what goes on within government firewalls. This is *huge* for us. You're doing splendid work here, man. Just keep your cool."

Matt sat back and glanced at Henke.

"Can you grasp the implications of this, Matt?" Henke said. "The thousands upon thousands of people whose lives you're about to ruin?"

"What do you mean?" Matt said uncertainly.

"Who are you talking to, Matt?" Faulk tried to cut in, but Matt ignored him.

"Why are you getting these journals?"

"Because my mom is sick."

"And do you think the genetic profiles of the wealthiest, most powerful people are going to make her better?"

"What?" Matt said.

"Stop talking, Matt," Faulk snapped.

"Do you know what they can use these genetic profiles for?" the doctor continued.

"Don't talk to him, Matt. Don't talk to him!"

"Treatment?" Matt suggested.

Henke shook his head.

"Matt, this is Zee. IGNORE the doctor! He's trying to trick you!"

"Shut up!" Matt yelled, looking down to his left.

"Genetically targeted biological weapons, manufacturing of DNA material. Evidence for framing people," Henke said. "The key to our innermost weaknesses."

"Matt, get out of there! The transfer has finished. Get out of there!" Zee's voice practically tore through his eardrum.

Matt looked at the screen. The process had been completed. He took out the earpiece and lifted it up to his mouth. "I'm coming back," he said.

Then he threw the device on the floor and stepped on it. With a sharp crunch, it shattered into a handful of tiny components on the expensive carpet.

Matt lifted the gun and took a step towards the tablet so he could reach the stick. He pulled it out and took a couple of steps backward, training the gun on the doctor.

"If you want to help your mom, this isn't the way," Henke said, taking a step towards him.

Matt raised the gun. Henke stopped.

"I can look at her file like we discussed. Would you like that?" Henke said. "Would you like to know? Aren't you curious about how I know your little brother is Kevin?"

Matt narrowed his eyes. Then he lowered the gun. "Talk. Now!" he demanded.

"Let me start by saying I haven't been entirely honest with you, and for that I apologize. You didn't seem ready for these kinds of revelations, since you seem to have quite a lot on your plate already. But I guessed that you're Matthew, judging by your age."

"Yes. How do you know?"

"I see a resemblance. I saw you riding your bike on our street so many times when you were a little boy."

Matt stared at him, utterly perplexed, and then suddenly, the realization hit him like a thunderbolt. The gray streaks in Dr. Henke's hair and the big, bushy beard had distorted the young, friendly, smiling face that Matt remembered from the old cul-de-sac. But now, noticing the similarities instead of the differences, Matt realized he was looking at the Turners' old neighbor.

"Mr. Waldhaven?" Matt said uncertainly. "Mr. Christopher Waldhaven?"

Henke smiled.

"Yes, that's correct. Christopher Henke Waldhaven. I use my middle name in my practice. Provides a bit of privacy from the noseys around here."

Matt felt like his legs were made of rubber. He pulled up the desk chair and sat down heavily, still keeping the gun pointed at the doctor. "You helped my mom with her pregnancy?"

"Yes. But I guess your parents didn't tell you. Your mom told me about her Alzheimer's a long time ago."

"What do you mean? It's not Alzheimer's, but something that looks like it. That's what everybody keeps telling me."

"How's your little brother?" Henke said, ignoring his question.

"He's fine. Do you remember him? He wasn't more than a year old when we moved," Matt said.

"Oh, I remember him. I remember all of you."

"What's he got to do with anything?"

"More that you'd think," Henke said.

"You need to explain."

"Then let's go back, Matthew. It might get a bit messy, so I need you to pay attention. For instance, do you know that Elizabeth isn't your biological mother?"

Matt stared at him. "That's... that's not true," he moaned, his face reddening with anger.

"I'm afraid it is. When Elizabeth came to me back before you were born and told me that she and Jeffrey were having trouble conceiving, I was fresh out of medical school. Since I planned to specialize in fertility issues, I offered to help them in every way I could. While sequencing her DNA, looking at her causative variants, I realized that using her eggs to conceive you would almost guarantee that you would inherit her fate. She couldn't bear that possibility, so we decided on donor eggs. She carried you in her womb, but you only have a genetic link to your father."

"So who donated the eggs?"

"I couldn't say, even if I wanted to. Anonymous donors were in high demand back then. But when she and Jeff returned ten years later, wanting another child, technology and science had made huge leaps forward in the field of in vitro fertilization."

Matt looked at him, uncomprehending.

"Uh, artificial conception, or *in the glass*, if you will. Anyway, at that point, we also had an excellent shot not only at treating her own impending Alzheimer's but at removing it from her germline so she couldn't pass it to her children. The topic was, and still is, shrouded in ethical debates. But the government approved most research projects that showed the ability to reduce the time and resources required for future endeavors. In the name of progress, of course. And boy, let me tell you, it certainly showed potential. I thought I'd succeeded, too, so I'm a bit saddened to see you standing here now, telling me otherwise."

"Are you saying that you did experiments on her?" Matt said.

"No, no, not per se. *She* wanted this. She had seen you grow up, seen the similarities between you and your father, and this made her want a true genetic descendant of her own as well. So we went ahead with engineering her germline, as it's called. We altered both her cells and the DNA that would be passed to her children. After countless trials, we produced a viable embryo. And so we impregnated her with her own egg this time."

"So Kevin is hers? And my father's?"

"Yes, very much so," Henke said. "Even more so than you are, the unkind would say."

Matt swayed under the weight of this new information, his eyes flickering as they had at Dr. Aldridge's. He bent over in the chair and put his head between his knees.

"You mother needs help, Matthew. And these charlatans have no interest in such a procedure."

Matt shook his head as his neurons focused again, his temper reaching boiling point. He stood, raised the gun, and pointed it at Henke. "You just want her back for testing and experiments. I'm not gonna let that happen, you sick fuck."

"I want to help, Matthew. This is of scientific value to me. And I can get approval for the electricity and the resources for one more treatment," Henke said.

"You're fucking lying. I should put a bullet in you, right here, right now."

"So why haven't you? I'm the only one who can save your family, Matthew." Henke had raised his hands in a defensive posture.

"No!" Matt shouted. "I'll take the data and her journal, and *they* will help me."

"But Matthew," Henke said softly, "there *is* no journal. There *is* no data on your mother. Why do you think I haven't shown it to you yet? I can't. Rebel hackers wiped all our data in a security breach, not long after Elizabeth gave birth to Kevin. I came back after two years of study in Shanghai, and you were all gone. You'd moved. The house was empty. I couldn't follow up because I couldn't reach you. And now I worry you're being manipulated by those same rebels."

"Shut up! SHUT THE FUCK UP! I need to think," Matt shouted, waving the gun frantically, backing towards the door.

"Don't go, Matthew," Henke said, still keeping his eerie calm. "Have you considered that your brother has the same genetic disposition as your mother does? He will suffer her fate if you don't act now. Leave the data here, get your family to the clinic, and I will secure approval for treatment."

Matt shuffled the data stick around his sweaty left palm. If he only knew what the fuck the data looked like. Then he could verify who was telling the truth. "Bring up your search console," he ordered, tightening his grip on the gun and taking a determined step forward, pointing the muzzle right between the doctor's eyes.

Then both men turned as there was a loud knock on the front door.

29

"Dr. Henke, this is the police. Open up!"

Matt cocked the trigger on the gun, aiming the barrel straight at the doctor.

"I didn't call them," Henke said, lifting his hands. "Let me go see what they want. Stay here—stay calm."

"No, I can't. I can't get caught."

"Dr. Henke, we will force the door open if you do not respond," the officer called. His voice echoed sharply in the foyer and carried up the stairs.

"Then go," Henke said to Matt, "but leave the data stick. The information it contains is much too volatile to end up with radicals."

"How can I know you're not lying?"

"Dr. Henke, this is your final warning," the officer called. "If you do not respond, we will use force. We have reason to believe there are unauthorized citizens on your premises."

"You can't. You take a leap of faith."

Matt stepped over to the office doorway, his back to the wall, and peered around it, down towards the front door. There were two loud crashes and a splintering sound as the officers broke the door down. Matt saw the tip of an assault rifle poke through the opening.

"This way," Henke whispered. He stepped over to the side of the huge window and opened the glass door to a balcony overlooking the garden.

"Consider this collateral," Matt said, stuffing the stick deep in his pocket. He shoved past Henke onto the balcony, leaped over the railing, and stood facing the doctor, balancing on the ledge.

"Ask them about 2056!" Henke hissed. "They're not telling you the truth, Matthew. And bring Kevin and your mother to the clinic. I will help them."

Matt jumped to the ground with a thump. The noise brought the beam of a flashlight through a nearby window. He sprinted out over the lawn; two rapid shots hit a tree as he flew behind it. Crouching, keeping his arms by his side, he glanced out over the darkened lawn. Then, taking a deep breath, he took off in a straight line, vaulting over a hedge. Beams of light crisscrossed over his head, followed by a barrage of bullets whining through the air, shredding the shrubbery. Matt flung himself to the ground and flattened himself against the moist grass.

Keeping out of sight, head down, he crawled towards a picket fence to the next-door neighbor's yard. Scrabbling in the gravel at the bottom of one of the fenceposts, he grabbed the largest stone he could find and hurled it to the opposite side of the yard. It hit a lawn chair with a clink, and the shots and flashlight beams changed course, attracted by the noise. Hauling himself over the fence, Matt dodged behind a shed and stood there, panting.

He heard a swooshing sound as a sliding glass door opened, and saw a man step out of the house onto his patio. He flicked a switch, bathing his whole backyard in floodlights. Matt held his breath behind the shed, still in darkness.

"Anybody there?" the man shouted.

Matt could hear the yells of the police officers, alerted by the sudden influx of light. He raised his gun and ran full speed towards the patio. As he reached the illuminated patch of grass in front of it, the man's eyes widened in fear.

Matt, lifting a finger to his mouth, kept running and aiming the pistol, grabbing the man by the wrist as he closed the distance. He whispered to him to kill the lights and close the patio door as they went inside. Matt looked out over the lawn. He could see the police officers pointing their flashlights over the fence, inspecting the garden. Motioning for the man to be quiet, he shoved him towards his front door. Shaking his head to indicate that this wasn't a time for an outcry or heroics, he opened the door, took three steps from the house—and stopped dead in his tracks.

A police officer was walking up the driveway. Startled, the man stopped and reached for his sidearm. Matt propelled his own gun upwards, now in a race against his opponent. His reflexes took over, and before he had a chance to think, his finger squeezed the trigger. The shot went through the officer's upper neck and shoulder, ripping at flesh and bone; blood spattered out over the cobbled driveway. The officer fell to the ground, his hand dropping away from the sidearm he was about to unholster. Matt froze, looking at the man lying on the ground, clasping his hands over the wound, his breath rattling as blood gushed from his throat. There was a crackle of noise from his radio, but Matt couldn't make out a message.

The sound of a woman's scream behind him snapped him away from the hypnotic spectacle of life draining away. Matt flew past the officer's still-twitching body and sprinted down the street.

Slipping into the dark space between two houses further down the streetlit road, he watched multiple police cruisers speeding towards the scene of the crime. Trying to muffle the sound of his terrified panting, he wiped the sweat off his forehead and tears from his cheeks. Matt had never seen a gunshot tear flesh, but he knew without a doubt that the officer he'd shot was dead. Closing his eyes only seared the horrible image further into his retinas, etched the gurgling and rattling sound into his brain. But he needed to keep going. He was his family's last hope.

Matt had no idea where he was. Mesmerized during the drive in, he'd lost his bearing. The streetlights seemed even brighter now. He longed for shadow, for darkened streets and abandoned buildings—the protection he knew best from the time he'd been a young boy. There were few people on the streets now. Other than the sound of officers in the distance, Matt was almost alone.

Controlling his breathing, calming its pace back to normal, Matt looked down at his clothes, checking them for blood. Finding none, he tucked the gun into the waistband of his pants again, concealing it under his shirt and jacket. By now, they would have his description broadcast through the airwaves—if not from Henke, then certainly from the neighbor. The entrance gates would be barricaded, so it made no sense for him to retrace his steps back there. He decided to head for the nearest wall, cross it somehow, and then maybe Zee and Faulk could locate him using the stick in his pocket.

Matt scurried from house to house, waiting for the occasional pedestrian to pass, watching for cars, listening for sirens. He was handpicking blacked-out houses, their owners either sleeping or absent. The evening temperature was plummeting steadily; the cold crept through his body now, leaving his sweaty skin clammy. He began to shiver. He ducked between two more houses and sat still, listening for the howling of nearby patrol cars. He had already dodged a few cruisers shining their flashlights down the rows of hedges and into the alleys between houses.

After rambling for a while, Matt realized that he was lost. He wasn't able to see the wall anywhere. The streetlights hampered his nighttime vision. *Think,* he told himself. He began to walk again; he took note of where the strings of lights ended and realized that the wall had to be close by. He followed the lights and found himself close to a road that ran alongside the encircling wall: it had two lanes of flat tarmac with no cover in sight.

The house closest to the wall had a wide lawn with a children's play area and toys scattered in the grass. Matt crept over the grass and crouched behind a wooden playhouse. He could see police cars passing at intervals, patrolling the perimeter, likely looking for him. The wall here was lit only by the surrounding houses; the passing headlights revealed cracks between the massive cinderblocks stacked on top of each other. Matt could see wisps of steel reinforcement mesh sticking out, exposed, from inside the deteriorating slabs of concrete.

"What are you doing?" said a tiny voice behind him.

Matt whirled around, bringing his gun in line with whoever had spoken. Instinctively, he began to squeeze the trigger, but the image transmitted by his eyes made his fingers halt just in time. There in the darkness stood a little boy in his pajamas, towing a stuffed bunny by its ears, looking up curiously at him. Matt released the pressure on the trigger and lowered his arm. He swallowed an enormous lump in the back of his throat and breathed out.

"Shh," he tried, not knowing what else to say. "I'm just out for a walk." It was worth a shot.

"In our garden?" the boy said. "Are you the man hiding from the police? The shows say you're dangerous, but I'm not scared. I'm not scared of anything, you see. Not like my little brother—he thinks there's monsters under his bed, but I know there ain't any. I've looked myself—"

Matt cut the boy off, grabbed him by his arm, and jerked him in close to the playhouse. The red and blue lights from a passing cruiser lit up its walls. Matt held a finger in front of the boy's lips. When the cruiser had moved on, Matt released his hold on the boy's arm.

"Thanks," he said.

"Don't worry," the boy said, grinning. "I'm always a bad guy when we play cops and robbers."

"Do you ever go outside the wall to play?"

"All the time. Mom says no, but Dad don't care much. Are you going outside? It's an easy climb, you know. I do it all the time."

"Could you do me a favor? Both of us being robbers and all."

"Sure. Is that a real gun?"

"Uh, yes. It is. Could you stand out on the road and stop the next cop car? Say that you saw me run that way?" Matt pointed.

"Sure. And then will you jump out and shoot them? And we win?" The boy's eyes grew enormous.

"Yes, something like that. But first, I have to go up on the wall, so you can't look my way. Think you can handle that?"

"Sure. Would you like to see my room after? I have dinosaurs, you know."

Matt smiled. "I would love that."

Guiding the boy with a hand on his back, Matt positioned the kid on the road, between the two lanes. Then he dashed over to the wall and started to climb.

It was quick and easy, just as the boy had proclaimed; there were grips and ledges aplenty. As he made it to the top, he heard the squeal of brakes as a police car made a one-hundred-and-eighty-degree turn and sped towards the little boy, who was standing on the dark road, arms crossed and a cheeky smile on his face.

"MOVE!" Matt yelled down, but the kid stood steadfast. The cruiser's tires whined as it raced towards the boy and his bunny. Matt closed his eyes; he couldn't watch.

The high-pitched wailing stopped. No thud, no bump. He opened his eyes.

"What are you doing, kid?" A police officer came flying out of the car, which had stopped just a yard shy of the child.

"NOW!" the boy yelled, and looked up at Matt. The officer turned, following the boy's gaze, but it was too late. Matt, a leg on each side of the two-foot-thick wall, grinned as he flung himself over and jumped down to the other side, silently thanking his little accomplice.

Disappearing into the comforting embrace of the pitch-black night, Matt made his way back towards downtown, following his old, familiar landmarks.

It didn't take long before a car pulled up alongside him. Zee rolled down the passenger side window.

"Get in," he said.

Matt, hands in his pockets, fondled the data stick and then his car keys, trying to decide.

"I want my pickup back," Matt said, and kept walking along the curb.

"Let's get back to the others with the data. We'll go get your truck later."

"No. I want it now."

"As you wish, then," Zee said with a sigh.

Matt climbed into the car beside him and they set off in silence.

They pulled up a few minutes later at the supermarket lot near the clinic; they still hadn't uttered a word to each other. Matt got out and walked over to the battered old truck, yanked the driver's side door open and climbed in. He started the engine, pulled out into the road, and trailed Zee back to the underground facility, taking great care to remember every little twist and turn along the way.

30

The hidden lift inside the containers rustled as it began its descent. Matt and Zee stood a couple of yards apart, still not speaking. Aside from the gears grinding away, providing a soft and heavy blanket of noise, there was a stagnant silence between the two.

Matt was just about to speak and ask what on earth the last few hours had been all about, but Zee cut in over him.

"I'm sorry," he said, turning towards him. "I should have told you about copying all their data, but we needed everything on your mother, not just her journal. I hope you understand."

"I trusted you," Matt said bitterly, still looking straight ahead. "But you didn't trust me. You didn't trust that I could handle the responsibility if I knew what you were really asking me to do."

"No. I didn't. Again, I'm sorry. I was wrong."

"So, will you tell me what the other data was? Or are you gonna keep treating me like a child?"

"Fine," Zee said. "I suppose it's only fair. That clinic you went to, that your mother went to? The staff there have connections to the government. They are tampering with genetics, and we need to know exactly how and why."

"But it's a fertility clinic. They are helping people get pregnant."

"To the public, yes. Your standard private company doesn't get clearance to circulate confidential government files. You think any business can employ armed guards the way they do? No, that requires connections to the government. And we are only scratching the surface of these covert connections. Don't you get it, Matt? We couldn't miss this opportunity for a peek at their research. When I told you that more than your mother's life was at stake, I meant it. But I didn't want to tell you anything further in case you got cold feet." He turned his head towards Matt. "I'm sorry, Matt. I should have told you the truth from the beginning."

Matt turned and looked at Zee. "Yes. You should have," he said.

"So, will you hand over the data now? We have to begin decryption immediately if we are going to find your mother's data in time."

Matt reached into his pocket and dug out the stick. He turned it over in his palm a bit, then put it between his thumb and index finger and stretched out his hand towards Zee. Zee reached for it, but Matt didn't let go. Feeling the resistance, Zee looked up, and Matt watched his reaction carefully.

"What happened in 2056?" he asked, still clinging to the little slim gadget.

"I don't know what you're talking about," Zee said without blinking. Not a flinch, not a twitch, nothing.

Matt let go of the data stick.

"Thank you," Zee said, withdrawing his arm and putting the stick in his pocket. He was still avoiding Matt's gaze.

The elevator door opened on the little underground hall, and there was a sudden roar of cheers from a small crowd that had assembled to meet them. Faulk and Ems stood in front of about twenty people gathered at the lift's door, both wearing big happy grins. At the back of the group, Kevin beamed.

Matt, ignoring all the others, plowed his way through a gauntlet of pats and claps on the shoulder towards his little brother and threw his arms around him, embracing him, squeezing him tight, knocking the air out of them both.

"I'm sorry, Kev. I should have trusted you more," Matt said.

"It's all right. I should've been there. I should've stayed, should've helped."

The two held each other at arms' length now, smiling broadly.

"That was fucking awesome," Faulk said, sticking his head in between the brothers. "This is so important to us. And your mom, of course."

Matt nodded his acknowledgment, and then Faulk darted off down the aisles, waving the stick like a triumphant little schoolboy catching the deciding touchdown, showing off a game ball. Kevin laughed.

Ems approached now, smiling from ear to ear.

"I'm so happy that you're back. I worried like hell," she blurted. "And I've got some good news."

"What is it?" Matt said

"It's Elizabeth. She's awake. I just came from her room. And she's talking. Would you like to say hi?"

Matt brightened.

Kevin grabbed Ems in a bear hug and lifted her off the ground, twirling her around and around and whooping with joy. They all laughed.

"For real? She's responding and all?" Matt said reluctantly as his brother put Ems back down.

She nodded and ran a hand through her hair, her smile widening even more. "It's the synaptic fluids, so I can't tell you how long it's gonna last, but it's a start, don't you think?"

"Thanks, Ems. You have no idea what that means to me," Matt said, giving her an impromptu kiss on the cheek.

She giggled. "I'm just doing my job."

Ems grabbed his hand and dragged him along the corridor towards Elizabeth's room; Kevin followed close behind. She stopped outside the door and leaned against the wall, ushering them in. "I'll give you guys some privacy," she said.

The brothers walked, uncertain what they would see. Matt stood on one side of her bed, Kevin on the other. Elizabeth still had tubes running in and out of her body, and several electrodes connected to the beeping monitors. A thick blanket covered her now. Elizabeth's eyes were closed, but as Matt brushed her arm, her lids flickered, and she opened her eyes and looked up.

"Hi, Mom," Matt said.

She smiled and inspected his face as if they had been apart for months. Then she tried to speak, but only a meager whisper came out.

"You all right?" he said.

She nodded, looked to Kevin, and smiled again. Then she spoke, gathering a bit more power behind her voice. "The doctor. Ems. She told me you had … run some errands. I've been waiting to see you. What day is it? How long has it been?"

"Since what, Mom?" Kevin asked.

"Your graduation."

"Practically two weeks. That's the last thing you remember?" Matt said, astounded.

Elizabeth nodded again. She took Kevin's hand and held it. She ran her fingers across the back of his hand, feeling his knuckles, turning his wrist over, running a finger down the inside of the palm.

"Mom?" Matt said.

She looked up at him.

"I have to ask you something," he said, looking over his shoulder and gesturing at Kevin to close the door. Kevin closed the door and stood beside it.

"Do you remember a Dr. Henke?" Matt said.

"Yes. Our old neighbor, Mr. Waldhaven. Christopher, right?"

"Yes. I went to see him today," Matt said.

"Oh. How is he? It's been so many years."

"He's fine."

"Ah, lovely. Be sure to give him my regards if you see him again."

"He told me something about how you and Dad struggled to conceive me."

"Yes, that's right. He helped us a lot back then. With Kevin too," Elizabeth said.

"So it's true you're not my biological mother?"

"Well, yes. We had to protect you, Matt. Give you the best possible future. I couldn't do that with my genes, of course."

Matt felt a tear creep into the corner of his eye.

"But Kevin *was* yours, and you never told me," Matt said.

"We thought very little about it, to be honest. You were always *our* son. Just as much as he was."

The tear slid down his cheek.

"Hey, Mattimouse?" Elizabeth said. "It was always about giving you kids a better future than we had," Elizabeth said. "I saw how Alzheimer's tore my mother apart. Your father and I didn't want you two going through that, too."

"But we *did*, Mom. We did," Matt said.

"I'm sorry I never told you. But for me, your future was all that mattered. Yours and Kevin's."

Kevin came over and, without saying a word, hugged Matt from behind.

"You knew?" Matt said, looking over his shoulder.

"Zee and Ems told me. While we were waiting for you to come online."

"But Mom?" Matt said. "You might still be sick."

"The doctor told me that was a possibility, yes," she said. "But she also told me you were out searching for information that would help them find a cure. Either way, Matt, I'm proud of you. Your father would have been, too. If it's my time, it's my time. Christopher always told me there were no certainties. It just makes me happy to see the two of you flourish together. And I'm so grateful I got to see that."

The three held hands in silence for a long moment. Matt was clenching his jaw, forcing a faint smile, but Kevin and his mother seemed genuinely happy. And he needed to savor that. As he watched them, his upper lip began to tremble. His father had always told him to be strong for his little brother. And now he couldn't anymore. Hot tears trickled down his face, darkening the sheets and the blanket as they soaked up into the fabric. Matt tried to wipe them away at first. Then Kevin hurried around the bed and enveloped him in his arms, then reached one hand back to Elizabeth.

"You're not him anymore," Kevin whispered, so that only Matt could hear. "And you don't have to be."

Matt began to shake with sobs as the tears flowed freely down his face.

It felt like hours before he finally stopped crying, although the clock on the wall said that only fifteen minutes had passed. Kevin brought over a chair for him to sit by their mother. For another forty-five minutes, they talked about the days back home, the summer they had all gone road tripping, and how they had all gotten the runs from a can of bad anchovies. Kevin tried to bring up the subject of college, but Matt nudged him and whispered to him to save it for later.

Eventually, Ems knocked on the door, opened it and stuck her head inside. Elizabeth needed rest, she told them gently. The boys hugged their mother a final time and got to their feet, realizing they both needed a good night's sleep themselves.

"Kev, how are you?" Matt said as they headed down the corridors towards the sleeping quarters.

"I'm fine, I guess. It's always hard to see your mom ill. It was nice to speak to her, though. Like we used to. You know, back before all this."

"No. I meant, how are *you* feeling?"

"Oh, me? I'm fine. Don't worry about me."

"Good."

"You know what? I'm better than fine. I'm happy, and it's so weird. I… I met someone. I can't tell you who right now because I want to keep her my secret. Until all this is over, I mean. And also, I don't know how she's feeling about me."

"Ah, one of those kinds of happiness." Matt smiled and gently punched his brother's shoulder. "I get it. Take your time."

"Thanks."

They reached their little room, and without even bothering to undress, they hunkered down on the hard mattresses, pulled up their blankets and closed their eyes.

31

Tossing and turning about in the bunk bed, Matt couldn't sleep. His body couldn't settle on a resting place his muscles didn't reject, and his mind raced along the eternal highways of doubt. He could hear his little brother breathing in the bed next to him, sound asleep. Matt squinted at his watch in the dark. It was hard to make out the time, but he knew he'd been lying there for hours now.

He got up and shuffled out through the heavy curtain, rubbing his eyes as they adjusted to the dim light in the underground hall. He decided to get some tap water in the mess hall. Everything was quiet. Up until now, he'd noticed no unified circadian rhythm at the facility, but now everyone seemed to be asleep. He drank another glass of water and then went back out into the maze of corridors.

By now, he knew his way around the complex, at least between the key points of interest. The monotone swish of the large fans at each end drew his attention, and Matt's feet followed the regular beat of their revolutions. He wandered down the hallway towards his mother's room and looked through the little window in the door. She lay still in her bed. The blanket rose and fell with the rhythm of her breathing as her lungs heaved in the musty air of the cellar-like surroundings.

For now, this seemed a necessary evil. Ems was working so hard, doing so much; Matt couldn't thank her enough for the hours of shared family time earlier this evening. It had felt almost like old times, being so happy together. And now Matt sensed a real possibility of getting it all back. But there were still a couple of things left that he needed to unravel.

Drifting further down the corridors, he found his way to the computer room. He glanced through the open door. Faulk was sprawled in his chair, feet on the floor and arms folded on the table, his head resting on top, one hand still clasping an energy drink. He was snoring loud enough that Matt could hear him clearly from where he stood. The stacked screens ran prompts and progress bars, but Matt was clueless as to the tasks unfolding; code and programming were utterly foreign to him. Although he was intrigued by the secrets spooling past, right before his eyes, in line after line of colorful glyphs and shorthand, he gave up on trying to understand any of it. He tapped the door, then tapped again, louder this time.

Faulk's upper body jerked upright, one arm flailing to save the energy drink from spilling over the keyboard in front of him. He searched around, disoriented, and saw Matt at the door.

"Can't sleep?" Matt said, knowing Faulk had been doing just fine before he arrived.

"Eh, no. I guess not," Faulk said. "Sometimes I just slip in a few quick winks when the machine is running its automation." He rubbed his eye with a clenched fist and took a large sip from his drink, shook the can to confirm it was empty, and threw it into the corner, where it rattled down a small mountain of recyclables. "How about you?"

Matt shook his head and stepped inside, grabbing an empty chair and pulling it up next to Faulk. He looked at the screens. "How's it going? Found my mom yet?" he said, pointing.

"Huh? Oh, no. Not yet. It's a slow process, and since we're emulating the doctor's machine in order to decrypt the data, we can't do it in bulk. He didn't have that kind of access. And with our equipment, brute force is not an option."

"Hey," Matt said. "I have no clue about what it is you're telling me. But it's all right. I just wanted to check in."

"Heh, sorry. I get carried away. And I even tried using the non-technical version there. Haha." Faulk laughed his weird little laugh.

They sat there for a couple of minutes, looking at the screens. Matt recognized names in one field, the sort order changing as the computer worked each journal. Decrypt, store, next. Decrypt, store, next.

"How many has it done so far?" Matt said.

"I can't really tell. I know we're about twenty-five percent through, but how much of that translates to journals, I don't know. So it might still be a while."

"And you're sure she's in there?"

"All logic says she has to be. That's about the best we can hope for, don't you think?"

"Guess so."

Matt looked around the room, and his eyes halted on the gun cabinet. It was open. The gun he'd been issued still sat on the table, where he'd dropped it when he'd returned.

"Why do you have all these guns?"

"Protection, mostly." Faulk swiveled in his chair, turning for a more conversational posture. "But we rarely need them. Just a precaution, you know."

"How long have you worked with Zee?"

"I don't know. Been at this place fifteen, twenty years maybe?" He thought for a moment. "Twenty's about right, yeah. I think Zee found me when I was nine."

"So you were here in 2056?" Matt tried

"Sounds about right."

"Zee told me about the incident." He was fishing for recognition.

"Huh?"

"The data breach, I think he called it?" Hook, line, sinker.

"Oh, yeah, that. Really went tits up, that did."

Bite. "Yeah. He didn't have time to explain the details, so…" Matt lingered on the last word.

"Well, it was a run a bit like yours," Faulk said, settling back in his chair. "We had a guy getting some data for us. He went to another building, of course, but that was before they decentralized everything. We hit the jackpot. It was a *huge* dataset. I remember watching Zee and our chief programmer in this very room. I was in training, you see."

Matt nodded, not wanting to interrupt.

"But something went bad," Faulk went on. "I couldn't hear what was going on, didn't have a headset. But suddenly, the mood shifted. The whole room filled with tension, like a rubber band stretched round too many cables, you know? They started arguing, and then they both started yelling. I remember Zee pushing Linus, that was his name, aside and seizing the board. Zee knows code too. Pretty nifty at it, actually. And then I got kicked out of the room. I think it was Linus who told me to beat it, but I'm not sure. But they kept yelling at each other; I could hear them right through the door. Something about corrupting the data."

Matt nodded; this time, he felt an urge to fill the lingering pause. "Yeah, I got that much from Zee," he tried. Faulk didn't seem to notice his dishonesty.

"Don't know how it ended," he went on. "They finally shut up. But our frontrunner? That's what we call your job, by the way. He didn't make it out. *Pow*." Faulk put an imaginary gun to his head. "So I was pretty stoked you did." Faulk chuckled.

"Yeah, me too," Matt said, trying his best to replicate the laugh. He felt a bit sick all of a sudden.

Faulk rolled to the desk's far side, opening a small fridge underneath. "Want one?"

"Nah, I'm good. Should be getting some sleep."

"I like to keep my own stash. Always cold, you see. Sometimes people forget to fill up in the mess hall, so..." Faulk rolled back to his former position, popping open a can.

"What about Linus?" Matt said. "Where's he now?"

"He left. Kind of tragic, actually. He died a few months later. Got involved in some drug shooting or something. I saw it on the news. Didn't consider him an addict, but I guess you never know before you know, right?"

"No. I suppose not," Matt concluded, turning over that last statement in his head a few times.

Faulk sipped at his drink, and they both turned their heads towards the monitors once again. A few minutes passed as the prompts and lines ran across the screens, sifting, tallying, harvesting.

"Is it possible that my mom's journal could have been among that data from 2056?" Matt said, breaking into the soft humming of the computers.

"No, I couldn't imagine that. If it was, I think Zee would have known. He knows what data center we breached back then. So, no, I don't think so. Patience. She'll show up, eventually," Faulk said.

Matt stood up. "I think I'll get some sleep, then."

"Got it. Think it'll do you good. You seem a bit distracted."

"Yeah. That might be it. Lack of sleep," Matt said, and left Faulk to his computers.

32

Walking back towards the sleeping quarters, Matt decided against trying to go back to bed. He swung around in the narrow aisle, turned a corner, and headed for his mother's room. From afar, he noticed the door was open. Someone was sobbing inside. Peeking around the frame, he could see that Elizabeth still lay in bed, her eyes closed, sleeping underneath the blanket. Matt dipped his head inside and peered around. Ems was sitting crouched against the wall, tucked into the far corner, crying as though her heart would break. She hadn't noticed him. He pulled back his head.

Matt felt embarrassed, as though he'd stumbled upon Ems grieving. Perhaps treating his mother had brought one of her own painful memories to the surface. He didn't know Ems's past, and he didn't want to intrude. He stood uncertainly in the hall; the sound of the doctor's sobbing kept persisting between the steady bleeps of his mother's monitors. Maybe she'd come in here because it was hard to find solitude in the complex. That was probably it. His mother could wait till morning. He tiptoed away from the door, but then stopped.

His mind was eager for Ems to have a moment of peace, but

his body seemed to feel otherwise. Ems had always been so cheerful, and even more so with Elizabeth getting better. Yet here she sat, in the dead of night, all by herself, bawling in a corner. It didn't add up. Maybe she wanted Matt to find her. Maybe she'd checked the bunks, looking for him, and then headed to the only place she was sure he'd be. Maybe, this time, she needed him. Needed his shoulder to cry on. He felt his face grow hot. Saliva gathered at the back of his mouth, lingering at the cusp of his throat. He dragged his suddenly sweaty palms against the bottom of his shirt, not able to rid himself of the uneasy feeling. Forcing himself to swallow, he swiveled his feet and took two quick steps back to the door. He tapped it and cleared his throat.

"You all right?" he said softly. He didn't dare look inside.

Ems sniffed. "You can come in."

She was still sitting on the floor, drying her eyes and cheeks. Mascara was smeared all over her knuckles. Matt walked over and stood on the opposite side, by his mother's bed. He didn't want to encroach.

"I'm sorry that I disturbed you," Matt said. "I was just going to see… You know, I couldn't sleep, so…"

"Hey, it's your mom. I'm the one intruding." Ems got to her feet; Elizabeth lay sleeping between them. For a minute, the room was still, other than the rhythmic beeps.

Matt glanced over at Ems, trying to catch her eye, but she was looking down.

"She's so calm. So peaceful," he said.

Ems didn't reply.

"You know…" he continued, uncomfortable with the silence and the turmoil of his thoughts. "I'm so grateful for everything you've done for us. I wish there was some way I—." He broke off, seeing tears streaming down her face again. A few damp locks of chestnut hair clung to her cheeks.

Matt tried to steady his breathing. Ems's sobbing now picked up from where she'd left off a few minutes ago, and now he was standing across from her like a statue, each passing moment affirming his inability to act.

Matt turned sideways to the bed, determined to move. He swayed, tilted forward, and then forced his feet to move, exploiting his reflex arcs to prevent a stumble, thus bypassing the roadblock of his brain and propelling himself into forward motion. He felt dizzy. And then, suddenly, he'd done it: he stood beside Ems, although he had no idea how each step had replaced the one before it.

Now for the tricky part: he urged his arm to move, then placed it on her shoulder, flattening the palm, calming the digits. Uncertain whether to squeeze or caress, he went with the latter. It worked. Ems turned and melted into his arms, into the more or less natural embrace he had hoped for. Matt snuck out a sigh between his deep breaths, not sure how she might interpret his relief. She tucked further into him, and Matt absorbed her, shivering slightly as her sobs turned to outright wailing.

Hours seemed to pass as he stood embracing her, gently stroking her back, but it was only a minute before she muttered something softly into his shoulder. Matt kept caressing her, trying not to squeeze, but still hugging her enough to let her know he cared.

"Just let it out," he said.

Ems suddenly stiffened and shoved her arms in between their bodies, breaking his grasp, lifting her head free of his moist shirt.

"I'm sorry," she said.

"Don't be. We all have our stuff. Can you believe it? I shot a cop last night. In the streetlights. By accident, I swear, but I don't think he'll make it."

"No, Matt. You're not... Listening. I'm... Sorry I got... You into this." She hiccupped miserably; the sentence came out chopped into lumps. "It's all. My. Fault."

"Relax," he said, trying for the soft embrace once again. "You're doing the best you can. That's all anyone can ask for."

Ems wrestled free and took a step back. She stopped crying, but her eyes were still full of distress. "No, you don't understand. I'm killing her. With the synaptic fluids. I can't take all these lies anymore."

Matt frowned. He couldn't make sense of it. "But... she's getting better, isn't she? We talked for hours this evening."

"No. She's not getting better. The fluids are destroying her tissue from the inside, accelerating her brain damage while covering up the symptoms. It won't be long before she can't even breathe without that stuff."

"You said it might work until we found the treatment."

"It could, but there's no treatment. We won't ever figure it out," she said and looked at him, waiting for a response.

Speechless, he realized the truth before she told him.

"There might not be a journal on your mother. There might not be any data on her at all," Ems said. "Zee knows it. He lied. And now, he wants me to fake a treatment to cover it up so that it looks like we tried. All while her brain turns to mush."

"Did *you* know?"

"No. I promise. He told me a couple of hours ago. But it doesn't matter—it's still my fault. I trusted Zee, and *I* convinced you to stay."

"It matters to me," Matt said.

Ems dragged the sleeve of her white coat across her face, leaving streaks of black mascara. She looked miserably back up at him. "I'm so sorry," she said. "I don't know what to say."

He grabbed her by the shoulders and held her out in front of him. Petrified, like a fawn caught in headlights, she cowered, awaiting her sentence.

Matt stood frozen for a moment. Anger and sadness battled inside him. It wasn't her fault. How could it be? *He* had asked for help, and she had done what she thought best. Restraining his rage, he forced himself to focus. He tucked her close, clenching her in a tight but loving embrace.

"I need your help," he whispered in her ear.

"Anything!" she blurted, her shoulders sinking, her body unwinding as she realized he wasn't going to harm her.

"Is there any way we can get her on the road?" Matt looked over at Elizabeth, still peacefully asleep.

"With the proper precautions and a reliable vehicle, yes. But..."

Matt looked back to Ems, expecting a continuation to fill the abrupt pause.

"Do you have anywhere to go?" she finished.

"I think I do. With your insight so far, what do you reckon is actually wrong with her?"

"To be honest, I don't know. I've never seen anything like it."

"Do you think it's related to genetics?"

"It could be, yes. I can see what the disease is doing, but I can't figure out the root cause. It doesn't look like she's sick; rather, it looks like the body is doing what it's programmed to do. And that points to DNA."

Matt released his grip on her; he needed to think. She drifted out of his arms, taking a small step back and then ducking to look in his eyes. She took his hand in hers, tapping it with her finger.

"What is it? There's something else, isn't there?" she said.

Matt nodded glumly. "The doctor, the one I held hostage? He told me all this. I just didn't believe him. I didn't know if I could."

"That's not it. I can see it, Matt. You can't hide yourself from me. I haven't known you for long, but you read like an open book."

He took her other hand and turned towards her, letting their arms hang down in between them.

"If it's genetic, what are the odds that Kevin will end up suffering from the same disease?"

"I'm sorry, Matt. I don't have an answer for that. I don't have odds," Ems replied sadly. "It's probable. If that's any help, but that means that you carry the gene as well."

"No," Matt said. "I don't. She's not my biological mother." She looked at him in surprise. "Could you treat it? I mean, could you treat Kevin?"

"I'm not sure. It would be near impossible for me to figure out which genome and which mutation is causing this unless you wait for the sickness to kick in. I would be stumbling in the dark."

"Do you think this Dr. Henke might know?"

"I don't know. But if you insist on odds, I'd say they'd be better at the clinic. It's their subject, and they have state-of-the-art machines and equipment."

Again, Matt's eyes drifted from Ems down to his mother. Ems snapped her fingers in front of his eyes.

"Hey? You there? You listen to me," Ems demanded, adjusting his head with a finger, fixing her eyes on his. "If you think that clinic will take you, if you have even the slightest hope of that, then go for it, Matt. Run the risk. The treatment there is the best you're going to get, and if you get your mother there in time, they may be able to save her."

"You're right." He looked over at his mother again, then back at Ems. "Okay, let's do this. How do I move her?"

They stepped over to Elizabeth's bed and began to inspect the monitors she was plugged into. Ems proceeded to give Matt a crash course on the function of each one, insisting that he would need some basic know-how on their usage. Some would need to be taken along; some could safely be disconnected. Ems went back and forth to a supply room, bringing out emergency equipment and simpler, portable versions of the monitors. She gave Matt instructions on each item, showing him how to use what and when.

As knowledge started pouring through his tired brain cells, Matt suddenly realized he was exhausted, desperate for a break to recuperate. He started to doze, but Ems caught him drifting off, nudging him at first, then slapping him. She underlined the importance of what she was telling him, but the terms and buttons and dials got mixed up in his head every time she asked him to repeat what she'd just told him. He tried his best, but it was futile. He needed to sleep. Finally, Ems gave up and put him in a chair next to his mother, tucking him with an extra blanket from supply. She bent down to his ear and promised him she wouldn't tell Kevin about the possible genetic connection, since Matt didn't want him scared.

■ ■ ■

Matt jolted from the chair. His feet and hands tangled in the blanket, and he fell heavily to the floor. He had no idea how long he'd been sleeping. There was a sharp beeping noise pounding through the room, much louder than before. He flung the blanket aside and jumped to his feet. Tremors were shooting through Elizabeth's body. She'd thrown the blanket off, and her arms and legs were thrashing wildly as she convulsed.

Ems was nowhere in sight. He looked frantically at the monitors, trying to sort through the new information in his brain, trying to make sense of the curves and peaks. He couldn't.

"HEEELP!" he screamed. Bending over Elizabeth's bed, he tried to keep his mother still to prevent her from tumbling off the edge of the bed. Bracing his feet against the wall, he pushed against the dead weight of his mother's thrashing body. He heard the sound of running feet as a nurse dashed into the room to assist him. Another nurse followed a moment later, and between the three of them, they heaved Elizabeth back to the middle of the mattress.

"You got her?" Matt said, panting. The two nurses were already turning knobs, adjusting IV flows, checking readouts. One of them nodded at him over her shoulder.

"Get Ems," he told them as he dashed out into the hall. "She knows what to do."

33

"Kevin, wake up. Wake up, Kevin."

The whisper sounded like a roar on the inside of his head. Kevin's shoulders were being thrust up and down, his gentle pulse forced into aggressive rhythmic pounding. He opened his eyes. Matt, shoulders hunched and head low, stared straight at him. Then his eyes scanned the room. Kevin tilted his head, trying his best to follow.

"Wha—" Kevin began, but Matt slapped a hand across his mouth.

"You need to be quiet," Matt hissed.

Kevin nodded. Something was up; there was a mix of panic and paranoia on Matt's face. Kevin nudged Matt's hand aside so he could breathe again.

Matt looked at his hand. "Sorry."

"What's wrong?" Kevin said, adjusting his tone to match Matt's.

"It's Mom. She's dying. And they've been lying to us. We have to move her."

"Stop it, Matt." Kevin sat up, annoyed.

"No, I'm serious. She's having a seizure or something. I just came from her room. Be quiet—let's go."

There was no reasoning with Matt, Kevin knew. He had become even more stubborn and self-centered than he usually was. He grabbed Kevin by the arm now and dragged him to his feet. Kevin followed him blearily down the corridor, trying to put his thoughts into some kind of order.

"Relax, Matt—please. I just woke up," Kevin protested as Matt flew down the hall.

At their mother's room, Matt flung Kevin up against the closed door, forcing him to look through the tiny window.

"See?"

Multiple nurses were at Elizabeth's bedside, looking at charts, adjusting dials, connecting tubes to new machines. In the middle of all the commotion, Ems leaned over their mother, preparing a needle for injection. A tube ran inside Elizabeth's mouth; her nose was covered in a transparent plastic mask. She lay utterly still.

Kevin's body woke suddenly, like a syringe had flushed ice-cold water straight through his veins. He stiffened. Matt whirled him around and pushed him up against the wall next to the door. Ten hours ago, she'd been fine. Talking, laughing, just like old times.

"See?" he said again. "We have to save her!" Matt insisted, still whispering.

"But how? We can't..." He bit his lip; a slight taste of iron dabbed his tongue.

Matt looked up and down the corridor. "Dr. Henke. He can help us. We just have to get her to the clinic," he said.

"What? You can't do that! She's dying, Matt! Don't you get it? I won't let you do this again."

"Listen to me, Kevin," Matt said, leaning close now. "Zee's been lying to us all along. They can't save her. There *is* no journal about her. The whole thing was a hoax to get me to steal the data—don't you see?"

Kevin shook his head in disbelief.

"Dr. Henke," Matt said again. "He can save Mom. He *knows* her. He knows *us*. I need you to trust me on this," Matt said.

"I'm not sure I can," Kevin said, blinking back tears.

"I can't do this by myself, Kev," Matt said, more gently now. "I need *you*."

Kevin felt himself wavering.

"Listen," Matt said. "We can either stay here and wait for her to die, which she will. Ems told me. Or we can give it one last shot. As for me, I truly believe *we* can do this. *Together.* So let me ask you again, Kev: Are you with me?"

At last, as though it had ignited from the inside, warmth burst through Kevin's body. From the fiery core of his pounding heart, confidence radiated out through his extremities all the way through to the tips of his fingernails. At the apex of his brainstem, cells magnetized, aligning all his thoughts into one, obliterating any doubt and fear.

"Yes," he said, straightening his back and squaring his shoulders. "I'm with you. So… What can I do?"

"We need a vehicle. There's a van up in the warehouse. It's white, and it's been retrofitted to carry a hospital bed."

Kevin looked doubtful.

"Ems told me," Matt said. "There's a little locker with keys somewhere inside the warehouse. Easy to spot."

"Okay, let's go." Kevin turned, but Matt grabbed him by the arm.

"No. I'm not coming. You must do this yourself. I have things to do here. Listen, I trust you. And don't let them see you."

Kevin nodded, speechless. *I trust you.* He couldn't remember ever hearing those three words from his brother. Matt released his grip.

Kevin darted through the corridors towards the emergency exit. Flew up flights of stairs, two steps at a time. As he pushed open the heavy metal door and ducked out of the main container, early-morning sunlight hit his eyes. Squinting, he stood still for a moment, waiting for his eyes to adjust, then made out the single-door entrance to the large warehouse. He moved steadily towards it, flattening himself against the cold steel sheets.

There was no one in sight. Walking sideways to the door and then passing it, he took a quick peek around the corner to the parking area. There was no one in sight. Grabbing the handle, he pressed it down until he heard the soft click of the latch bolt releasing. He waited. Listened. Nothing. He opened the heavy reinforced door just a few inches, enough for a glimpse inside. The warehouse was empty. He opened the door wider and slipped inside, closing it behind him with a soft thud. Then he let go of his breath.

At both ends of the vast hall, huge ventilation ducts extended up through the floor; Kevin could hear the faint humming of the complex echoing in the cavernous space. The lot was crowded with vehicles, all neatly parked. There were two vans, but only one was white. The old paint was faded now to a yellowish hue. Rust had eaten along the edges; Kevin prayed that it drove better than it looked.

Down one aisle, alongside a couple of wide garage doors, he spotted the small locker next to a panel of buttons on a center column dividing the roll-ups in two. He jogged down the wall of doors, taking care to tread lightly. Reaching the column, he noticed that the button layout matched the doors: up and down arrows for each, a single red one in the middle. He smiled: now he knew how to get the van out.

Opening the metal locker, he saw a long grid of nails, with keys hanging from most of them. Kevin turned around and squinted at the van to clarify the make. Three keys matched. Grabbing all three, he ran back to the van.

He found the correct key and pulled the driver's side door open with some difficulty; the hinges creaked as flakes of rust shed from the steel. A crack in the windshield split the view in half. Kevin closed the door and sank into the cracked pleather seat. His breath made little clouds in the cold, stale air of the old van. As he tried to calm his panting, it dawned that he had no idea what to do next. Did Matt want him to drive the van up to the container? Or did he want him to wait in the warehouse? Why hadn't he explained? Kevin dropped his head on the steering wheel as his little bubble of confidence burst, leaving only that old, familiar doubt. Heaving a sigh, he tried to calm his pounding heart and gather his thoughts, hoping reason would reassert itself.

He sat there for a long time, looking out through the cracked windshield, focusing his gaze beyond the confines of the vehicle. Against the walls of the warehouse, the forked-lightning shape of the crack was nearly transparent.

Finally, Kevin snapped out of his empty thoughts. His palms were clenched on the steering wheel; there were imprints on his palms from the grooves. He adjusted his weight; his pants clung to his butt, sweaty now against the plastic upholstery. How long had he been drifting?

He turned the ignition and tapped the gas, setting the wreck into motion. As he rolled out of the parking space, he passed their old pickup, which someone had parked at the opposite end of the row. Kevin jammed on the van's brakes. Even though the pickup was banged up and trashed, it still carried a familiar little knickknack in the glove compartment. He wasn't leaving without it.

He put the van in park and got out, leaving the door open, and sprinted between the cars towards his brother's trusty old truck. He pulled on the handle; the door was locked. Fuck it, he thought. They'd already shattered most of the windows. He smashed the passenger side window, unlocked the door and reached for the glove compartment.

Rummaging around among spare keys, pocket tissues and a packet of Tic Tacs, Kevin pulled out his toy crocodile. Smiling, he ran his fingers down along its serrated tail. It used to calm him when he was younger, whenever Matt acted too bossy, too much like a father. But now, he was learning that Matt was also a brother, an ally. It seemed like years since they'd packed up the apartment; he realized with a start that it had been just a couple of weeks ago. He remembered sitting on his bedroom floor, deciding to keep the little crocodile in case, one day, he wanted to pass it along to a child of his own. And now, maybe, he would get the chance.

"Anybody here?" someone shouted.

Kevin stood up, his heart hammering. He looked around the inside of the truck and spied the old metal rod Matt used to park it on slopes. He grabbed it with one hand, tucking the crocodile into his pocket.

"It's just me," he yelled.

A man in battered charcoal overalls, with grease and oil stains up and down his bare arms, walked towards him. Kevin kept one arm inside the truck, holding the two-foot metal rod inside, just below the glassless frame.

"What the fuck are you doing? I heard glass shattering."

"Sorry. This is my brother's truck. He lost the keys, and I came out to get the spare from the glove compartment. Silly, right?"

The man was scrutinizing him, not falling for his lame excuse. Kevin tightened his grasp on the steel bar in his hand, shifting the weight, adjusting his grip.

"You going somewhere?"

"No, we just needed the keys. I was gonna hang them in the cabinet." Kevin nodded over towards the center column, hoping the man would shift his focus. Sure enough, the man took a few steps sideways and turned to look. Kevin assessed and slid his weapon out and held it behind his back.

"Hey, what's that van doing out?" the man said.

Kevin shifted his feet silently forward to close the distance.

"Who put it there?" The man turned. "Did you drive it out?" he asked. His eyes shifted as he noticed Kevin's hand was behind his back. He took a step back.

There was a sudden crack, followed by a resounding boom that thundered up through the ventilation shafts, then a deafening echo that exploded off the steel walls of the garage. The man ducked, shifted his weight, and turned towards the ducts. Kevin sprang forward, swinging the rod with all his strength. He struck the man across his head with all his might, and he fell with a thud at Kevin's feet, then lay still, a pool of blood gathering around his head.

34

Matt watched his little brother sprinting down the hallway and then set off into the complex. He had one stop to make before they could leave with Elizabeth, something he needed to make sure of. Dodging the trickle of early-morning traffic through the hallways, he turned a corner and closed in on Faulk's work room.

"Have you found her data yet?" Matt demanded as he slammed the door open.

Faulk jolted upright from his slumped position in the chair and swiveled around, flustered, trying to get his bearings.

"Do you have her DNA profile?" Matt said, taking a couple of steps forward and towering over Faulk.

Faulk's eyes filled with distress; a small tic began under the left one. "We've found *some* data. I told you. But we're not finished searching and indexing yet. Calm down, Matt," Faulk said, raising his arm in defense and shrinking in the seat.

"Did you know?" Matt said, leaning over him, his eyes wild.

"Wha—"

"DID YOU FUCKING KNOW?" His voice echoed off the walls.

Zee stepped through the door behind him. "What's going on here?" His voice was soft, collected, relaxed.

Faulk wiped the sweat from his face.

Matt turned around and took a deep breath, composing himself. Now was not the time to lose it, he sensed.

"You've been using me," Matt said, stepping up to Zee. "To get your fucking data."

"No, Matt. You helped us get a lot of data, *including* your mother's," Zee said. His restraint was overwhelming.

Matt took two deep breaths, shaving further notches off his racing heartbeat. He turned and pointed up at the screens. "But she's not there, is she?"

Zee looked down at Faulk, still cowering in the chair.

"She hasn't come up yet." Faulk's voice trembled.

"But she will, Matt. You need to be patient." Zee's voice was steady, almost hypnotic.

"How can I be patient? My mom's fucking dying down there." Matt pointed back out to the corridor.

"Ems has got it under control. I checked in with her earlier. She knows what she's doing," Zee said.

"You came from there? From my mom's room?"

"Yes."

"You're lying. I was just there, and I didn't see you."

"I had some errands to do on the way, so maybe we missed each other."

Zee's tranquility was baffling. Matt couldn't get a read on him. He was so temperate. So eloquent. There was nothing, not even a faint stutter, to give Matt any indication of what he was up to. Matt looked at the screens again, watching counters and prompts shifting at sixty frames a second. Every so often a single tick appeared on a bar, confirming some process or other.

"How long now?" Matt said, looking accusingly at Faulk.

"I—I don't know."

Matt frowned.

"It's sifting the data," Faulk explained, "but the files seem to have been stored in a random pattern. I'm getting tremendous variations on entry dates; it's not consecutively ordered. I think they did it this way to prevent algorithmically optimized searches based on only a few decrypted files. We have to decrypt them all before we can see the full puzzle. So it's hard for me to say when your mother's journal will appear. But I'm scanning as we go so that it will pop up as soon as her name shows."

Matt looked down at the floor, away from the numbers and screens. He needed to focus. And he needed to know the truth. Who was telling the truth? He was sure of Ems, and also of Faulk, somehow. He didn't seem like he could tell a lie, even if his life depended on it.

"So journals are randomly distributed across entry dates?" Matt asked him.

"Yes. That's right."

"Bring up the data that you already have. On the screen."

Matt noticed a tiny twitch in Zee's neck, his eyes glancing down at Faulk, who turned to his keyboard. A flash of uncertainty leaked through Zee's stoic facial expression now.

Faulk tapped the keys, entering commands. "Here."

"Sort by entry. Oldest first," Matt demanded, turning his attention to the screen.

"Done."

"Where's the entry date?"

Faulk pointed.

Bingo.

"Thanks. And now, I'm getting my mom. We're leaving," Matt said.

"No, you're not," Zee said. He took two steps closer to the door, blocking it. Still calm and collected. "I can't let you do that."

Zee's calm demeanor had rubbed off on Matt. "She's not in there," he said calmly, pointing to the screen. "Tell Faulk the truth."

Zee turned to Faulk. "It's true. She's not," he said.

Faulk looked flabbergasted, turning his gaze from Matt to Zee.

"Tell me you knew about that clinic before we met? Tell *him*." Matt nodded down to Faulk, keeping his eyes fixed on Zee. He wanted to hear the truth; he wanted Zee to admit it. And he wanted the others to know. Faulk. Ems. Everybody in the damn fucking complex needed to know about this enormous fraud.

"Well, of course I knew it," Zee said evenly. "It's *the* most prominent place for genetic engineering. And it has very close ties with the government. How was I not to know?"

"So tell me you didn't breach and destroy their data back in 2056." Matt pointed to Faulk. "Tell him."

Zee was silent. For the first time, he seemed to be without an answer.

"Tell him why, of all the random entries up there, not a single one's from before 2056?"

Still no reply. Zee stood motionless in the doorway.

"You destroyed my mother's data back then, and you fucking

knew it when you sent me in there, didn't you? You just wanted more data for your shitty political agenda."

Zee smiled coldly. "Are you finished, Matt? Are you happy now? Remember, we took you in; we patched you up. We gave you food and shelter. Believe me, I hoped I was wrong. I didn't know if your mother's data was backed up on some remote server. But *you* wanted hope, and so I gave it to you. But now I'm sorry I did, you fucking little ingrate. I should have let you rot to death in that community center. 'Cause you sure as shit wouldn't have come this far without me. And after all that, after all I've done for you, now you want to leave? Well, no. I can't let you do that." Zee took one step forward, raising a finger. "See all this, Matt?" He gestured around at the screens. "I have a responsibility. I'm responsible for keeping these people safe. If I let you go, if I let you walk out of here, crawl back to the government on your knees, they will hunt us all down and execute us. And I won't have that."

"I'm not gonna tell," Matt said, realizing how lame he sounded. "I just want treatment for my family."

"They'll force you to tell them, Matt. Don't be naive. I can't take that risk."

"You'll have to."

Zee looked from Matt to Faulk and then gave a nod to the side. Faulk gaped at him, uncomprehending.

Matt understood perfectly, however. He spun around and lunged towards the gun, which still lay on the desk. Grasping the handle of the gun, he turned back to Zee and Faulk. Zee had his back to him, one hand inside the gun cabinet.

"Stop!" Matt yelled.

Zee froze. "Don't do anything stupid, Matt," he said. "Nobody wants this."

"Get your hand out of the cabinet. Slow!" Steadying his right hand with his left, he kept the pistol aimed at Zee. Zee lifted his hands and turned to face him.

"Lock it up," Matt said. "And throw the key to me." He nudged the gun a bit towards the latch on the cabinet; the keys still dangled from the padlock.

"Easy now." Zee closed the doors, locked them, and tossed the keys towards Matt. They jangled to the floor.

Matt crouched and rummaged with his left hand on the bare stone floor, still training the barrel of the pistol on Zee. Faulk sat still in his chair, arms raised, watching the standoff. Matt found the keys and stood upright again, stuffing them into his pocket.

"I'm leaving. I'm leaving with my mom," Matt said.

"You know that's a bad idea, Matt. There's still a lot we can do for you."

"Fuck you. You're just killing her. And you just tried to kill me."

"Put down the gun, and we'll forget about this little incident."

"Fuck you. We're leaving," Matt said again.

"I'm not sure you heard me, Matt," Zee said calmly. "I can't let you—"

Matt reached for the armrest on Faulk's chair and jerked it towards him. The tiny wheels skidded across the floor and Matt put the gun to Faulk's head. Faulk sat frozen in the seat.

"Now Matt, we both know you don't know firearms," Zee said.

"I shot a police officer in the neck. So at this range—point-blank, isn't it called?—I'd say Faulk was a goner. Thought you didn't want to risk your buddies?" Matt said. He prodded Faulk's temple with the barrel. "Get up, Faulk."

Faulk got to his feet, keeping his hands in the air.

"Do as I say, and nobody gets hurt." Matt grabbed Faulk's shirt. There were wet streaks of sweat across his back. "Not if you let us leave." He nodded to the corner. "Get over there, Zee. Keep your hands up."

Zee did.

Matt glanced across the computer desk and saw the data stick connected to a cable.

"Faulk, unplug the stick."

"No. I can't. I have to—"

"Rip out the stick. Now!"

Faulk cowered, then carefully lowered his hands, grabbing the end of the cable with one and the stick with the other. "Don't make me, please," he said. "The transfer's not complete. A failsafe program will destroy what's already been decrypted. Everything we've done so far will be wasted, Matt."

Zee spoke up again. "Think things through, Matt, please. I know I lied, and I'm sorry. But if you take that data, nobody will ever know what they're up to in there. And it's not good. The government is more corrupt, more nefarious than you can ever imagine. We have to fight it. Fight back. At least help us with that. I know you agree. I saw that when we were at Yamada's together. You recognize the inequality in this system, Matt. Leave if you must, but let us keep the data. Don't be selfish. Everybody can still win."

"Don't lecture me about selfishness. Do it," Matt said, poking the gun into the back of Faulk's head. Faulk ripped out the cable and stick.

35

Matt edged his way into the corridor, dragging Faulk by his shirt and leaving Zee behind. As he cleared the doorframe, he thrust his back against the wall and dragged Faulk in front as a shield. Faulk was scrawny, unlike Matt—easy to hold and wrestle with one hand if he were to make a move.

Continuously ducking and swiveling his head, Matt tried to keep his eyes in all directions. Moving with tight, short steps, they neared a corner where two hallways crossed. Matt glanced backward and saw Zee halfway out the door.

"GET BACK!" Matt yelled. He spun around and aimed down the wall, stopping Zee in place.

"Easy," Zee said again. His hands went into the air. He waved them so that Matt could see they were empty.

"Turn around. Slowly!" Matt, still holding onto Faulk, waggled the gun back and forth, motioning Zee. "Against the opposite wall," he demanded as Zee walked closer.

Following him with the nose of the gun, Matt guided Zee in a half-turn. "Stay in front. Walk, slowly, to my mom's room."

There was a high-pitched shriek behind him as a woman

turned the corner and spotted the gun and the three-man hostage situation. Zee spread his fingers, waving his hands a bit, as if to say everything was under control. She inched backward, the way she had come, as Matt moved into the open, still keeping Faulk in a tight grip. Clearing the crossing, shielded by the drywalls once more, Matt was back to safety. He exhaled.

With stiff, stuttering steps, they shuffled their way through the damp, dimly lit corridors. Matt could make out the patter of feet scurrying from room to room, quiet voices on telephones and intercoms, as news of the situation began to spread. Heads peeked at them from every corner, every section, every doorway, then ducked back, disappearing into the maze. If a head lingered too long for Matt's comfort, a quick swivel with the gun ended any curiosity.

Zee, still moving forward, craned his neck and turned his head back towards Matt. "You can still stop this. Give me the stick, and I'll let you and your mother leave, no strings attached."

"Shut up."

"There is no need for th—"

"SHUT UP!"

Zee went quiet and resumed looking forward.

Matt's arm fluttered back and forth as he nervously tried to shoo away the curious. "Zee," he called, "tell them to stay back, get away. Tell them." Sweat poured over his forehead now.

Zee commanded the next gawker to keep clear and make sure the order spread. The man darted down the dark corridor. Matt heard a murmur echoing through the maze, and the snooping stopped. Finally, they reached Elizabeth's room.

Zee went in first and calmly informed a nurse of the situation.

Matt peered around the door to get a glimpse inside. Ems wasn't there; only a single nurse was tending to his mother.

"Make her ready to move," Matt ordered through the door.

"What? I—I can't," the nurse said. "She's on life support. We shouldn't try to—"

"Just do what I say! Those monitors go under the bed, and so can that oxygen tank. Make it happen!"

"Yes, all right. I'm sorry."

"Help her," Matt ordered Zee. "Anything she says."

Zee nodded, and Matt turned his attention to the corridor. It was eerily quiet now. There was none of the usual running, none of the chatter; all he could hear was the beeping and hissing from the medical equipment fastened to his mother's bed. He took another look at her; she lay still, her chest heaving to the rhythm of the machines. Where the fuck was Ems? He needed her. Wanted her reassurance. She was the only one he trusted.

A sudden flicker of red light strafed his eye. He blinked and ducked reflexively. He looked down the corridor and saw a red dot wander across Faulk's shoulder and disappear.

"Hey!" Matt screamed. The sound echoed off the walls. He tucked himself in behind Faulk, peeking out from behind his head.

Zee rushed out the door, hands waving frantically.

"Tell them to stay back," Matt whispered. "If I see guns, I'm gonna start shooting. Ask the dead cop if you don't think I have it in me."

"Take it easy, Matt. They don't know any better," Zee said. Then he leaned past Matt and Faulk and yelled down the corridor. "LISTEN UP! Do NOT, I repeat, DO NOT, shoot! He has Faulk hostage and is armed and dangerous! He IS NOT, I repeat,

IS NOT government. DO NOT execute contingency plan and evacuation."

"She ready?" Matt said, tilting his head towards the doorway but keeping his eyes on the corridor.

"Almost, yes. What do you want me to do?"

"Push her. To the elevator."

"Listen," Zee cut in. "There is still time. Leave the stick, and my men will stand down. We won't follow; we won't fight. But if you don't, you're not leaving us a lot of choices."

"Don't threaten me. Remember, I'm the one pointing a gun at *your* head. Now move."

Zee sighed and went back into the room. In a moment, there was a rumbling sound as Elizabeth's bed began to move into the corridor. The nurse steered it carefully through the doorway and began to push the bed down the hall. Matt motioned Zee to follow her, and then, dragging a terrified Faulk behind him and trying to stay in cover, began to follow along behind the little procession. The nurse took it slow, checking that the tubes and machines all stayed in position.

The corridor widened as they approached the entrance; overhead bulbs provided more light here, eliminating the shadows and the nooks that might hold potential threats. His heartbeat stopped its continuous climb, but still beat well above his comfort level. For the first time, he became aware of the sweat pouring over his fingers as they clung to the gun and Faulk's shirt.

"Matt!"

He swiveled, thrusting his back to a wall, panicky eyes scanning to see where the voice had come from.

"It's me, Ems. I'm coming out."

From a corridor off to one side, Ems moved into sight, hands raised, walking steadily towards him.

"Get her to the elevator," Matt said to the nurse, motioning to Elizabeth. "Now."

"Matt, you can't do this. Your mother is in a coma. She's on life support." Ems walked closer and closer.

"You told me I could. We have the car ready."

"That was before. It's too risky now."

"Listen to what she says," Zee chimed in. "Give me the stick and we'll be good. And Ems can help you with your mother."

"No. You're lying. She can't do anything. It's too late."

"Too late? For what, Matt? Where are you going to go? This is your mother's only chance." Zee held a hand out towards, Ems who stopped. Then he took a single step closer to Matt. "*We* are her only chance."

"Wrong." Matt pierced Zee with his eyes, tired of his constant lies. "I have a doctor standing by."

"The doctor from the clinic?" Zee barked out a laugh. "What makes you think he'll help you?"

"He knows my mother. He knows her illness. He wants to do right."

"No, Matt. Don't you get it? To them, to the system, to the government, you're nothing but a calculation. An equation with a result. A number. A return on investment. Didn't you learn anything at the hospital?"

"It's different. He knows what to do. He's got access. He's honest."

"Matt, I'm telling you, the guy's lying. They only want what's best for them. Always have, always will."

"Shut up." Matt aimed the gun at Zee.

"Don't make this mistake, Matt." Zee shook his head. "You know better. I know you do."

Matt saw the commiseration in his eyes, heard the pity in his words, and realized with a sickening feeling that Zee had nothing but contempt for him—as a man, as a son, as someone who could take care of his own family. Matt struggled to find words to rectify himself.

"Put down the gun and let go of Faulk," Zee said. "I'll forgive you—"

The shot cracked, booming from end to end of the long, dug-out cave complex. One scream overlapped another, howls and shouts rattling through the pipes and vents. Matt could hear Zee's desperate panting over all of it, strangling the soft swishes from the large turbine fans up above. Faulk stood to one side, hands on ears, veering away from the muzzle by his ear. The smell of gunpowder tickled Matt's flaring nostrils, somehow calming his nerves, steadying the whole of his body, satisfying mind and soul.

Matt still kept the gun aimed towards Zee's slumped body. Zee was grasping his shoulder, writhing in agony, wincing like a rat. Matt savored the moment for a split second. Towering over this fraud, this liar, he considered his options. He had a golden opportunity to put this pest out of its misery, once and for all. Free all these people from its menace.

"Don't," Ems said, as if she'd read his mind. "You don't want to do that."

"Why? I've already killed a cop," he said again. He didn't take his eyes off Zee.

"That was an accident. You told me. This would be something else. You don't want to be that man. *I* don't want you to be that man," she said.

Blood flowed from the wound in Zee's shoulder, expanding its reflecting pool of crimson in the amber glow from the overhead bulbs.

"You," he said, looking at the petrified nurse, who had stopped dead in her tracks. "Take care of him. Ems, you're coming with me." He swung the gun point-blank into her kind face. It distorted in terror. "Take my mom. You must keep her alive."

Ems was silent. Tears trickled down her cheeks as she wheeled the bed across the floor into the elevator.

Matt followed her in, dragging Faulk with him, and pushed the button for the ground floor. As the elevator clanked into motion, he turned and gave Faulk a push in the back, releasing his shirt as he stumbled out of the freight elevator. Grabbing Ems by the arm, he yanked her in front of the door, just in case anyone tried to get off a shot before they disappeared into the shaft, and then pulled the safety grille down.

As soon as they were out of sight, Matt lowered the gun, giving Ems room to breathe.

"I'm sorry. You've only been kind. But… I have to save my mom; I hope you understand. I'm not gonna hurt you, I promise. But I needed them to believe I'm capable."

She nodded, her hands rubbing the tears away. "I just hope you know what you're doing," she said. "He's going to come after you, you know. He won't give up on that data. I know him."

When they reached the ground floor, Matt raised the grille and turned to Ems, grabbing her shoulder.

"Listen, Ems. I won't force you, but I could use your help getting my mom to the clinic. If you don't want to, it's okay. I understand," he said, suddenly wracked with guilt.

Without a word, Ems grabbed hold of the end of the bed and

began to push. The bed made a slight clanking sound as it traveled over the bump in the floor where the elevator ended and the container floor began. "Promise me to take it slow," she said.

Matt nodded and opened the large metal door.

36

Bright light hit Matt like a slap in the face, scorching his retinas. The warm early summer air blasted away the underground chill. He shaded his eyes with his free hand, still keeping the gun at eye level. A battered van stood parked ten yards from the container, its tarnished yellow finish glinting dully in the sunlight. Matt turned to Ems with a questioning look.

"That's not it," she said.

Matt sighed. His little brother nowhere in sight. Suddenly there was the sound of an engine roaring from inside the warehouse. Matt whirled and looked at the door, which was already raised. He recognized the sound of the engine: it was his old truck.

Wheels skidding, brakes shrieking, the battered old truck came drifting through the wide hole in the steel frame of the building, with Kevin at the wheel. He sped past them, across the yard, and slammed on the brakes. The old pickup skidded to a halt as gravel sprayed from underneath the wheels and came to rest against the exit doors of another container. As the dust settled, Kevin burst out of the driver's side and dashed towards Matt and Ems, a thick metal pipe in his hands.

"I blocked the emergency staircase," Kevin panted as he stopped at the three. "Sounded like trouble down there, so I'm trying to buy more time." He waved the pipe.

Matt gaped at his suddenly resolute little brother and muttered in disbelief, "Yeah. Sure, Kev. Good thinking." He noticed blood at the steel rod's tip. "What's that?"

"I'll explain later. Let's go!" Kevin looked down at Elizabeth, motionless in the bed, tubes sticking out of her body and an oxygen mask on her face.

"It's not the right van," Ems said, looking at the yellowed wreck parked near them. "There are other exits, but they're through tunnels, so they're far away and probably dangerous." She looked uneasily at Elizabeth.

"What? This was the only one that was even close to white," Kevin said.

The elevator behind them started clanking. Someone was coming. Matt grabbed the pipe from his brother's hands and ran back into the container. He jammed it between two of the elevator's drive cogs, bringing the gear train to an abrupt halt.

"Aw, shit. Zee must have figured out what you were up to," Ems said. "Wait—I know where the van is. This way. Hurry." She set off at a brisk pace, motioning for them to follow.

Matt flew out of the container and positioned himself behind the hospital bed. He began to push, his feet almost sliding out from under him before it began rolling. Kevin joined him, and together they followed Ems, Kevin steadying the bed as much as he could as their mother's body vibrated between the safety straps.

The yard lay quiet; the only sound was their footsteps and the wheels of the bed crunching on the gravel. With Ems leading them, they passed through the entire warehouse, headed towards a couple of large sheds standing at the far end of the lot. Ems sprinted ahead to them and began peering their tiny window slits, positioned a foot from their tops.

"It's here. Come on," she said, pointing to the second shed. As Matt and Kevin neared, she started jumping up and down, trying to get a better look through the window. "I can't see if it's in workable condition. I helped Zee empty these sheds a couple of years back."

Matt hauled himself up and looked in. A sparkling white van was parked inside the striped, oversized shed.

Ems went around the shed.

"I can't see. Kevin, give me a leg up."

Kevin sprinted over and knelt with his hands together so that Ems could get a better view.

"Hah!" she said triumphantly. "The key's in the ignition. Idiot always keeps emergency vehicles prepped."

Matt went around the back of the shed, where there were two steel-plated doors fastened with a large padlock.

"But the shed is locked," he said.

"Think I can fit?" Kevin looked up at the windows.

Matt shook his head. He looked back at their tracks leading around the corner of the warehouse. Deadest of giveaways, like a sled through snow. "Fuck. How long have we got?"

"Five minutes tops, if they haven't gotten past the pickup and the elevator's still stuck," Ems said. She rummaged through the multiple pockets on her coat.

Matt banged on the metal doors, kicking at the padlock. It was new and not budging.

"Fuck. Fuck, fuck, fuck," Ems said. "I can't find my key. I think it's in my bag."

"What—you've got a key for this thing?" Kevin said incredulously.

"Yeah. All trusted personnel have one. All of the locks—padlocks, doors, cabinets— use the same key. How would we manage otherwise?"

Matt stopped banging. "All the locks are the same?"

"Yes, but I can't find my damn key."

Matt reached into his pocket, past the data stick, and pulled out the key from the gun cabinet. "Like this one?" He waved it between two fingers, a smug grin on his face.

She jumped forward, kissed him on the cheek, and grabbed the key from his fingers. In a moment, she had unlocked the doors, swung them open, and was halfway in before Matt had even comprehended the fact that she'd kissed him.

Ems climbed in through the driver's side and squeezed through the front seats, then threw open the back doors of the van. "Get her in!" She unfolded a metal ramp, which clattered to the ground.

The two men wheeled their mother up into the van's cargo bay and locked the wheels of the bed into grooves in the floor. Matt looked around and gave a low whistle: the interior of the vehicle looked like a fully equipped ambulance, only without any paramedics' logos. Ems pulled the rear door closed, flung down a folding seat beside Elizabeth's bed, and strapped herself in. The two men scrambled up front. Kevin climbed into the driver's seat and Matt took the passenger seat, placing his gun in his lap.

Kevin turned the key in the ignition and the engine came to life. He shoved the gears into reverse and, with a chirp of the tires, propelled them back out onto the compound lot. As Matt watched his brother effortlessly working the manual transmission, he wondered how many times Kevin had snuck off for a drive in his old pickup. He shook his head and grinned to himself.

They sped across the gravel yard, headed back towards the elevator container and the gated entrance.

"How do we open that?" Kevin called back to Ems.

"Ram it," Matt cut in. "Seems flimsy."

Kevin floored the gas.

"NO!" Ems screamed from the back.

Kevin switched his foot to the brake, and the van trembled as the anti-locking braking system kicked in. With a shudder, the van came to a halt.

"Your mother's back here. In a coma. You'd be doing her a favor if you remembered that."

The boys looked at each other, and then Matt turned sheepishly to Ems. "Sorry. My bad. So what do we do?"

"There's a big red button that slides it open. It's inside the warehouse."

"Saw that on the center column," Kevin added.

"Got it." Matt jumped out of the van, leaving the door ajar, and dashed across the courtyard towards the wide roll-up doors, tucking the gun into his waistband as he ran.

Halfway across, a sound made him stop. The elevator's gear drives were moving again. He looked up and saw that the pipe he'd jammed into them had broken. Sprinting as fast as his legs could carry him, he skidded into the warehouse and ran to the little metal cabinet on the column.

He reached for the door and was suddenly hit from behind by something heavy. Matt fell against a car and fell to the ground as someone kicked him in the kidneys. He gave a howl of pain as he felt his stitches burst. Rolling to one side, he looked up and saw a man standing over him, bleeding from a slash that stretched from his temple to his cheek. Half his face was covered in blood, which streamed down onto his bare arm. The man kicked him again and Matt curled into a fetal position, the gun sliding from his grasp.

Matt reached for the gun, but the man kicked it away, sending the weapon spinning across the concrete. He wound his foot back and sent his boot into Matt's ribs. Blood gushing from his side, Matt watched as the man walked to the gun, picked it up, and turned towards him, a horrible smile on his face.

Matt raised a bloodied hand weakly and suddenly saw something move behind the man. *Kevin.* Moving on silent feet, he sprinted up behind Matt's assailant and launched himself through the air. There was a dull thud as the man was shoved onto the hood of the car, then a sharp crack as the gun went off, sending a bullet into the roof. There was a clattering sound as the gun fell to the floor beside the car.

The air was filled with grunts and shouts as Kevin wrestled the bigger man and pinned him against the car, then a sickening crunch as Kevin smashed the man's head through the windshield.

Matt got to his knees with difficulty, his left arm wrapping his abdomen and his hand pressing on his right side. The floor spun under him as he got to his feet and limped around the back of the car. Grabbing the handle of the gun, he fumbled to find the trigger. Turning towards his brother, he pointed the pistol straight between the terrified eyes of his assailant as Kevin raised his arm for one more punch.

"Shoot him!" Kevin demanded.

Matt cocked the trigger. Blood was making his hand slippery.

"Do it!" Kevin screamed.

Matt took his finger off the trigger and lowered the gun. "No," he said softly. "You don't want to see that. Nobody wants to. He's finished, Kev. Let's go."

Kevin let go of the man's collar and the man slumped backward, blood pouring from his mouth. Kevin slid off the car and ran to the box, mashing the big button in the middle. Then he hurried back to Matt.

Slinging Matt's arm across his shoulder, Kevin steadied his gasping brother as they began to move towards the exit. Matt kept applying pressure to his wound; blood was flowing freely through his fingers as he staggered out into the yard, leaning heavily on Kevin. The gates were sliding off to the side; the white van was still idling, just fifteen yards away.

Then they heard the clunking of the elevator cage reaching its pinnacle.

"Go!" Matt pushed his little brother away. "Get in the van. I'm right behind you."

Kevin ran towards the van, and Matt, gritting his teeth against the pain, turned and aimed the gun at the container. The elevator door opened. He fired towards it twice; the light inside was too dim to make out any hits. He turned back towards the van and a wave of nausea rolled through him. Gasping, he fell to his knees in the gravel.

"Come on!" Kevin yelled at the top of his lungs from the driver's side window as shots rang out across the gravel from inside the container.

In rapid succession, three bullets thudded into the ground a yard from Matt's feet, sending up puffs of gravel. The sudden shock flung his adrenaline into overdrive, pumping Matt's body back into action. As he scrambled towards the van, Ems opened the doors at the back.

"Get in!" she yelled, as bullets whined over their heads.

Matt ducked behind the open door and returned fire. Then suddenly, the gun clicked. *Empty.* For a second, the yard fell silent; the only sound was the van's engine and his own labored breathing. Gritting his teeth, Matt heaved himself around the door and went to climb up into the van. Bullets pinged off the ground behind his fast-moving feet and suddenly, people flooded out into the yard brandishing guns and rifles.

He grabbed Ems's outstretched hand as a hail of bullets punched holes in the van's side panel. Ems ducked in time, but one struck the frame of Elizabeth's bed with a sharp clang. Matt threw himself inside and onto the floor of the van.

"GO!" Ems screamed in terror.

Wheels spinning to gain traction, the vehicle accelerated towards the opened gate. Matt could see the first cars pouring out of the warehouse, picking up the armed men in the courtyard. He looked at Elizabeth, who lay unconscious, oblivious to the chaos around her. Then at the bullet holes in the side of the van.

He reached inside his pocket. His bloodied hand closed on the data stick and clenched it tight. Dragging his hand out and raising his arm, with one last effort, Matt lobbed the blood-covered data stick out onto the dusty ground. Ems slammed the van's doors shut as Kevin pulled it into a sharp ninety-degree turn. The wheels skidded as they hit the tarmac.

"They're stopping," Kevin said from up front. "They're not following us." He gave a little whoop of triumph.

Matt exhaled and then sank to the floor beside Ems as she tore open a packet of bandages.

37

Matt sat in the back of the van, propped on a seat now, while Kevin drove expertly through the early-morning traffic. Matt let the route unwind on the insides of his eyelids, prompting Kevin at every intersection like a human GPS. Every sign, every landmark unspooled in his mind from memory as he replayed the route to Kevin, trying his best to provide feedback. Matt told him to keep a lookout for old cars, abrupt lane shifting, high-speed passing. For vehicles that were not run by automation. There were none.

Ems rewrapped Matt's wound in clean bandages, tidying his stitches as best she could to alleviate the excruciating pain that shot through his body every time he twisted his torso. Her touch was gentle; her nimble fingers slid carefully his injured skin, applying gauze and dabbing him with wipes. Every so often she turned her attention to Elizabeth, checking her, and then went back to work on Matt. When she was done, she sat back in the little fold-out chair and pulled Matt sideways to rest his head in her lap. Matt obeyed without a second thought. It felt natural. It felt good.

He caught her glancing down at him, and she gave him one of the faint crooked smiles he'd seen so many times before. It was, he realized, the exact smile Stephanie had given him that first time when he'd made a pass at her, and that he'd enjoyed seeing on her face so often when they'd been dating. He closed his eyes and kept reciting directions to Kevin.

"I think we're here," Kevin said at last.

Matt opened his eyes. Ems looked down at him.

"I have to go," she said. "Do you mind stopping here, Kevin?"

"What?" said Matt, struggling to sit up. "No, you can't. Why?" His heart dropped to the bottom of his stomach.

"My work here is done. The people we left behind, Matt—they're my family. And just like you, I need to take care of my family."

Matt sat up carefully as Kevin pulled over.

"Don't you think Zee will punish you for helping us?"

"No. When he calms down, he'll realize why you did what you did. He's pretty reasonable, actually. And more to the point, he got his data back."

"Do you know your way back?"

"I'll figure it out," she smiled. "I don't want to get caught on the clinic's cameras, though, which is why I need to get out here."

"We won't tell. Right, Kev?"

Kevin turned his head and nodded from the front seat.

"I'm sorry I had to do this, Ems," Matt said. "I never meant to put you in harm's way."

"I get it." She smiled at him. "I'm just happy I could help. But without your mother's medical history, I ran out of options. So I hope you're right about these guys."

"I'm sure of it. After all, they made me and Kevin, so we'll just pluck the blueprints from the basement." Matt laughed nervously at his own little joke.

Ems kept smiling.

He smiled back.

"It was nice meeting you guys," she said, still looking at Matt. "Everything aside, and all."

"I think so too," Matt said. "Maybe we'll meet again… Some other time, in some other place perhaps."

Ems nodded. She leaned in to give him a hug, but stopped. Then, as though she had decided something, she kissed him. On the lips. Quick, like a peck, but enough for Matt to know.

"Some other time," she said, and touched his cheek gently. "Now, get her inside. I've written a brief note here." She shoved a piece of paper into Matt's palm. "Give it to the staff. They'll know what to do."

Without another word, Ems opened the back door, climbed down and hurried off down the street.

Matt watched her go, willing himself not to cry. He still needed to focus. He closed the doors again.

"Let's get Mom in there, shall we?" he said, turning his head towards Kevin.

Kevin sat looking at him in the rear-view mirror with a smirk on his face. "You liked her, didn't you?"

"Shut up, Kev."

Kevin put the van in gear once more, pulled up and parked it in front of the clinic's entrance. Two armed guards watched impassively as Matt opened the doors and extracted the collapsible ramp, and he and Kevin rolled Elizabeth's bed onto the ground.

The front doors slid noiselessly apart, and they pushed the

bed into the clinic on its tiny, squeaky wheels. Air was still pumping steadily through the tubes in her nose; the life-support machines beeped quietly.

"Help," Matt whimpered as they approached the counter. "Dr. Henke told us to come."

"Right away, sir," the receptionist said. She was already on the intercom, and moments later, the hall flooded with nurses and staff, tending to Elizabeth and transferring her into a new and clean hospital bed. Matt handed Ems's note to the head nurse. She read it, looked at him and nodded. Then she started issuing orders to her colleagues, who swarmed around Elizabeth. Finally, their preparations complete, they wheeled her off down a corridor. Matt and Kevin made to follow along, but the nurse told them to stay put. They slumped down on a couch in the waiting room.

Matt, almost sick with exhaustion, looked around at the pristine white walls, the wide skylights, the high ceiling. A large painting of a wooded glade hung on one wall, a circle of trees lining a soft velvety patch of green, rays of sun shimmering through the trees, shining on a single red apple lying in the grass. The room was quiet; there was no noise, no ticking or whirring of industrial fans. Indoor plants and trees, stretching their leaves, wound their branches towards the panoramic windows, providing a flickering shade under which Matt lay back. A breeze passed his nostrils; the air was fresh, not stale. He sniffed. No moisture, no mold, no mildew.

A door opened and Dr. Henke stepped through it. Matt sat up.

"I'm glad to see you, Matt," he said. "You made the right decision." He turned to Kevin. "You must be Kevin? It's so nice to meet you after all these years. I'm Dr. Henke."

Matt could see Kevin was uneasy; he laid a calming hand on his shoulder.

"I know this is a bit weird," Matt said to him quietly.

Kevin nodded and then met Dr. Henke's gaze. "Likewise, I guess," he said, shaking his outstretched hand.

"Your mother is in good hands now," Dr. Henke said. "I was told she is in a coma, but rest assured, we are stabilizing her as we speak. I'll get back to you two as soon as I have updates. This could be hours, so why don't you stay here, Kevin, and get some rest. And meanwhile, Matt, let's get you fixed up." He pointed to the impromptu bandage and the bloodstains on Matt's shirt. He motioned to a nurse who had been standing by the intake desk. "Please follow our nurse," he told Matt. "She will take care of you."

Matt spent the rest of the day being tended to. His wounds were cleaned; his stitches were redone by a surgeon, and this time anesthetics were administered to make the procedure bearable. Afterward, Matt was given painkillers to keep it that way.

He washed them down with two cups of vitamin water with added electrolytes; he gulped the first in one go. The sweet yet chemical taste of the bright translucent red beverage still lingered on his tongue as he was tucked into a clean bed and nestled under a warm, snug blanket. His brother lay in another next to him; the staff had given them a private room, simple, yet sufficient for relatives. Matt placed his empty cup on the side table and lay back, exhausted. He was soon asleep.

■ ■ ■

"Matt, I was hoping to find you before I left for the night," Henke said.

It was late evening. Matt stood in front of a cafeteria vending machine, looking at an assortment of health bars, nutritious snacks, and single pieces of packaged fruit.

"Where's your brother?" Henke said.

"Asleep again," Matt said, punching in the number for a bag of roasted nuts. "Should I go wake him?"

"No, let him sleep. It's only you that I need to talk to."

Matt turned towards him. "Is there something wrong, Doctor?" he said, worried.

"Let's go to my office, where we won't be disturbed."

Dr. Henke's office was sparse compared to his extravagant one at home. There were no sculptures of DNA strings and no lavish views. The walls had only a few modest science posters on the human reproductive system, a couple of backlit embryos, and a large screen behind a large oak table.

They sat on either side of the desk in two comfortable leather chairs.

"I thought you didn't have kids," Matt said, pointing to the only picture frame on the desk. In it was a photo of two girls wearing identical red dresses.

"Oh, that. Yes, lots of people make that assumption. But they're not mine."

Matt looked closer.

"That's Lulu and Nana. I met them once; few others have. I keep the picture to remind me of my commitment and my responsibility," Henke continued. "But let's not get bogged in the past. There's a future we need to attend to," he said, laying the frame flat. "So, have you decided?"

"Decided?" Matt said.

"Have you decided who gets the treatment?"

"What do you mean?"

"I didn't want to bother you while you're still recuperating, but now I need to know what you've decided."

Matt shook his head; he had no clue what Dr. Henke was referring to.

"You do remember the genetics we talked about at my house, don't you?"

"Yes. The root cause of this, right?"

"That's right. And I told you that your brother has the same genetic disposition. That same flawed set of genes," Henke said.

"You told me you could fix him too, yes?" His memory from the study in Henke's house was a bit vague.

"And I can. But I can't fix them both, Matt. You knew that."

Matt sat back in his chair, his lips drifting apart.

"I told you at my house. I thought you'd remember," Henke continued after a pause.

Was Matt forgetting something? Hadn't he paid attention?

"If they suffer from the same disease, why can't they both get the treatment? I don't understand," Matt said.

Dr. Henke avoided his gaze now, his eyes drifting out the office window.

"Think of it like this, Matt. The DNA region we manipulated cured your mother's Alzheimer's, but the process introduced unintended side effects. This is what we are now witnessing in your mother, and thankfully, it is treatable. And since Kevin's embryo was transformed with similar guide RNA, it's likely to have introduced those side effects into his cells as well. But because of possible mosaicism, where he has genetically different sets of cells, there is no telling how this will evolve."

"It's all mush. I don't understand."

"All medical terms aside, then, it means your brother could become extremely sick, with ramifications never seen before, and we wouldn't have a known treatment for him. If we treat him now, we could prevent this progression." Henke paused. "But then I can't treat Elizabeth."

"Why?"

"I told you. I need approval for funds. These are two separate, expensive procedures, and I can only petition the government to supply the funding for one."

"What?" Matt's heart was hammering in his chest.

"Listen. Didn't they tell you at the hospital? It's all based on algorithms, and your mother's life is just not valuable to society anymore. But I'm doing you a favor here. I can treat one of them, expense it to our research budget. But I can't do them both. The government simply won't allow it."

Matt gaped at him in disbelief.

"It's a near certainty, Matt," Henke tried to elaborate. "Kevin will get sick. I can't tell you when, I can't tell you how, but my professional guess is sooner rather than later. Now, if you want to let him wait, give his genetics the benefit of the doubt, so be it. But if, or rather when, he gets sick, he will need a hospital assessment too. And let me tell you, your mother stood no chance of getting admitted. This is expensive, uncharted territory, reserved for the best and the brightest of candidates, for those who will go on to become a benefit to our society. I suspect that in time, your brother may become such a man. Wasn't he college-bound? The fact that he has obtained an education and a graduation certificate will reflect very positively in his evaluation, as will the fact that he is now headed for college."

Matt's eyes filled with tears. "He won't go," he whimpered. "And I don't think I can make him."

"Oh dear. I'm so sorry," Henke said. "But remember, Matt: you have a choice. Most people do not get this opportunity—one could almost say 'privilege.' So, what is it going to be?"

"Do you need an answer now?"

"I need a decision by tomorrow. We need to start whatever procedure you choose by then. Right now, we're spending a lot of energy and resources on idle time. You can have the night to decide, if you'd like."

Matt sat in the chair, looking at his feet. His wound had begun to bleed again; he watched each drop bleed into the white fabric of the hospital gown they had given him.

The doctor got up and gestured him towards the door.

"I have to get going. Long day tomorrow. Long night, I suppose, for you. You are welcome in the cantina if you need a place to collect yourself."

Matt walked to the door.

Dr. Henke shut the door behind them both and locked up.

"See you in the morning," he said.

38

Kevin turned to the side, the warm, comfortable blanket turning with him. His one leg protruded, sending chills running up his calf. He wiggled his toes, freeing them from the dampness of night, letting the air squeeze itself through the crevices between each one. Sunlight stroked his eyelids, the warm orange kindling his mind. He opened his eyes.

In the little room that the staff had given them, his bed doubled as a couch; sometime in the night, he'd kicked the foam cushions to the floor. Matt's bed opposite was empty, the blankets a mess, not like his brother usually left them. Kevin looked at his watch. It was still morning, though he'd slept well over ten hours; time to stretch his rested legs. And he wanted to find Matt, to see if he'd gotten any news about Elizabeth.

Standing, straightening his back, he wrestled his bones into shape. His muscles ached from the many hours of inactivity and insufficient blood flow. He put on his clothes, tapping his jacket pocket; the little rubber croc was still inside. Then he made both beds as his brother had taught him. He hadn't done it for weeks, he realized. The last time had been back at their apartment. It was weird. Such a short time, but already a distant memory. He didn't even miss it. Thinking of it reminded him of that feeling of stagnation. Now, it was as if saying goodbye had catapulted him into unknown yet electrified hopes and dreams. He felt invigorated. He felt free.

Kevin went to reception and asked where his brother was; a pleasant woman pointed him towards a courtyard. His brother was sitting on a bench, under the shade of a tree. Kevin regarded him at a distance through a window. Matt looked a mess. His eyes were red, the skin from cheek to nose to above his eye socket an angry pink blemish; the rest of his face was ghost white. His eyes were empty as he stared at the ground.

Kevin went to the cantina. Staff members were making small talk at the tables. He poured two large cups of coffee, leaving one black and adding milk for himself. Then he strolled back to the courtyard, taking great care not to spill. Matt hadn't moved an inch.

"Looks like you could do with a cup," Kevin said, extending one of the coffees.

Matt, startled, gave him a bewildered look. "Yes. Thanks," he said, taking the cup. It steamed in the crisp morning air.

"Sorry if I disturbed you. Rough night?"

"No. Well, yes. Don't worry about it."

Kevin sat down next to his brother, blew on his coffee, and slurped his first sip. "Did you get any?" he asked Matt.

"What?"

"Sleep?"

"Some."

He seemed reluctant to share, so Kevin decided to fill the silence.

"I slept like a baby. Can't really remember the last time I did that. Worry free and all."

"Hmm."

Kevin took another sip. Matt hadn't lifted his cup yet.

"Anything about Mom?"

Matt shook his head.

"Guess it's too early, huh?" Kevin tried to prompt his brother for a conversation.

"Guess so," Matt muttered.

It was ages since he'd seen his brother like this. So devoid of words. So inert.

"Wanna tell me what's wrong?" Kevin tried.

Matt seemed not to hear. Or maybe he was ignoring him. It was hard for Kevin to tell the difference.

"Think you're gonna see her again," Kevin said, poking around. Maybe Matt was missing Ems.

He recalled Matt being like this years ago, on the day Stephanie had married her husband, Robert. Kevin knew she had invited Matt to the wedding, but his brother had opted to pass. That evening, Matt had shown him a text from her. It was pretty basic, saying just *I missed you here*. But Matt couldn't stop staring at it. The following morning, Kevin had convinced him to delete it. Move on. And now, here they were again—his brother, sitting still once more, at a loss for words.

"You know where to find her, don't you? So, go for a fucking visit when this is over. Ask her out. I'm not gonna sit around looking at your moping ass for weeks on end."

Kevin drained his cup of now-tepid coffee. "I'm gonna go see Mom. You wanna join me?" he said. "I could use the company." Kevin stood, took a step, then turned back to his frozen, silent older brother.

"Hey, Matt," he said irritably. "Snap out of it, will you? If I can ask a girl out, so can you."

Again, Matt seemed to jar himself out of a distant train of thought. "Yes. I'm sorry," he said, taking a sip from his cup. "I'm coming." Then he rose from the bench and followed Kevin inside.

Elizabeth's hospital room was miles from the underground complex. Clean, airy, bright. She lay still and silent on pure white linen, covered in a blanket and wearing a breathing mask. The life-support machines made faint, regular beeps and clicks. Everything was spotless and shiny.

They stood at her side for minutes, just watching. Kevin felt somehow at peace among the steady beats of the monitors. He took his brother's hand.

"I'm happy you got us here. You were right. This is the best chance she's gonna get."

Matt stood silent. Kevin could see tears forming in his eyes. He knew how Matt hated to cry in front of him.

"Hey, it's okay," Kevin said. "You did everything you could. Now it's up to the doctors."

The drops slid down Matt's cheek to the bottom of his chin.

"Let's talk about something else," Kevin said. His brother seemed petrified. What on earth was going on in his head? Trying to distract him, Kevin angled his face in front of his brother's. "Her name is Ruby."

Matt turned and looked him in the eye for the first time that morning. "What?" he said.

"Her name. The girl I like. It's Ruby. Isn't it beautiful?"

"Oh, shit. I forgot. Yes. From the community center?" Matt brightened, and a bit of color returned to his cheeks.

"Yes. I think I'm gonna go work there for a bit."

"Sounds great."

"That means, Matt, that I might not go to college. You do get that by now, right?"

"Yes. I get it. And it's your decision. Has to be."

They stood quietly for a while, contemplating, at their mother's side.

"It's also what Mom would have wanted, I think," Matt said. "For you to be you."

"Hey, and likewise for you, you know?"

"Yeah. I get that now." Matt turned suddenly and hugged his brother hard. The little rubber crocodile dug into Kevin's hip, and he pulled it out, holding it out to Matt.

"Still got that?" Matt broke into a laugh.

"How could I not? It's the best gift you ever gave me."

Silence.

Kevin shuffled the toy around between his fingers. Then, with his free hand, he picked up his mother's hand and held it, raising her arm so that the sleeve of her hospital gown slid down. Not a single one of her muscles resisted. The bones in her forearm protruded beneath her skin, which was loosened by the lack of muscle tissue. Her knuckles stuck out, raised like the tail of the plastic crocodile in his hands. Kevin ran his thumb across the back of Elizabeth's hand.

Matt was watching him. "What's the last thing she said to you? I mean, what words will you remember if she doesn't recover from this?" Matt said.

"I don't remember. But when she woke after her seizure at the graduation, she looked at me and said, 'You were so beautiful up there.' I'll never forget that," Kevin said. He warmed inside.

Matt was silent.

"What did she say to you?" Kevin asked.

"She said 'Take care of your brother.'" His voice trembled. He didn't know if it was true, but he wanted it to be. Kevin stroked his brother's arm and sighed.

There was a knock on the doorframe. Dr. Henke stood in the open door, asking for a minute with Matt. Matt followed him out into the corridor, leaving Kevin alone with Elizabeth. He figured they were discussing her treatment and was glad for a bit of time alone with his mother.

Kevin walked around the bed and sat down in a chair beside her. He picked up the remote hanging at her bedside and lowered her with a slight buzzing sound. Wiggling to get closer, he took her hand.

He looked over the monitors. The rhythmic beeps had already disappeared from his inner ear. Streaks of blue and yellow ran across the screens like the veins visible up and down his mother's neck. A single pearl of sweat gathered momentum for a marathon down her pale forehead, then finally began to trickle down.

Tenderly, at the will of the minute creases in the complexion of her skin, leaving a soft, moist trail, it struggled its way through the thin hairs of her eyebrow and into the corner of her eye, resting up against her eyelid.

Kevin watched as it once more grew in size, until mass and gravity forced it further.

Along her nasal bone, it crept, pausing at the slight cavity before taking on the corner of her nostril. Running free from nose to upper lip, it took the last dip before settling in the corner of her mouth.

Kevin couldn't stop staring.

And then it jerked—her mouth. Ever so fast, ever so slightly,

Elizabeth's lips snapped open and closed again to let the tiny droplet rejoin the insides of her ecosystem.

Kevin gently tightened his grip on her hand, with all his muscles converging on the single mission not to let go. He closed his eyes.

"She's sick," Matt mumbled behind him, and he started. He'd spoken so softly it was hard to make out the words.

"She won't make it, will she?" Kevin said. He opened his eyes.

"No. But that's not what I said. I said *you're* sick, Kev."

"What?" He must have heard wrong the second time.

"You're sick."

There it was again. *You're.*

"No, I'm not."

"You have the same genes. You have the same flawed genetics."

"But I'm not sick, Matt." Kevin turned around. His brother stood a yard from him; Dr. Henke lingered in the doorway, watching them.

"You're gonna be. It's inevitable," Matt said. He shook his head.

Kevin stood up and took a step back, stumbling into Elizabeth's bed. He looked at Matt, narrowing his gaze. "What the fuck are you talking about?" he said.

Matt took in a deep breath. "You're gonna end up the same way." He inclined his head gently at Elizabeth.

"Shut up. I'm not dying," Kevin said.

"You have the same genetic defect. Don't you see?" Matt said. "It's going to kill you. But we can save one of you."

"So save Mom!"

Matt shook his head sadly. "I was worried you wouldn't understand. She wouldn't want that. She told me."

"No, Matt. That's not what *she* told you; it's what *you* heard, what *you* interpreted! Don't I get a say in this?"

Dr. Henke took a step into the room and sauntered towards Kevin. A couple of broad-shouldered male nurses stepped through the doorway behind him.

Kevin took another step back. "Fuck you, Matt! You can't decide that. I'm perfectly fine, and Mom's the one dying." He watched Matt's face. "You're listening to your dad again, aren't you?"

"No," Matt said.

"Easy now, Kevin," Dr. Henke said.

Fast as lightning, the two nurses stepped around Matt and grabbed Kevin's shoulders. "Get your hands off me!" Kevin cried.

"It's for your own good," Matt said. "It's what she wanted—don't you see? All this, this whole trip, this attempt at saving her? All of it was for your sake, for the betterment of *your* future. But what future is there if you end up hooked to a machine, ticking towards this same fate?" Matt pointed to their mother.

"Kevin, you need to come with us," Dr. Henke said.

"You can't do this," Kevin screamed. The two nurses were wrestling him into submission, his scrawny arms and body no match for the fit, sturdy men. Dr. Henke stood to one side, trying to explain.

"Kevin, you're not of legal age. We have to follow the decisions of your guardian. And we have provided him with the best possible grounds for a decision. We all believe this to be the best cause of action for you and your wellbeing," Dr. Henke said.

"You're not doing this. Matt!" Kevin screamed, as the nurses forced him, feet off the ground, out through the door. "Matt!" he screamed, as they shoved him onto a stretcher. "MA—" he screamed, as a syringe flooded his veins with an anesthetic.

39

Water streamed down Matt's face as he stood there, expression-less, emotionless, flatlined. His eyes blinked from time to time. He had been standing resolutely in the pouring rain for almost an hour now. He was drenched to the skin, shivering, as the wind cut through his sodden clothes. Matt took no notice; his mind had transcended the elements. Above, the branches of the huge oak tree provided little shelter, the leaves only barely mitigating the heavy drops that plummeted from the sky.

Jeffrey D. Turner. The letters were etched in stone, beveled, inset, and polished to contrast with the rough granite surface. *Turner.* Every year, Elizabeth had brought the boys here, to this little cemetery on the outskirts of WDC 8-5, to place flowers and a candle. Every year, choking back tears, she had reminded them how their father's legacy had dissolved, told them that their last name was now free of its terrible burden. How ironic, Matt thought, that after all, his father had left him exactly those two things: a legacy and a burden. And a ragged old armchair.

The ground next to his father's grave was freshly turned; it had been a mere fifteen minutes since the gravedigger had patted the last of the soil. The minister had advised Matt that, because of the rain, it was best to cover the hole immediately. Matt had agreed. Otherwise, rain and mud would cover the white lacquered coffin and drown the few daisies he'd bought. Yellow. Her favorite. Like the dress she'd worn at Kevin's graduation.

The trees lining the cemetery were all oak. Spaced apart, their wide crowns stretched their branches over the outlying graves. Following his father's funeral, Elizabeth had claimed the spot beside him in preparation for when her own time arrived. Each year, she had provided a small payment towards the plot.

At their father's funeral, the cemetery had been crowded with people paying their respects. Nobody had shown for Elizabeth's. Matt stood alone now, close to home and yet home no more. Kevin was in a coma. The clinic staff had induced it so that his body would relax and his immune system wouldn't reject the genetic therapy. It had been a week now, but Dr. Henke had told him to expect this, reassuring him that they had years of experience with these procedures. Matt knew no reason not to trust him.

Dr. Henke had helped put Elizabeth's funeral arrangements together. Transportation of the body, obituaries in local news feeds, arrangements with the clergy. He had even provided a car for Matt and given him a decent black suit, which was soaked now.

"Ah, you're still here!" It was Stephanie.

Matt turned.

"I was hoping you'd still be here," she said, tiptoeing across the gravel path, avoiding the deepest of the puddles. She had the baby wrapped up on her chest, sleeping. A large, heavy raincoat, open in front, covered them both. "I'm so sorry I couldn't make it. Can you believe it? We were just about to get in the car, and this little rascal blows his trousers off in the biggest dump I've ever seen, shit oozing out all over the place. I fucking had to change the both of us. What's up with that? Anyway, I'm really sorry I wasn't here."

Matt smiled for the first time in days. "It's fine," he said. "I'm glad to see you."

"The others already left?"

"Yeah, you could say that. Nobody came, truth be told."

"Oh. I'm so sorry, Matt." She leaned in and hugged him, drawing a disgruntled snort from the baby in between. "Who did you expect?"

"I don't know. Maybe her old boss, coworkers. Those kinds of people. Dr. Aldridge, perhaps. He wanted an update, and I'm certain he scans the obituaries."

"Shit, haven't you heard? He died. Car crash a couple of days ago. I read it on a feed somewhere."

"Oh. I'm sorry to hear that. He was a good man. Always helped us, always cared."

"Yeah, we wanted him for little Jeffrey here. But I guess we'll have to look elsewhere now. Oh, have I told you?"

"About the name? Yeah, you told me last time."

"Yeah, but Rob's agreed. So we're gonna make it official sometime soon. I still hope it's not too weird? I just really like that name. I think it suits him." She looked down at the bundle.

"No, no, it's fine. You go ahead. I'm sure he'll make an excellent little Jeffrey."

Stephanie looked around the cemetery, her face suddenly creased in a frown. "Hey, wait a minute," she said. "Where's Kevin?"

"0-1."

"Still? Shouldn't he be at his own mom's funeral?"

"He's in a coma."

"What?"

"It's a bit of a mess, to be honest. But he'll be fine. The doctor promised."

Stephanie waited in silence. Matt didn't know how to follow up.

"You want to talk about it?"

"No. Not right now," he said.

How could he? How could he tell her that he'd ripped his little brother away from their dying mother against his will? How could he tell her he needed treatment for something he couldn't even explain? Kevin could get hit by a car two months from now, and all of this would be for nothing. Second-guessing tormented him every waking minute. Precognition produced no blessing, Matt reckoned, only burden.

"Well, I'm here. Whenever you're ready," Stephanie said, putting an arm around his shoulders.

Matt smiled. "Thanks."

"Want to come for dinner? Rob's away on business."

"Thanks, I would like that. But I can't stay. I have to get back to the hospital, in case Kevin wakes."

"I understand."

They stood for ten more minutes, making small talk about his future and what it entailed. He leveled with her, confessing his cluelessness. For now, his only thoughts were on making amends with Kevin.

40

Matt spent the next couple of days on the bench in the clinic's courtyard. He had nothing else to do. Nowhere else to be.

Every so often, he looked up at the glass door. Replaying Kevin joining him that morning with a coffee. Over and over. Pausing the image. Kevin smiling. The two of them sitting together, laughing over their steaming cups. Sometimes, Kevin would drop his cup when Matt told him that their mother was getting better. Sometimes it was Matt who dropped his coffee, as Kevin told him about Ruby. Sometimes they'd be laughing so hard that one of them would drop his cup, which just made them laugh even harder.

Silence echoed off the walls in the yard now, despite the images that crackled before his eyes. With a deep sigh, Matt pulled his thoughts back to the present. There was a flower patch beside the bench. The petals were still dormant; the flowers had yet to stretch and show their full colors to the world. Some sort of fall variety, Matt guessed.

He went and got coffee. Made one for Kevin, too. Brought them both back to the little garden. He didn't know what day it was. It didn't seem to matter. He saw patients, relatives and staff trundle along the corridors, but to Matt, they were ghosts. Pure figments of his imagination, a remnant of a real world, a world he tried his best to escape in that little bubble of his. He reckoned he was, in fact, the ghost. A faded image of a once lively, hard-willed, full-spirited fighting soul, dead set on saving his family from obliteration. He had succeeded in mind but failed in heart. And now here he was, sinking, slumping, listening as the seconds ticked their slow tocks to the beat of his lackluster, pounding heart.

Dr. Henke came out the door. He sat down, moving aside the now cold cup of coffee next to Matt.

"Good news," he said. "We're ready to wake him."

Matt turned. The spark lit the fuse.

"In fact, he is being woken as we speak," Henke continued. "But I have a matter to discuss before you go see him."

Matt frowned. Part worry, part confusion.

"You told me your brother graduated with honors, am I correct?"

"Yes?"

"You told me he wouldn't be going to college, that he wouldn't be pursuing higher education? Is it still safe to assume this?"

"Yes, I believe so," Matt said, his interest piqued.

"How would you like to take his place? Go off, get an education for yourself? No reason letting his seat go to waste."

"What?" Matt felt as though lightning had hit him. "Why? You can do that?"

"If you would like to, yes."

"I would *love* to." His thoughts began to tumble over one another. "Of course, I have to confirm with my brother first. Can't bypass him again."

"Yes, I understand," Henke said.

"You're sure I can do this? I mean, aren't there thousands of students in line for an opportunity like that? Wouldn't I have to take tests or something?" Matt's head was spinning. How could this be?

"I have some connections in the educational department. Let me pull a few strings. We could use men like you, Matthew Turner. And besides," Dr. Henke smiled at him, "you've already passed the tests that matter." He stood and stretched out his hand.

Matt took it. To his recollection, this was the first time they had shaken. He had a firm grip, and Matt tried to match it.

"A nurse will be out to fetch you when he's fully awake. Come see me afterward."

"Yes. I will. Thank you," Matt said.

Dr. Henke went back inside.

An hour later, Matt stood in front of the closed door to his little brother's room. But this time, he didn't dare look through the tiny window. His heart rate was elevated, his breathing shallow. A small but significant part of him was still hoping for Kevin to come to *him*. But the onus was on Matt: who wouldn't want to visit a sibling who had just awakened from a coma?

He stepped aside and leaned against the wall. The nurse had told him Kevin was in full recovery, that both his short- and long-term memory were impeccable. Matt had guiltily hoped for parts of it to be blurry, that the details persisting in his own head had not been rattling around in his brother's. For so many days, time had dragged, the seconds seeming to span eternities; now, each tick of the clock seemed microscopic in comparison.

Matt grabbed the door handle, regretted it, and realized that he already pushed the damn thing halfway down. Kevin would have noticed. What else was he to do?

He opened the door and went through, keeping his eyes locked straight ahead, avoiding eye contact, each stride heavier than the one before. There was no sound besides the soles of his sneakers squeaking on the polished epoxy floor. Reaching the room's center, he took a deep breath and looked at his little brother.

Kevin sat upright in bed, a blanket covering his legs. Tubes from both sides of his head joined a nasal cannula. He was peering at a flatscreen TV hanging on the wall, remote in hand, the volume turned down. Matt glanced at the screen. Baseball. Kevin never watched sports, as far as he knew.

"So, the nurse told me you were awake," Matt said. He had no clue how to cut through the glacier ahead.

Kevin didn't even blink; he just kept staring at the screen.

"How are you feeling?" Matt asked, trying to be jovial.

Still nothing.

"I buried Mom the other day."

"You did? How thoughtful." Kevin didn't turn from the game.

"I had to. There's a limit to how long you can postpone a funeral, you know."

More silence.

"Stephanie said hi," Matt said.

Kevin shifted his head and looked at Matt.

"They'll name their newborn Jeffrey. Bit funny, right?" Matt said.

Without moving a muscle in his face, Kevin rotated his head back towards the screen. Said nothing.

Matt stepped in front of him. Kevin staring through him as if he was transparent.

"Hey, I want to talk to you. How long are you gonna keep doing that?" Matt snapped, annoyed.

"As long as it takes," Kevin said.

"Takes to what?"

"Takes for you to leave this room, get out of my life, and never return."

"You don't mean that."

Nothing from Kevin.

The ice hadn't melted, but a crevice for communication seemed to have opened up. Matt grew tired of waiting, of being ignored.

"Can't you see that I did this for you? Don't you get it? It's what Mom wanted."

"What?" Kevin looked him in the eye now. Matt averted his gaze under the sheer force of his brother's piercing stare. "Think she wished that her older son—you, Matt—would have her younger son, me, dragged off, anesthetized and put in a medical coma, and then subjected to treatments and procedures to which he never consented, and which were never explained to him?"

Now it was Matt's turn to be quiet.

"Yes, Matt," Kevin went on, "I'm certain, now you remind me, that everything went *exactly* as Mom hoped it would."

There was a long pause.

"But I guess we can't ask her now, with you having killed her and all," Kevin said.

"Fuck you!" Matt yelled, grabbing the rails of the bed. "*I* made mistakes, *I* fucked up, absolutely. And I answer to that every day now. But don't you *ever* fucking dare say that *I* killed Mom!"

The last syllables resounded off the walls as Matt leaned forward and towered over his little brother.

A moment passed as they locked eyes with each other. Matt was breathing heavily. This time Kevin looked away first.

"I'm sorry," Kevin said. "I didn't mean it like that."

Matt grunted and stepped back. He turned around, stared at the television. Commercials were rolling.

"Dr. Henke asked if I wanted to go to college, get myself an education," Matt said, still keeping his back turned. "It's odd, me being so old and all."

"Can he do that? It's all you ever wanted."

"Yes, I know."

"So why hesitate?"

"Because the opportunity is yours, not mine."

"What?"

"It's your spot I would be claiming."

Kevin sighed. "Do me a favor and leave, Matt."

"Well, I'm not gonna take it," Matt said, turning. "It's yours. I wouldn't—" He stopped mid-sentence.

Kevin shook his head. "What do you want from me, Matt?" he said quietly. "My life? My love? What the fuck is it I have that you constantly want to control? What did I ever do to deserve this?" He gestured down at the bed, the blanket, the tubes and wires.

Matt exhaled. "But you said you didn't want it. The college spot," he whispered, exasperated.

"Where does that leave me, Matt? What am I supposed to answer? What if I changed my mind?"

Matt looked to the floor. Kept quiet. He knew he'd fucked up.

"Don't you get it, Matt? Just like always, you're snatching the decision away from me just by putting another possibility out there. What if I say I've changed my mind? Suddenly I'm the vindictive asshole, once more stopping you from reaching your goals and dreams. And you get to walk away guilt-free. And if I say it's yours, you get to have your dreams fulfilled, and I just *did what was expected of me.*"

Matt felt the familiar lump growing at the back of his throat.

"Not this time. You don't get to do it this time." Kevin snapped his fingers. "Look at me, Matt. Look me in the eye!"

Matt lifted his gaze and stared bleakly into Kevin's eyes.

"I'm gonna let you have that spot. But I want you to know it's because I have the capacity to do the one thing you cannot do, couldn't ever do: to think about others before myself. So pay close attention now. *I'm* giving you my spot because it's what *you* want. This time, you get to live with the nagging torment of wondering if *you* stripped *me* of my dreams."

Matt had nothing. His tongue felt like a stone in his mouth. He closed his eyes. For the first time, he understood Kevin. What it had been like living with his older brother as a father figure. The pressure, the burden, the exact same worries Matt had been struggling under ever since the crash. And he had nothing in terms of remedy.

"Get out." Kevin turned up the volume on the television. The game was back on. "I wanna watch this."

Matt turned away, his eyes still closed. He moved to the door, unable to stomach another look back before he left. Without another word, he closed the door behind him.

41

Dr. Henke took his little dictation device from the drawer in his office desk and sat down, leaning back in his reclining leather chair. He turned the device over a few times between his fingers. He smiled. Then he turned it on.

"Message to the Council of the Judicious," he started. "I have regained a location on Embryo Zero. This time, I'm not letting him out of my sights. Also, I am covering our tracks from the recent incident and am taking measures to eliminate any ties back to us and any of our facilities."

There was a knock on the door. He pressed the pause button.

"Who is it?"

"Matt."

Dr. Henke went to the door and opened it wide. He waved Matt inside.

"Hope I didn't disturb you," Matt said.

"Nothing that can't wait a bit. So, did you have a friendly chat with your brother?" Henke said. "How is he doing?"

"Well… He's fine, I guess." Matt looked at the floor.

"And so?"

"So I think I'm off to college," Matt said.

"Now that is excellent news." Dr. Henke looked Matt up and down from head to toe, then smiled broadly. "I'd hate to see all that opportunity wasted."

END OF BOOK ONE

Get the Free Prequel

Would you like to know who invented the ruthless government algorithms?

Wondering who envisioned the streetlighted enclaves?

Then I've got just the story for you!

I wrote a prequel for fans of The Streetlighters Trilogy centered around the essential elements of this near dystopian future. It's set at the time where the Energy Efficiency Act is brought forth by the government.

Since I wish to build a lasting relationship with my readers, this novella is exclusively available for subscribers to my newsletter.

Sign-up to claim your FREE copy at
www.trevorwynyard.com/streetlighters-exclusive

Help the Author

Independent authors, like myself, are responsible for all the steps in publishing and marketing their work. It's a lot, but I'd never trade it for anything, as the joy of delivering the final story to my readers is worth every bit.

Honest reviews of my books helps them find their readers. Not all stories fit all people. But reviews help both authors and readers find their right match.

So, if you would like to help me, and other readers like yourself, I would be grateful if you could spend a few minutes leaving a review (it can be as short as you like), where you got this book.

Thank you very much—every word and star is much appreciated.

Acknowledgements

Nothing lives in a vacuum, and so too this book has it own little world of contributors.

A huge thanks goes to my editor **Jennifer McIntyre**. Was it not for her keen eyes and sharp notes, this story would only be halfway to readable. Also a thanks to **Garret Schnackenberg** at Status Quill for his hard work fixing any last errors. It's been a joy working with you both.

I would also like to thank my family. **My wife** who took on the burden of our home, when I was buried behind the screen, to **my children** who during writing made me rediscover the magic of a keyboard putting letters on that screen, and to **my parents** for their continued support through out.

To **my friends** for their interest and encouragement from start to finish.

And at last to you, **my dear readers**. You keep me on my toes, and I wouldn't have it any other way. In the end, it is all for you.

About the Author

Trevor Wynyard writes dystopian fiction for an adult audience. From the egotism of oppressive regimes to the intricacies of everyday peer pressure, he has always speculated about the darker sides of humanity. He believes the only way to mitigate an ever-encroaching dystopian future of our own is through an understanding of the underlying, basic emotions and behaviors at play between human beings from all walks of life—themes he explores tirelessly in his writing.

Trevor lives in Denmark, where he eagerly awaits a utopia chock-full of craft beer, indie rock and pistachio ice cream.

You can keep in touch with Trevor by visiting his site, www.trevorwynyard.com, where you can learn more about upcoming books and sign up for his newsletter.